The Metal
Shredders

BLUEHEN BOOKS
a member of Penguin Putnam Inc.
New York
2002

The Metal Shredders

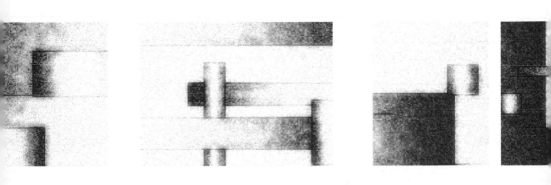

 Nancy Zafris

BlueHen Books
a member of
Penguin Putnam Inc.
375 Hudson Street
New York, NY 10014

Library of Congress Cataloging-in-Publication Data

Zafris, Nancy.
  The metal shredders : a novel / by Nancy Zafris.
    p.   cm.
  ISBN 0-399-14922-8
    1. Family-owned business enterprises—Fiction.   2. Scrap metal
industry—Fiction.   3. Brothers and sisters—Fiction.   4. Columbus
(Ohio)—Fiction.   I. Title.
PS3576.A285 M47   2002   2002018571
813'.54—dc21

Printed in the United States of America
10   9   8   7   6   5   4   3   2   1

This book is printed on acid-free paper. ∞

Book design by Stephanie Huntwork

For Sam and Jim

I would like to express my gratitude to Betty McDaniel who introduced me to Freddy Loef, a generous man who shared his amazing knowledge of the scrap recycling business with me. I also want to thank my editor Greg Michalson, my agent Gail Hochman, Michelle Herman, Gretchen McBeath, Anesa Miller, Michael Sweeney, and my father Stephan Sydor—with a special thanks to Heather Schroder. For editorial advice and emotional support, I am fortunate to be able to rely on Julian Anderson, Keith Banner, Sharon Dilworth, Joe Freda, Bob Harrist, David Lynn, Jean Reinhold and, last in the alphabet but first in everything else, Jim Zafris.

Portions of the manuscript were written under the financial support of the National Endowment for the Arts, the Ohio Arts Council, and the Greater Columbus Arts Council. Aspects of this novel were based on the short story "The Metal Shredders," published in *The People I Know* (University of Georgia Press), and *The Flannery O'Connor Award, Selected Stories* (Charles East, ed., University of Georgia Press).

Prologue

John Bonner is the only living John Bonner currently on the scene, so it's his job to solve this problem: Allman's Nightrider is blocking the entrance to the church parking lot.

It's a humongous thing, this twenty-two-wheeler, Allman's little bitty baby, and inside its cab is a regular apartment—bed, hot plate, coffee roaster, interloan library, camcorder, gun rack—nearly everything a bubba hippie of the road and proud owner of Franklin County's biggest overload (forty-two thousand pounds' worth of an infraction) could want. But it's blocking the church parking lot, that's the main thing right now.

John has leaped out of his pickup and is already sprinting down the sidewalk. Fortunately Allman is early, so the assembling cars are few in number. John spots a Pennsylvania license plate idling in front of United Methodist. Pennsylvania must mean Murray Kempleton has arrived. Soon the other metal shredders from the tristate area will be here, and they are strange wealthy men for whom the wide world is either ferrous or nonferrous. Nothing else. Except on special days like this, when things can also be alive or dead.

The Nightrider has corkscrewed itself into *hopelessly stuck*. Why did Allman think he could wend his parade float of a truck down a side street, much less into a small church lot? Probably due to the imagination built up through long hours of night driving, and other things. Enough time on the road, John has noticed, and the independent haulers start thinking their big rigs are Fiats. John is relieved to see that Tony, always ahead of time for work, has the same habit for funerals. He is here, he is one leg up on the running board and shouting over the engine noise to Allman behind the steering wheel. "We're backing her out!" Tony yells over to John, and then he does something he probably shouldn't, but it doesn't matter, nobody sees him, he stands on someone's car roof. His vigorous semaphore indicates he has seen a way to untangle the knot. The suit Tony is wearing hides the welding burns up and down his arms, but John can see a burn on the back of his hand, maroon and perfect as a caste mark, while Tony summons Allman two hand waves forward, straightens him, then motions him backward. The truck bucks in place, moves one crashingly loud inch after another. The noise turns everything else into a silent movie, and John finds himself watching it, the only sound the flapping of the sixteen-millimeter film, it seems so dated and jumpy and everybody looks a little weird, as if the ancient technology can't capture how things really are today. Tony has wet-combed his dark hair straight back, and the stark white forehead makes him look like somebody else. John has the sensation he is someone else, too. And he guesses that he is, actually. From this day forward he is sort of somebody else.

John turns to find his father silently by his side.

"What's going on?" the Senior asks.

John doesn't answer. It doesn't really need an explanation. Does it? The Nightrider is so loud that maybe the Senior will think he has spoken.

"I see," the Senior says.

John is about to ask where his mother and sister are, but realizes if he speaks the illusion that he has already spoken will be ruined. He pulls his tie out of his shirt pocket and begins to loop it around. He's just read about eighty-five ways to knot your neckwear. He mentioned it to his dad—just something interesting—and all the Senior said was, *Eighty-five ways to tie a tie. That's eighty-four things you don't need to know.*

As John straightens the knot and pushes it into place over his Adam's apple, he's aware of the Senior studying him. All of a sudden he feels this tremendous urge, it overtakes him. *What the hell are you looking at?* he demands of his father. He wants to say it so badly. He just wants to say it, that's all. His father is looking at him as if he can't recognize his own son, and now his son simply wants to say what the hell are you looking at?

But he doesn't, of course.

John and his father are still out in the middle of the street, keeping it clear for the violently bucking but hardly moving at all Nightrider. Then, miraculously, like a wedding ring soaped off a finger grown too fed up, the truck slips clear and free and escapes. Except it doesn't run off to Telluride, Colorado, where it decides to live with its sister and get a job substitute teaching. It goes down the street to a Columbus, Ohio, grocery store. The Big Bear supermarket has plenty of parking room for Allman's Nightrider.

With Allman gone, the cars pour in.

"That was easy," his father says. They head toward the church. They won't get inside, however, without properly acknowledging the tattered summit flags waiting for them at the top of the steps. The old guard, down to three. And a zealous three it is. Aluminum walker, nurse's aide, devoted daughter acting as crutch be damned: these elderly men are the celebrities in this crowd and they're not heading in to sit where their shrunken bodies will be hidden by the pews.

Jacob Kolski from Youngstown raises a hand from his walker and offers his condolences. "He caused trouble," Jacob says.

"Jacob, glad you could make it," the Senior says, shaking his hand.

Next to Jacob is Happy Lazar, down from Cleveland. "Thought he'd never die," Happy Lazar says.

"Happy, glad you could make it."

Happy is looking poorly since the last time John saw him, having developed the turtle-ish slouch—shoulders high, head low—that John recognizes from his grandfather's last months. Clasping Happy's hand, now thin as a girl's, he feels a sadness at the fan of finger bones plucking through his palm like four sharp piano keys.

The last of the old guard is Murray Kempleton, all the way from Lebanon, Pennsylvania, home of the first gas cutting-torch. In the world of scrap, the gas cutting-torch was an invention equivalent to talking movies. Murray probably tries to take the credit for both the torch and the talkies. He's about eighty-five, eighty-six. He had John's grandfather beat by a couple of years.

"Murray, great to see you. Dad would be happy you came."

Murray grasps the Senior's arm and pulls himself close. He gets up into the Senior's air space. "I told him many times. I told him, listen here, John Bonner, just because . . ." Murray Kempleton twirls the air, doesn't complete the sentence, lets the important advice hang in the sunless September breeze. His daughter is there next to him, holding his forearm. The daughter, with that stockiness that sometimes turns linebackerish in fifty-something women, seems nice enough, but John can see from the ironing lines that Murray's shirt has been sent to the dry cleaner's. John's mother wouldn't wash his grandfather's shirts either. Nor would she pick them up off the floor for him. It's true, he had begun to smell a little, but his mother's distaste for the man had settled in long before that. Although he dressed neatly, the clothes didn't necessarily have to be clean. His grandfather was a man who tried to turn his scrap yard into an obsessively organized and disinfected medical tent. He would stand under the wet scrubber and watch the iron drop into a bin until he spied a small piece of magnesium tangled in with the ferrous. He'd yell, There's sixty cents in here, get it out! But he was also a man who would stand in his bedroom among a sea of dirty socks, and a pair from the floor was the same to him as a pair from the dresser.

John Bonner & Son Metal Shredders.

A proud business for three generations. Three generations of John Bonners. The ghosts of scrap metal past, present, and future, John liked to joke. He used to milk the Shredders as fodder for all his funny anecdotes. Especially at dinner parties. He'd talk about his Strange Job. He'd talk about his Strange Employees. People loved it, especially the husbands, with their dragged-here-forced-to-do-this faces. He'd weave a few Shredder tales and suddenly he was the center of attention and loving it. Of course Elise was always there to throw him a look. She'd heard all of the stories before—the wild dogs, the live-body shredding, the various perils of the various night watchmen, the attempted scams of the father-son hillbilly teams who make their living scouring the blue highways for road-kill scrap. Elise didn't find the human condition illustrated by these stories something to brag about. The high school English teacher in her, the spelling-test roll-call schoolmarm part, came out in times like this. She didn't find any of the employees particularly amusing—not Tony or Greenslade or Worm or Ada or the hapless octogenarian Don Capachi. She didn't throw her head back and howl like the others. She looked elsewhere, out the window, where her own thoughts were gathering until they formed a riot and she left. First the party, then him.

Nancy Zafris

Everything made of metal contains scrap
And everything made of metal eventually becomes scrap

from the pamphlet *Don't Ignore Scrap, It Won't Ignore You,*
written by John Bonner and passed out free at the
weighmaster's station.

An invisible force is at work. The mourners have self-classified in their seating choices. The church has turned into a scrap yard with the mourners ranked like grades of metal, best to worst. The purest grade, the family, are here in front: John's mother, who hated his grandfather with the purity of No. 1 copper; his mother, whose coiffed hair has never moved in the thirty years John has been alive, not even long ago when it hung in a ponytail and she was pitching a softball to him. His sister, Octavia, home from Boston—for a while, she says. His cousin, Rory who's decided to quit the business. Presumably Rory's mother, the Senior's sister, will be here at some point, since she's the sister. Nobody's heard from her. She lives in Florida.

The finest alloys come next, the old guard, his grandfather's peers in the business; then business colleagues in other fields, Judge Cotter from the federal court among them, and some guy who looks like the ex-mayor, not that being an ex-mayor of Columbus is any great shakes, but it's enough to get him into the alloy seats.

Iron, the scrap yard's tumbleweed, sturdy but rusty, takes up the middle ground of pews: Ada, the weighmaster cashier, sits here, as do Tony and their night watchman, Joe Greenslade. There's Dooley, the Linkbelt and shredder operator. He's either hungover or green with grief. Worm is here, too, that's sort of a surprise. Marcus, the yard boss, looms head-and-shoulders above poor aged Don Capachi. And the Welbargers are in attendance, the hillbilly entrepreneurs of the blue highways, who've forgone a day of scavenging the roads to pay their respects and no doubt stockpile some good food from the reception afterwards.

The self-classification continues all the way to the rear where, hiding behind the sturdy iron middle, sit the contaminants. Here begins the sprinkling of lead, the Hispanics and the Cambodians who draw their salary in cash. Some stragglers John might have recognized had they not gone further downhill from the last time he barely recognized them—in fact, if he knew who they were he'd be surprised they weren't dead. And now some older folks, black men and women gone gray and white, people John doesn't quite know but suspects he might have long ago, people from a bygone era; some old ghosts whose loyalty his grandfather bought when such things could be purchased—Thanksgiving turkeys and Christmas presents and school shoes and paid-for medical bills. They liked his grandfather and they're not afraid to say so.

At the back of the church Tommy Landers from Indianapolis has just made his entrance in Olympian fashion and he could be a clone of the Senior: good looks, big body, eyes that can ripple with emotional depth or cut like a shear. As if hearing John's thoughts, Tommy poses at the back of the church to let the sun's rays beam off him in a holy crown.

Like the Senior, Tommy's been wanting to redirect his scrap business into white goods. The scrap yards won't take refrigerators, or washers and dryers any more, too many fluorocarbons and PCBs, it's now classified as hazardous waste, so there's a market out there that Tommy wants to exploit. The Senior seems to be in some kind of race with Tommy to get his up and running and profitable. It's personal, John is sure of it. Each is too used to being the only one who parts the sea into two behaving halves.

Distracted by Tommy Landers, John doesn't notice Hayley Badecker until she's gripping his biceps with—he could swear—a flirtatious squeeze. She looks very good in her tight black suit. She's a rep from the railroad company but she looks more like the woman behind the Clinique counter, the one who's actually beautiful with or without the makeup, the one heads above the rest in commission. John notices his sister checking out Hayley Badecker with a who the hell is she type gawk, startled, he can tell, at Hayley's modelesque aura with the edge of trashy tartness the blond hair gives. John undertones an abbreviated introduction. Hayley Badecker reaches out to shake Otty's hand, smiling broadly at his sister before remembering *funeral! sad!* and abruptly shutting the curtain on her sparkling teeth. She goes back to regulation sympathy, mouth closed, lips together. She takes her leave with a clamped, tragic smile, using both hands to enclose the Senior's grip. "Such a wonderful man," she whispers to his father.

"Thank you, Hayley," the Senior says.

Tommy Landers now approaches, his mouth aimed only at John with a bit of an Elvis twitch to include John's mother. The Senior is shut out. Shredder etiquette demands at least a handshake, but each of them looks elsewhere as their fingers intertwine, the Senior's nod directed toward Jesus' cross, Tommy's nod toward Ada, the weighmaster cashier, who waves back.

John looks at his watch, wondering when he'll get home. It's ten A.M. right now. That means it's eight A.M. in Telluride. She'll probably call later in the day, after five, which is perfect because he'll be home around seven. If he misses her call, the answering machine will pick up. Elise's message on the machine plays in his head. *Call me, okay?* He'll have to stifle a laugh at that one. *Call me, okay?*—the poetess, not so good with the spoken words. *Look, there's a letter in the mail explains it all.* He knew the message would end with that. She's lost without her pen, her spelling books, her attendance sheet. Plus she's got to get in the last word.

When he comes up for air, he realizes he's been talking to himself. It's okay, no one has heard him. His muttering has been drowned out by the argument taking place at the coffin. The old guard, naturally, still up to their tricks. Who helped them up there? John was sure rheumatism would keep their spines soldered to their seats this time. His father is fighting through a Tommy Landers blocked aisle, but it's too late, and besides, nothing will stop them now. The magnets attached to their key chains are already out and testing the coffin for any pull. Happy Lazar slaps the coffin with his bony palm and triumphantly shouts, "This is yellow brass!"

"Yellow brass!" Murray Kempleton grrs, raising his tiny fists, ready to fight.

John sighs, excuses himself past this mother's knees, and strides up to the coffin to join Tommy and his dad.

"Sit down," his father says to Happy, not in a mean way, but in a comforting, almost gentle way. He settles his palms on Happy's frail shoulders.

"Let him have his say." Tommy Landers pushes the Senior aside, pleased to order him around.

The Senior is quickly roused and squares off against Tommy. He and the Senior look like brothers. It's Romulus and Remus with those two. Before John can think to act, Tony steps in. He sees Tony's hand, castemarked with its perfect maroon burn, slip between their almost butting chests and push them apart. John is not sure it's really needed, this peacekeeping of an actual physical sort. What's going on is more or less a tradition, sort of a summer-stock production, and it's usually reserved for equity actors only. Tony the welder is not quite welcome up here but he doesn't know it.

"There's a five-percent pull on this," Murray Kempleton croaks. He turns to make his announcement to the church at large. "Five percent pull!" he proclaims to all the mourners, smacking his lips with satisfaction.

"Let it go. Let it go," the Senior says.

This time Jacob Kolski pounds the coffin. The dwindling arm that lifts away from the walker and falls upon his grandfather's corpse is still a touch too strong to be engaging in this kind of punching, but that's what makes it edgy theater as well.

Murray Kempleton declares, "Your grandfather wanted copper, not yellow brass, and what a metal shredder wants for his coffin a metal shredder gets."

He has a point.

It's all happened before. And will again, with Romulus and Remus trying to save the day. Who cares about a nice send-off to Heaven? Not these guys. Heaven is just some aggravating regulatory commission the federal government has dreamed up.

John checks his watch. 10:15 A.M. 8:15 in Telluride. Ten, twelve, possibly fourteen hours for her to phone. The machine can pick up if he's not home.

Call me, okay?

Call me, okay?

To Shred or Not to Shred

 Part One

In the farthest corner of the Shredder yard sits a late-model LTD with fifty-one thousand miles on it. It should be slated for shredding, but it's not. It's going to get a beauty makeover instead. John tries to explain why to Octavia, but it's hard to come up with a reason since there is none— at least no reason that makes sense. The car runs, but it isn't driveable. A discouraging odor has seen to that. Which is how the Senior referred to this death bouquet: a discouraging odor. A challenge, he offered with the meagerest of fist pumps. The Senior even skimps on fist pumps.

The smell is more than challenging. It's overwhelming. For three long summer weeks two murdered bodies lingered undiscovered in that car and they've left an eternal afterlife. It's completely upsetting, the way a smell that you've never smelled before can awaken some part of your brain that instantly remembers it. John is worried about the effect it might have on his employees. What startling behaviors will result from their false recovered memories awakened by this smell? Later, at some party, the antics might find their way into a new entertaining anecdote, but the actual anecdote-generating experience has never been pleasant. *Quit pissing on Ada's car **right now,*** for example. It's not that John has actually found himself saying this to a worker, it's that he's found himself saying this more than once. A favorite winter sport, resulting in funny yellow icicles, sure to provoke a laugh or two when he recounts it. But it's not amusing at all when Ada is getting into her car.

Whether or not Octavia can make it here at the Shredders is an issue that awaits her down the line (and she's the one who wants to be here—at least "for a while"). For now there's the LTD. John wishes his father would stop doing this kind of thing. Now and then, from the county attorney's office, these sorts of vehicles come their way. A car that's been victimized. Usually it's some unsalvageable wreck left over from a getaway crash, or else an abandoned hulk of untold secrets winched from a lake. Nothing this gruesome before. The Senior is always happy to take the vehicle off the county's hands. It's the type of favor he gladly does. The Shredders tow it, strip it, take out the battery, tires, and exhaust system, haul the worthless stuff to the landfill and pay the fee themselves, and for all their trouble they get about seventy dollars' worth of iron hunk and one chit of goodwill redeemable at the county attorney's.

It's not worth it.

The LTD should go pell-mell headfirst into the shredder, forget about stripping off the tires, forget about making a few cents on the radiator, engine, and exhaust. Throw it all in and get rid of it. The smell has already trashed the car.

John's opinion. Not the Senior's, clearly. According to him, all it needs is to be cleaned, deodorized, and upholstered.

Which is a little bit hard to do since no one can get near the LTD without gagging. Tony has tried rags dipped in other foul-smelling solvents, wrapped them in layers around his mouth and stuffed them into his nostrils. He always comes stumbling back, blinded by the smell. Though Tony is the welder, functioning as a maintenance man, the Senior has assigned this chore to him. Checking out the office window, John sees that Tony has now switched to the protection of welder gear. After wrapping his head like a mummy, he fits on his welder's helmet and lowers the face shield. He ventures down the path toward the car, hits the smelling wall, stumbles back, lifts his face shield for a deep breath, lowers it, squares his shoulders, and tries again, only to be turned away once more.

Meanwhile, John's up here in the office trying his best to explain the basics of the business to Otty. She's always been the smart one, so somehow he assumed an hour would do it. He didn't realize until he got started how much there is to learn. Otty's face has grown blank. Her eyes, tired and swirling, tell John her brain is fainting away.

He pulls out a can of fizzy water from the minifridge and hands it to her. "Maybe we've done enough for the day. It's almost five anyway."

Octavia doesn't answer. She takes a first sip of the water and presses back a burp. She's put some blond streaks or something in her hair. Not quite blond, not quite noticeable. Just makes her hair look shiny.

"Did you do something to your hair?" he asks her.

"I was a hair model at a haircutting school."

"You were? Great idea."

"Saves on costs." She shrugs. "I had a friend in Boston who's a guard at a women's penitentiary."

"What's that got to do with a haircutting school?"

"That's where it was."

"Oh." Then John asks her, "Weren't you afraid of having a sharp pair of scissors pointed near your eyeballs?"

"None of them were in there for eyeball crimes," Octavia says.

"Well, it looks nice. They did a good job."

She leans into her hands, covering her eyes, and rests.

"We have a women's prison pretty nearby. You could try them."

"I don't mind a normal salon," she mutters through her fingers. "Now that I have a decent salary. Thanks to Daddy. Just as long as it's not the one Mom goes to." She looks up, runs her hand through her hair and fluffs it. She says, "I've had all types do my hair, and I think female cons have it all over gay hairdressers."

The clumping of feet rings on the metal stairs. Octavia jerks, then settles herself into an attentive position. Awaiting the Senior. John, however, knows the clunking is too fast and heavy.

The door kicks open. Tony walks in. Octavia yawns.

"Any luck?" John asks.

"No." Tony plops on the couch and throws his feet up on the table. If the couch weren't some beat-up piece of junk from Goodwill and the coffee table made from particleboard, John might take some offense. As rich as metal shredders might be, they can't have nice stuff in a working office. One of the things John has stressed to Octavia is keeping the computer and keyboard covered when not in use.

"You'll never get that smell out," Tony tells him. "I can't even go near it."

"Go near it anyway."

"Go near it anyway he says." Tony turns to Octavia. His arms, tracked with welding burns, implore the air. "Go near it anyway he says."

Octavia responds by studying her can of fizzy water.

John checks out Tony, sitting on the couch with his legs propped up. For John the issue has always been the quality of the furniture when they sit in his chairs in their dirty clothes and put their dirty boots on his tables, but for Octavia it's something else. That much is clear from the shutdown look on her face. It must be the kingliness of Tony's repose, the *get me a beer, woman* way he's kicked back. If she meets his kingliness with her own, she'll just come off as a dyke. If she tries to flirt, she'll cheapen herself and end up like Rhonda. The Senior's sister is sort of the family embarrassment, an alloy of barfly and upper crust. Putting the women in the family business—it's never been a good idea.

But this is what Otty wants—"for a while." She'll have to figure out her own way. She stares down at her can of water.

The thing is, Tony's not really like that. He looks like the rest of them, but John has learned how different he is. He's a corporate wannabe from the trailer parks. He's like a little kid in the innocence of his belief that he's going to climb the ladder. He's going to school nights at Columbus State, business administration, he's a killer on the computer (well, compared to the rest of them anyway), but he looks like a welder, he walks like a welder, he eats like a welder. He even smiles like a welder. John had wondered whether a suit and tie could wash it away, but when he saw Tony all dressed up at the church, that answered that question: he looked exactly like a welder attending a funeral. Especially with his hair combed back *with water*, as if for a school photo, exposing the raccoon tan lines around his face. Tony follows John constantly. He makes sure he's by John's side, hoping for his trust, hoping for a shot. He already has the weighmaster tasks down cold. But it doesn't matter what Tony does, he's not coming into the inner circle. It's all family.

"I'll tell you something else," Tony says. "Dogs."

Octavia glances up.

"Dogs," Tony repeats. "Mark my words."

Octavia plucks a pen from the chicken noodle soup can cleaned into a pencil holder. "Okay," she says meanly.

"Coming around in a big way. Thinking there's a big pile of rotten food."

Tony gets up from the couch and goes over to the Bunn coffeemaker, inspects the insides of various mugs until he chooses the one mug he shouldn't, the Ohio State University mug belonging to the Senior, and pours himself a cup of scorched brew. Then he kicks at John's old desk, the desk where Octavia now sits, and jerks the unbudging bottom drawer. He remembers to crack open the top drawer to unhinge it. "Excuse me," he says to Octavia. The bottom drawer releases and he rummages inside. "She know about the dogs?" he asks. Octavia swings her thigh away from him so he can get what he's after. She shrinks into her body. A parade of expressions comes and goes on her face.

Tony pulls out a Little Debbie oatmeal cookie from the box. "She know about the dogs?" he asks John again.

John is too mesmerized by Tony's odd behavior to respond. Flirting? Not a very good job of it.

"You could ask me that question," Octavia says.

"I just did," Tony says.

"No, you didn't. You asked John."

Tony rolls his eyes wearily. He digs into the box for another oatmeal cookie and offers it to her.

"No thanks."

Tony shrugs. He moves back to the couch. John doesn't like the tension in the air, because there is definitely tension in the air. He doesn't want to have to deal with this kind of stuff, the trouble caused when one or the other, usually the female party, wants to get angry over semantics or little gestures. He got enough of that from Elise. It wasn't just him—she wasn't perfect either. *Ready to pounce.* That's how he'd describe it. Like a fourth-grade teacher waiting, even hoping for a misspelling, she was there ready to correct every nuance in his sentence structure and body language. Every time he spoke he was watching himself speak, every time he lifted a fork he was watching himself lift a fork. And wondering: am I doing this right? Is the angle of this fork correct? Is it even the right fork? Are there wrong forks? That's why, toward the end, when they made love, this other self, the super-self-conscious Frankenstein she had created, rose from him and took up watch by the bed, criticizing his every move until he barely had a move left. That's why he stopped talking to her as he licked and stroked—*Love talk sounds really stupid, Stupid!* his other self critiqued—and all the passion he wanted to express was swallowed and held inside until one night all he could find was a man silently, ever so silently churning away. Lovelessly churning away. At that moment it was loveless.

"In fact, that's a great idea. He's perfect for the job."

He hears Tony but he's lost the thread of conversation. He doesn't care. He's locked inside his favorite activity, Elise, thinking about Elise, getting angry with her, scoring points against her, imagining ways they'll make love when they see each other again. He's addicted. He's addicted to his own Web site, Elise dot com. All he can do is hope that over there in Telluride, Colorado, she's addicted, too. God forbid she's logged off the message board to seek healthy ways to get over him.

You know, she could have worked some on her sense of humor, he tells the remaining message board addicts. A little too moralistic in her stance whenever he told his work anecdotes. Everyone else at the party laughed—why not her? She could have attempted at least a chuckle or two. How about the story of his much younger grandfather and Don Capachi—when a worker broke his bottle of Old Grand-Dad whiskey over Don Capachi's head to get everyone's attention, then climbed up the crane that fed the cars into the shredder and dropped like a spent Corvette right into the churning maw, whether drunken suicide or drunken accident no one was quite sure—about how the shredder hammered him at a rate of 950 times a minute and turned a horrible sight into absolutely no sight at all? Okay, maybe that one wasn't so funny. He remembers how Elise couldn't sleep the first time she heard it. Later she noted with disgust how people reacted to the story of a human shredding by laughing their heads off. What do you want me to talk about instead? John once asked her. Do you think they want to hear that aluminum's down to sixty-four cents a pound? Why not? she said. I think that could be interesting in the hands of the right narrator.

"What do you think?" Tony asks him.

"I don't get it," John says.

"Why not? He's perfect for the job."

"Who?"

"Greenjeans."

"No, Tony, don't get started on him again. He's an old man."

"The smelling section of his brain is gone. He had an operation knocked it out."

"What operation, when?"

"Brain surgery, I don't know."

"I didn't hear about any operation. I think I would know if there's been an operation."

"It wasn't recent," Tony tells him.

John watches his sister exit the conversation. She goes to the little kitchenette area and fills a bucket with detergent and water, puts on Playtex gloves, and heads into the bathroom.

"What's she so pissed about?" Tony whispers.

"Drop it," John says.

The stairway rattles with a crisp autumn hollowness. Clung thump, clang hump—clung thump, clang hump. A little slower than usual, but John recognizes the left-foot sound, the right-foot sound. Tony doesn't get it. He's unprepared when the Senior strides in. He leaps up from the couch with the electric shock of panic, but it's too late.

The Senior stands at the entrance, doing a stomping routine as though it's snowing outside. "Do I pay you to sit there?" he asks Tony.

"Hi," Octavia greets listlessly from the bathroom doorway.

The Metal Shredders

"Hi, honey," the Senior says, not shifting his gaze from Tony. "Been welded to those cushions since yesterday."

"No, I've been . . ."

The Senior's eyes wrestle Tony to the floor. "What?" he asks Tony, his hands twisting toward the sky in aggrievement. Then he picks up his OSU coffee mug from the particleboard table. "Anybody using this?" Tony shakes his head vigorously, back and forth, back and forth. As if the stare-down weren't enough, the Senior moves to straddle the desk, sending Tony a casual crotch shot. "So I guess this means the car's all done? If this is a victory party, I'd like to join in." Again his hands twist out, ready to catch the good news.

This is really stupid, John thinks. Your dick in our faces, your friendly-prosecuting-attorney act.

"What?" the Senior asks.

"No, it's not done," John says. He doesn't like watching Tony squirm. Tony, who'd be the Senior's most loyal lapdog if he'd let him. It'll never happen: The Senior's got it in for Tony ever since the knock-down fight he and Cousin Rory had about two years ago. The Senior had to physically intervene. Ever since, he's been treating Tony like this, the object of his serene, royal sadism. No matter that the blame belonged to Rory.

Rory was such an immature jerk, the worst Generation X had to offer, but he was Rhonda's son and he was family. Now that he has chosen his grandfather's death to mark his own retirement from the business at age twenty-five, John is left to take over Rory's job in addition to his own duties. His cousin will be back, John imagines, the money's too good, but it might be five years down the road. For the foreseeable future John will be working the weighmaster station, tallying the haulers' loads at the ferrous and nonferrous scales. He'll be locked in there with Ada and her kachina dolls and skeet-shooting trophies. He likes Ada, he truly does, but she never stops talking, funny and harsh, dispensing her country justice. One week she's bringing down the boys who pee on her car. Next week she's threatening to call the FBI on Worm. Every week she's giving insulin shots to husband number three. Sometimes there are diapers involved with number three. He gets to hear about that, too. If and when this marriage ends, the search for number four will begin. He'll hear it all. He's not looking forward to being glass-caged with her, but no way can he give the weighmaster job to Otty. You have to know the business too well, be able to spot-grade the irons and metals, and know the prices, and work the spread. There's always the buyer's discretion, which makes it one more job that can't go outside the family.

John tells his father, "You know, we're having a real problem with the car."

"What problem is that?"

Fake mafioso fake naïveté. Works like a charm on Tony. But he's not Tony. "One of the five senses has totaled the car," he's driven to shoot back.

"What sense is that? Lack of initiative? Lack of drive? Lack of the entrepreneurial spirit?"

"Yeah, that's right. All of those things."

"We tried," Tony says. "I don't see what the big deal is about just junking it."

". . . Not to mention I'm a welder," Tony stupidly decides to add when he gets no response.

The Senior allows the darkness of his displeasure to settle over Tony. He takes his time because his displeasure is gourmet displeasure; it needs time to ferment.

The silence begins.

The Senior is dressed in a red golf cardigan with a breast logo of Ohio State University. He wears a white dress shirt underneath. He is a handsomely featured man, conventionally good-looking, with a thick head of hair parted on the side. And what he looks like is what he is: a member of Scioto Country Club with its $32,000 initiation fee and $450 monthly dues; add a hundred to that for every round of golf. He's a loyal alum with season tickets to OSU football. He's a member of several corporate boards. He's a man whose vision is vast, on the one hand, and yet goes no farther than the Ohio border. A man who's not embarrassed to still be wearing his college signet ring. In short, a local boy embracing riches and the status quo. With some breeding, with some natural class. Tony will never be able to join this club.

The silent displeasure is now exquisite. It has aged properly and it's time to take a sip. The Senior says to Tony, serenely, royally, sadistically, "I'm sure you don't see what the big deal is. That's my job, to see what the big deal is. It's not your decision. I asked you to do something and it should have been done."

Such mild sentences so mildly put, and yet they can bring a grown man to his knees.

The Senior waits and waits, and finally Tony says, as if trying them out—are these the words that will finally get him off the hook?—"I'm sorry," he says.

"You'll get to it?"

"Yes I will, Mr. Bonner."

The only thing John can figure is that this nasty car-cleaning detail is some sort of punishment the Senior is doling out to Tony. But Tony hasn't done anything lately except be himself, nothing out of the ordinary. John goes back to the reception after the funeral, checking over the details of that. He remembers seeing Tony in the buffet line, but that's all. It was those others who caused the problem. Tony *did* come up to the coffin at some point during the yellow brass/copper donnybrook and try to help. Maybe it was the proprietary assumption in that, like Tony's part of their family. Trying to steer Tommy Landers away: that's probably what did it.

Tony came between the Senior and his archrival. In trying to help the Senior, Tony showed him up for a sap who can't wage his own war.

Quick, clumping footsteps sound a reprieve to Tony's further humiliation. In a second the door opens and one man after another moves quickly to the time clock. John takes advantage of the noisy flow to defend Tony without being overheard by him or the others. "Look," he tells his dad, "this doesn't make any sense. From a cost-benefit point of view, it's absurd."

"It's not absurd."

"It is. And it's not our job. It's outside the metal-shredding sphere."

Clearly the Senior is aware of the presence of these men. He looks cool and calm—except to John. The Senior has only one unattractive feature on his face: a too-thin upper lip that curls under and disappears during stress. Why is he stressed over this? It's just a car. They shred eighty thousand tons' worth of cars every year.

The workmen notice that the Senior isn't greeting them as he normally does. They get the message and scurry out. One after the other. All except Ralph Dooley, the crane and shredder operator. He slumps nearby and pauses. They each throw out a handshake. "Dooley," the Senior greets.

His dad is so hard to figure sometimes. The Senior adores Dooley. To John, Dooley is a blob.

When the men have left and it's back to the three of them and a bathroom-stowed-away Octavia, the Senior pulls out a desk chair and slowly sits down. He allows himself a sorrowful gaze, but John won't meet his eyes and neither will Tony. He straightens the scattering of industry magazines on the desk, then arranges each *Phoenix Quarterly* according to date. He stops to study the lead article in this month's issue: "Scrap Ahoy!"

It's quiet enough that Octavia opens the door, but she closes it immediately.

The Metal Shredders

"What game level are we on now?" John says this aloud but no one seems to have heard.

Tony is drumming his thighs. He sends John panicked signals. When the Senior isn't looking, he swings up his hands: *what now?*

John says, "Well, I guess we'd better get started, Tony. Come on, I'll give you a hand."

Now the Senior seems to have heard. He pushes against the chair and stands up.

The Metal Shredders is no place for girls. Octavia knows this, but here she is. When they finally leave, she comes out. She'd take a deep breath, but the air's too dirty. First thing, clean the bathroom, then put up a sign: GIRLS ONLY. That means one person—her. And maybe Ada from time to time, if she can stand climbing the steps. Ada wears two-and-a-half-inch heels, and the metal steps have those holes in them just the right size to capture the spike of a pretty dress shoe. Just another way to keep women out. Trap in hole, break ankle, replace with man. Subtle.

She checks out the window. Ada, who could miss her, is hanging out down there with the men. Wobbling around in those shoes. Her hair is piled up high on her head like everybody's favorite pedicurist's. Her smile is lit up toward the Senior. What is she now, like sixty? and still acting out her crush. It's so obvious: only her father couldn't perceive it. If he says jump, she'll say how high. She's worked here forever, probably without a pay raise. He doesn't know how lucky he's got it with her loyalty. Ada is not someone you want as your enemy. Already Octavia is dreading the work that will be involved in getting Ada to like her.

𝕵𝖔𝖍𝖓 𝕭𝖔𝖓𝖓𝖊𝖗 & 𝕾𝖔𝖓 𝕸𝖊𝖙𝖆𝖑 𝕾𝖍𝖗𝖊𝖉𝖉𝖊𝖗𝖘. She reads these words, flopped and backward, off the front gate. The whole place is musked with metal powder. It's there, everywhere, even in this office, even on her desk—no, *in* her desk. The metal dust, its tinge of iron red, is inside everything, and soon it will be inside her. But, as her grandfather used to say, Metal shredders are born, not made.

It's like having the thrill gene or the alcoholic gene. She's got the scrap gene.

It's coming to get her.

How do you stand it? she'd asked John. You get used to it, he'd said.

What she really meant was *them.* How do you stand these awful men?

But she knew his answer to that question, too: a shrug, then, People are people. He seems to really like them. Or maybe he's just gone weird since Elise left him. She doesn't actually know him too well even though he's her brother. She likes him of course but it's hard to tell what he's thinking, at least on a personal level. He never mentions Elise, so she doesn't know if he's happy, sad, celibate, or screwing his eyes out since the woman left. Most of their adult lives they've been apart from each other. He stayed in Ohio, went to Ohio University in Athens; she went east to Wellesley. Then he started at the Metal Shredders and she lived abroad in Madrid for almost six years. It sounds exotic, but living abroad was like sharing a house with a bunch of people—it kept her from growing up and time passed too quickly. Like the expatriates she hung out with, she just got by with various impermanent jobs. *Being in Spain* was their real occupation. She never got around to doing anything remotely professional involving art, her major.

She has nothing much to show for those six years. She's fluent in Spanish but so's even the dumbest Spaniard. Big deal. Now she's thirty-four and she feels like she's wasted everything. She wasted time in Spain on American men for whom being in Spain meant no obligations. She wasted time on Spanish men for whom being with an American meant no obligations. She then wasted time in Boston on a married man for whom being married meant no obligations to the single woman he finally charmed into bed. That was the worst one. That went beyond wasting time and into something that felt close to ruining her life. She had finally moved into a real job as an arts administrator and then immediately screwed it up. She did something wrong, really wrong, in being with him, she can't get clean of the morality issue. She can't stop seeing his wife and child, the way he poked his head into her office one day and said, Hey you want to meet the two girls? The two girls were the wife and kid, she knew about them. What she didn't know about was the third girl, marinating for, oh, about eight months now, she guessed from the wife's protruding stomach. That's so funny, isn't it. Got that third girl ready to pop. Keeping the car running so he has an excuse to dash out to the hospital, the birthing room, to a place where she can't go.

Checking out the wife's tummy, she did a bit of calculation: his friendliness turned ardent about the same time when—well, she'd never been pregnant but she could figure when screwing might not be so fun. If she'd known about the car running . . . too late for that. That he really really really really loved her and wanted to stay but the car was running and the birthing room awaited. Too late. She couldn't stop loving him, too late for that. She simply added on hatred of him and they were fine side by side, Love and Hate, two overpowering emotions that nearly killed her, and don't forget Guilt, which made her wish they had. That's her current opinion of herself.

And so she's here. Now she's a Metal Shredder.

So now she knows what to do with her life.

Hurray.

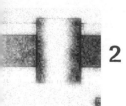

2

Joe Greenslade has arrived. He stands beside Marcus. Marcus tries to talk to him, but Greenslade just grins at whatever Marcus says. Old Joe's got it into his head he can't understand black people and so he never does. John hears Marcus say "How you doing, Joe?" but that's black talk for "How you doing, Joe?" and Greenslade shakes his head with an indulgent smile. Joe likes Marcus, just can't understand him is all.

"Now is there anything else I can do for you, anything at all?" Ada asks the Senior and when the Senior says no, have a good night, she departs in her picante strut, her hairpiece a dark saucer sliding loose from the hairpins. She manages to master the high heels up all the way to the gate in case the Senior is watching. He's not, but John is. Right before she turns out of sight, she breaks down into a limp, and John shakes his head at what she puts herself through for his father.

"Joe," the Senior acknowledges, adding a salute so he won't have to repeat himself.

The Metal Shredders

Joe Greenslade bows. He has slow, elaborate manners. He bows too deeply and grabs for Marcus's forearm.

"Come here, you idiot," Tony says. He pulls Greenslade away from Marcus. He pushes him toward the LTD. Greenslade is stranded without support and for a few moments his arms breaststroke the air. Then he catches himself. Balance has always been a problem with Greenslade, but today it seems worse. He's seventy-one years old, looks eighty, acts ninety, and John assumes that's because his health isn't so great. He's slow, and the density of his thought process makes him even slower.

John has arranged for the county nurse to come on-site to give flu shots to everyone; he hears this season's strain is a bad one, and he fears Greenslade is going to get it. If that happens, maybe Greenslade will bag it and quit like all the rest, and maybe like the others he won't even bother to tell them he's quit. He'll just stop coming. Despite his age, his slowness, his general uselessness, John needs him. His eyes still function, his fingers can still dial 911. His car out front lets people know someone is inside the gates keeping watch.

It might not seem like a big deal having a night watchman at all, but what most of the world doesn't know, including his own employees (except Ada), is that the Shredders at all times has at least forty thousand in cash on hand. It used to be one of Rory's jobs to go to the bank and make a deposit but the bank bag he carried was always extra-thickened with Monopoly money. He swung it in the air a bit to make sure everyone saw him. No one realized how much of the money was actually staying on-site.

"Hold it right there," Tony orders Greenslade. "Don't run away." Tony readies himself, buries his nose into his sweatshirt collar, runs to the LTD and pops the trunk. The odor is released like a malevolent genie. Everyone except Greenslade makes a dash to escape it. They're shooed farther and farther back until they're at the warehouse porch. Even the Senior, John notices with satisfaction, winces and withdraws.

Greenslade looks around with an agreeable smile on his face. The shrunken flannel shirt tucked into the baggy painter jeans accentuates his ladder in a barrel build. He's always at least slightly bent over, at the exact angle of a stepladder.

"Go on!" Tony shouts. He holds his breath, makes another run, and nudges Greenslade forward. Again Greenslade strokes the air to get his balance back. He steers himself back on course and suffers through his own dizzy inner-ear landmines until he's made it to the car. He smiles again.

"See I told you!" Tony screams excitedly. "His smeller's gone."

"I got vertigo is all," Greenslade says, leaning on the car.

A wave of nausea hits John. He wishes everyone would hurry up and leave so he could sit and figure this thing out. It still doesn't make sense to him, this odious task. Even as punishment to Tony, it's just too gross. Yet the Senior shows no signs of yielding. The only thing that might save them is Greenslade.

"S-s-something went on here," Greenslade stutters out, looking down into the trunk.

"There were a couple of bodies in there for a while," the Senior informs him. Greenslade cocks his head. "I SAY THERE WAS A CORPSE IN THERE, JOE."

Greenslade still can't hear but he grins appreciatively. He shuffles over to the group. Everyone waits quietly for him. They hear the sound of his boots scraping dirt. Marcus pulls on his jacket and fits on a black Pittsburgh Steelers cap and gives a wave so-long.

The Senior begins the story of the murder. Marcus, already backing away, hears the opener to the bloody tale and decides to return.

John steps up to the cement porch of the warehouse and pretends to check on something. He hates the story and he hates the way the Senior works his audience. He acts like such a good guy when he tells it. Sure, he can afford to be the good guy: he's the man in charge. John watches his father's studied version of the common touch, the way it sucks them in. They're believers; they think the Senior really likes them. Even Tony, who will never learn. He keeps trying and trying to get the Senior's affection and that makes him screw up everything in the Senior's presence, big things, little things, unimportant things that become important once he screws them up. Physically strong, with the inherent confidence this weapon gives him, Tony nonetheless melts into a little boy in front of the Senior. "Sorry for your loss," Tony finally managed at the funeral, mangling "loss" into "lose." The Senior, a centurion of impervious calm, bobbed in acknowledgment and dismissal.

The Senior's deep, well-modulated voice invites intimacy, commands it, and now here in the yard, surrounded by his employees, he uses his voice and purposeful bits of friendliness to further his own cause. It's these kinds of moments that aggravate John most; he doesn't like his father during such times. Maybe it's because on these occasions he sees his grandfather rising to the surface. What John relives is the manipulative way his grandfather passed out free turkeys, grocery certificates, Christmas presents of new workboots, the way he used gifts to keep people happily in their place. Secretly, John worries he does the same thing, in ways he doesn't yet recognize. It's hard not to think yourself superior when you work where he works with the people he works with.

The Senior's bold gray hair, the tan against the blue eyes, the devilish, charming Zorro smile when he decides to flash it—these things make his father shine as the focus of the group huddled around him. This year marks the year the Senior is old enough to get his Golden Buckeye Card. Not to worry—fifty-five is hardly old these days, and the Senior has lost none of his vigor or strength. Though Marcus at six-foot-four is the tallest man in the group, the Senior at a couple inches less still exerts that magical quality of always seeming to be the tallest. John knows how that optical illusion works. John is over six foot tall as well, but next to his father everyone mistakes him for five-nine. He's the same exact height as the Senior except a lot shorter.

John pauses as his father lays out the scene for Marcus and Greenslade and Tony. "A man and a woman are in over their heads," he tells them, his hands circling in the air, spreading the paints he'll need to color this story. "A couple from a small Ohio town, thinking they're really something. Imagine the setup. They're going to make a sale to big-time drug dealers. They're going to start doing business with these big shots, become big shots themselves."

"Mafia?" Greenslade asks.

"No way," Marcus says.

"What'd he say?" Greenslade asks.

"This couple pulls up to the farmhouse where they had agreed to meet, trying for the right image, both man and wife wearing sunglasses and black gloves. This is their moment. They're going to step up to the big time. Become the drug lords of their own little hamlet."

"What happened?" Tony asks, forgetting he's already heard this story.

"They walked right into a trap."

"Figured that," Marcus says.

John moves inside so he can't hear. He knows the rest. Stupid Man from Smalltown, Ohio, goes into the house with his briefcase of money and meets a man with an Uzi. Stupid Woman from Smalltown, Ohio, sits in the car, with sunglasses on, and is met by another man with an Uzi. Both of them shot a thousand or two thousand times.

In a dark corner of the warehouse John spies a slumped body. Given the story he's been hearing, he's momentarily startled. Closer, he makes out Don Capachi, curled over a stool. Asleep, he figures, but no, Don Capachi is just sitting there, staring at the sawdusted floor.

The Metal Shredders

"Don?" John calls to him. "Mr. Capachi?"

Don Capachi lifts his head. John reaches out his arm to help him stand. He sees the forehead scar from the bottle of Old Grand-Dad whiskey that went crashing across Don's temple nearly twenty-five years earlier on the day of the infamous human shredding. Some said it was because he tried to stop the man from killing himself; others said Capachi was coldcocked for no good reason other than it being the second to last stupid thing the man ever did. Don Capachi is the only one who really knows. Though probably John's grandfather knew, too. Probably Capachi told him.

"Everything all right?" John asks.

Don Capachi nods, not exactly in his direction. He slides toward his office corner where he has a desk and shelves, a cubicle wall, and a square of carpet remnant. It was an official stamp of appreciation given to him by John's grandfather. Don Capachi has been here from the very start, since before it was a shredders. When it was nothing more than a hubcap emporium. Don and his grandfather went way back. At one point, so the story goes, they were almost partners.

Don Capachi laboriously wipes his feet on the cement before stepping upon the carpet remnant that covers his office area. He moves over to the freestanding coatrack and unhooks his jacket. Although thrown over greasy cement, the carpet, through Don's proud efforts, has managed to remain somewhat clean.

Don Capachi is eighty-two years old and has become dispensable to the point of being a liability, but John knows his father will show him the same Bonner loyalty his grandfather showed. Don Capachi can do whatever he wants until the day he dies or decides to quit. Moving at the speed of an iceberg, he sorts their nonferrous metals into fifty-five-gallon drums. Tin, lead, zinc, yellow brass, red brass, cocks and faucets, copper. He approaches his barrels with a type of reverence. Anyone knows enough to remove the brass fittings from copper pipes, put the brass into the brass barrel and the copper into the copper barrel, but not everyone makes the effort to sort copper itself into No. 1 and No. 2 grades. They'll just throw electrolytic wire into the No. 1 drum and the copper tubing into the No. 2 drum and forget about it. But Don Capachi checks the No. 2 tubing: often there's a joint of No. 1 copper he can salvage. Of course, if it takes you a half hour to salvage it, you've lost about three dollars instead of gaining fifty cents.

John waves good-bye to Don Capachi but there's no point. Dragging his jacket, Don Capachi refuses to turn around. He scrapes away, curled over into a question mark, without a glance to any of them. John steps out onto the porch in time to hear Greenslade squawk like a bad clarinet as the Senior finishes his story about the shooting. Greenslade nearly knocks himself over with his own laughter. His squawking dries into a rasp. He leans exhausted against his knees.

"How long were they in there?" Marcus asks.

"About two weeks," the Senior says.

"Which is why it stinks so bad," Tony feels the need to explain.

Greenslade's head juts up. "It smells?" he asks.

John continues to watch Don Capachi. He diagnoses mournfulness in Don's eighty-something sluggishness. Two weeks after the funeral, he is still displaying the symptoms of immediate loss.

John remembers how in his last days his grandfather returned to work side by side with Don Capachi, sorting the nonferrous, saving thirty-five cents here, eighty cents there. No matter how rich his grandfather became, the sight of a wasted nickel could provoke a tantrum. When his grandfather first started the Shredders, he took in cars whole, milking them for every penny. Sometimes he fixed them up and resold them; sometimes he stripped them down to sell off the parts. Down to the hubcaps and tires and door handles.

The Metal Shredders

Nothing is outside the metal-shredding sphere, the Senior told John.

Nothing *used* to be outside the metal-shredding sphere, back when his grandfather rode the scrap cart and knocked on people's back doors. Now, like everything else, it's highly specialized. Which is why fixing up the LTD makes absolutely no sense. Which is why, finally, it begins to make some sense. Fixing up the LTD is the Senior's nod to the past, a posthumous Oscar to the man who started it all.

Of course the Senior could have saved all of them a lot of trouble if he'd just told the old man he appreciated him before he died. Now they're into symbol therapy, and the whole Metal Shredders has become the Senior's shrink. With all the different kinds of scrap, and all the ways to interpret scrap, cleansing the Senior's psyche could be endless.

John draws closer as his father finishes up to loud laughter. The purposeful friendliness and camaraderie he has displayed while providing storytime to his employees has worked its way to this final hurrah: "Okay, let's get to work on that car!"

Tony, the man in need of a father or at least a high school coach, twitches with an eager-to-please enthusiasm.

Then the Senior takes his leave. He tucks himself into his Trooper. He sticks his arm out the window and slaps the roof as a good-bye. Marcus, driving a rust-spotted cargo van, pulls out after him.

Tony drags out several bags of lime. He knifes them open, then goes off in search of something. Greenslade rummages around in the trunk of the LTD. He pulls out the jack. He gets the spare tire halfway out before giving up. Then he takes the hose to it and starts spraying.

A fountain of water shoots into the air. It takes John, watching from the office steps, a few seconds to perceive that the water spraying everywhere is a fountain of confetti. He reaches down and picks up one of the pieces of paper that has landed near his feet. Another moment passes before he registers that the confetti is a fifty-dollar bill. He's picked up a fifty-dollar bill. Okay, he can comprehend that. He knows what a fifty-dollar bill is. He scoots over to another piece of confetti: another fifty-dollar bill. Then a twenty. A twenty again. A fifty. A twenty.

The confetti comes raining down on him. He collects the pieces. Money. He finally gets it. Money. It's raining money. He notes the sum growing larger and larger in his hand, he sees the carpet of plenty-more-where-that-came-from spreading across the ground. So . . . Stupid Man from Smalltown, Ohio, only put some of the money in his briefcase. The rest was hidden in the trunk. How that was supposed to prevent what inevitably happened from happening to him belongs to the criminal small-brain department. But the upshot is this: a lot of money has landed at the Shredders in the arms of a welder, a night watchman, and himself. He doesn't grow excited or change expression. In fact, he mostly wishes it hadn't happened. He doesn't know why. But he tries to look at it this way: another event in the day.

Tony returns swinging a bucket. "Look at this," John says to him.

Octavia is still sitting up in the office. She's left Boston for this, well, not really Boston, one of those outlying places that are pretty depressing and still cost a fortune, but people here don't need to know that. Just say Boston. Close enough. She's left Boston for this. And it's perfect timing: to others it looks exactly like she's here to help out after Grandpa's death. She's sacrificing herself.

Serious second thoughts about joining the business, however, darkened into very serious third thoughts while she sat watching the scary movie that was her grandfather's funeral. In the middle of a—well, the service wasn't nice exactly but it was passable, it was at least turning into get-throughable—in the middle of the service these three ancient probably been dead for years probably mummies actually, metal shredders of course, who else could be so weird, get up from the pew and start shuffling toward her grandfather's casket. She's fooled (but she won't be again). She thinks they're going to go up and rasp out "Amazing Grace" or something, that they're too old and overcome to abide by the etiquette of a funeral service. All three of them have something in their hands, those little tuning pipes so they can get on key for their grief-stricken Irish dirge, but no (she finds out later), they're magnets. They keep tapping the coffin with their magnets until one of them lets out a victory whoop as if he's just raised the dead. Judging from the pushing and shoving at the buffet afterwards, it worked up everyone's appetite.

Lots of yelling. Not at the funeral but outside, down below in the yard. She's not going to look. Let them yell and yell and yell. She's not going to look.

And another thing. Everybody thinks it's so great Cousin Rory's going back to college at age twenty-five or twenty-six—as if she doesn't know what that means. It means he'll take one course per quarter and screw off the rest of the time, but people will still buy that he's working toward his Future. And if he ever, though she doubts it, pulls close to the finishing line, he can just change his major and begin again. She ought to know. She kept the Future out there for several years. Sometimes she'd get a little close but then she'd always pull back. Finally something hit her: the speed at which she was not moving toward her Future. She left Spain, came back, got a regular job in Boston. She finally sucked it up and got brave and stopped wasting time. She took the plunge. She allowed herself to meet her Future head-on and now she knows why people don't do that. Love, hatred, guilt. It's so much better just to have fun.

John bursts in the door and runs to the sink and begins scrubbing his hands.

"You guys are yelling," she says. "Is someone hurt?"

"No." He turns to face her. "This might be something you want to see. You're not going to believe this."

"Nobody's in pieces, are they?"

"Come on, you've got to see this."

"Is Dad gone?"

"Yeah."

So she gets up and goes outside. Her tennis shoes tamp against the metal steps. That useless night watchman is here. He's got mush for brains, he can't move, he's ancient, he tried to sit next to her at the funeral, and now he's directing an addled delight toward her. Stay away from me, she says, which is fine, it's not rude because he can't hear her. With his arthritic hands he delivers the thumbs-up sign. She doesn't smile back. Absolutely no encouragement for this guy. She's seen from the funeral the damage that old men can do if you give them a little bit of slack. She sits down on the steps. "What is it you wanted to show me, John?" she asks.

Then she sees it.

A mound of what appears to be dollar bills has been raked into a circle. She sees Tony sprinkling something on it.

"And this is just half of it!" Tony yells over to her. His foot kicks at the pile, mixing it up; then he sprinkles more stuff on it. Is he going to burn it? His hand waves Greenslade over. "You need to count this," he says. "Put it into four even piles." He looks over at her. "Right?"

She shrugs. "Don't look at me," she says.

"Three, I think," John tells Tony.

She shrugs again. They can do what they want. She's going home.

Tony squeezes by her and runs up the steps. John comes over to her and explains about the car disgorging money. The LTD, the one the county attorney gave them.

"Who does the money belong to?" she asks.

The Metal Shredders

"Us," Tony says, running back down the steps. "The people it belonged to are dead, and it wasn't their money anyway." He hands Greenslade three trash bags. "You need to start counting. You're not busy this evening, are you?"

Greenslade chokes on his silent laughter.

"Come on, don't be an idiot. Just count."

"You're keeping it?" she asks John. When he doesn't answer, she says, "You're kidding."

He shrugs.

"You can't keep it," she tells him. "John," she semi-pleads.

"If I can't keep it, they can't keep it. Greenslade makes minimum wage and he's got a family. Who am I to tell them they can't keep it? I'm not in charge of the money."

"You own the car. You're in charge of what's inside."

"You sound like Grandpa," John tells her.

"No I don't."

"Yes you do."

"At least I take baths."

"Now now, let's not speak ill of the dead."

"And who started this again?"

John comes over to sit with her so they can talk without being overheard. Tony is making a racket anyway. Now he's dressed himself back up in his rags, nostrils stuffed. Yanking on some gloves, he wades into the money with Greenslade and starts doling out the bills into three piles.

John says to her, "What is the county attorney going to do with the money if we return it? Just keep it for themselves. It's nowhere money. It doesn't matter where it goes. It might as well go to them."

"And you, too, I notice."

"It's too much noblesse oblige if I refuse."

"Oh, right."

"Hundred hundred hundred!" Tony shouts out. "Hundred hundred hundred! Fifty fifty fifty! Twenty twenty twenty! Twenty twenty twenty!"

"We get the picture," Octavia calls over.

"Just trying to be fair," Tony yells back.

Octavia's starting to feel suffocated. A feeling she's had before, a pair of existential hands at her throat. It pops up from time to time. She says, "You don't want to get involved with them."

"What do you mean?"

She shrugs.

"What do you mean, Otty?" he asks again.

"It's hard to explain." She stares at him to make sure the question is sincere, that he's not waiting to pounce on her.

"It's okay," he says. "You can tell me. I won't get offended."

"You don't want to share important secrets with guys like this. And I don't mean that in my I'm-being-like-Grandpa sort of way. Did I ever tell you about how I was robbed at a 7-Eleven?"

"No."

"I mean the 7-Eleven was robbed but I was there. And right before that, standing in line, I had this feeling like I shouldn't be here, and everybody else in line was like buying Colt 45s, it was dark out and cold and snowy and I just had this lousy feeling about the human race, and I had this picture of the world ending and me being stuck with these people in line as the only survivors. And then of course I instantly felt guilty for making a value judgment about people who buy Colt 45s—and by the way, why did I feel guilty? Because I am *not* like Grandpa, that's why. Or Mom, god forbid."

"I didn't mean it."

"But then we were robbed right at that moment, and a gun was pointed at my head and I saw it go off but it didn't and I still don't know if that part was real or . . . and then it all changed for me somehow with everyone showing their true colors—mine was yellow naturally, but a very high-class yellow. Anyway, that was it, I'm just not going to feel guilty for—you know—class distinctions. I'm not going to pretend they don't exist. And that . . ."

"I understand what you're saying." John gives her knee a pat.

"Okay. Well, thank you."

"Are you all right?"

"Yeah I'm fine."

"No nightmares or anything?"

"No!" Octavia scoffs.

"I know what you mean. Working here . . . believe me. You can't survive here as a boss without understanding all the class issues hurled around this yard like bricks through windows."

"John!" says Octavia.

"What?"

"A metaphor."

"Yeah. Anyway, it's never hey rainbow coalition, let's love our differences. The one thing that keeps us together is that we can all earn a living at this. It's about money. And that's where I keep the focus."

"Naturally. That doesn't make you a bad guy, John."

"Where there's money, there's exploitation."

"Or is it that based on certain things, people have a certain place. They might act like they want to be the boss, but they really don't. Or they couldn't."

Both John and Octavia turn to watch Tony and Greenslade at work on the three piles. John says, "That money over there I don't care about. Tony and Joe, they're not in a position not to care. So who am I to say you can't have that money? It's not really fair of me. Is it?"

"Your upper-middle-class guilt is not really the issue."

"I'm not feeling guilty," John tells her. "I don't have upper-middle-class guilt."

"Yes you do."

"No I don't."

"Yes you do. That's why you make such a big deal about being their buddy."

"I'm not their buddy and I don't try to be."

"Yes you do."

"No."

"I've seen you."

"Otty, look at those two, it's like the best thing that's ever happened to them. Now me, I'm feeling a whole lot less excited than they are. In fact, I wish it hadn't happened. So how is that making me one of them? If anything, it's making me *not* one of them."

"Semantics isn't going to get you out of this. You're slumming."

"The money means a lot more to them."

"And now you're slumming as Mother Theresa. Forget it, I can't win with you. And well, I'm sorry, I don't care about saving the world, because ninety percent of the world is full of crappy people."

"No gun at your head nightmares destroying your perspective?"

"I don't want to argue about it," Octavia says. "Maybe it's eighty-five percent of the people, but whatever, it's way too high."

"I got it divided," Tony shouts out, running toward fresh air and tugging off his rags.

"Did you get a count?"

"Have to do that later when the smell dies down. Maybe like five thousand each or something." Tony turns to Greenslade. "Or you can do that tonight up in your cubbyhole."

Greenslade leans back and coughs.

The Metal Shredders

Tony shout-speaks, "YOU CAN COUNT TONIGHT BEFORE YOU FALL ASLEEP."

Greenslade picks up one of the trash bags filled with money. He rears back and laughs as loud as his old dry throat will allow him.

"Do those sounds mean something?" Octavia asks.

"COME HERE," Tony says. He prods Greenslade's chest. "AND DON'T TELL ANYONE!"

Very deliberately Greenslade zippers a line across his lips.

"And I'm sure he's absolutely trustworthy," Octavia says. "Is this really a good idea?"

"Let's lock up," John tells her.

Octavia says, "I don't really want that bag of money upstairs in my office."

"All right," John says. He walks over and pats Greenslade on the shoulder. "Joe, let's put your money in your car. That way you won't forget it. We don't want a bunch of people, you know, seeing it. And it smells pretty bad. WE'LL PUT IT IN YOUR CAR. SMELLS TOO BAD."

"It smells?" Greenslade asks.

The four of them go to their cars. Tony and Greenslade put their bags in their trunks. Greenslade goes back inside the gate and John locks him in. Octavia points John to the watchful sign above the gate, John Bonner & Son Metal Shredders, where perched within the coiled lettering there appears to be a gargoyle staring down at them. "What would Grandpa say about all this?" she asks.

"He'd say, 'Why are you sharing it?'" He throws his own Hefty bag of money into the back of his pickup.

"Yeah, that was Grandpa all right," Octavia says.

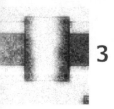

3

The garbage bag of money flaps in the wind the whole way back. John avoids the highway and keeps to the back roads in case it flies out. It's two miles to the nearest small town, Jefferson, one of those depressing time-warp repositories of money-worried, all-white, down-and-out family values.

He creeps in second gear through Jefferson. The town is four blocks long with a streetlight at every corner. He notices what looks like Marcus's cargo van parked in front of Tail Lights Tavern, but he doubts it's the same van, not in this all-white town, not with their sort of fundamentalist patriotism, and not with the Confederate flag decal he now spies winking in the windshield's shadows.

Ten more miles to Columbus and a reentry into the present day.

Money.

Money from dead people that smells like dead people.

What to do about the money.

The Metal Shredders

He'll blow it. He'll do his usual, he already knows it. Nothing. The same thing he did when Elise left. Things weren't bad between them, not exactly passionate, just in a lull, that's all. He doesn't understand why she had to leave just because things were treading water. Elise wanted it *bad* or she wanted it *good*. Bad she could handle—it could give her a focus, rungs to climb on a ladder of improvement. Bad was not such a bad thing when you actually thought about it (Elise's opinion). Great poetry came out of bad, after all. But a lull. A lull was nothingness, it was the void (also Elise's opinion). Lull she couldn't handle. Middling stuff came out of a lull and she didn't want to be a middling person caught in a middling marriage. This was the sort of vague, cloudy stuff surrounding her leaving. He keeps waiting for the fog to lift in the same mysterious way it descended and for her to return. Yes, that's it, he's in a lull, waiting for her to return. In the meantime he does nothing—which is the same thing she left him for.

Easier to think about the money.

At home he finds a flagstone rock and throws it on top of the Hefty to keep it weighted down. He doesn't bother to bring the money inside for the obvious reason, although it is somewhat amusing to think of the black garbage bag as another piece of what passes for decor in his living room. A stuffed black Hefty—it could pass as one of those beanbag easy chairs. God knows he could use some more furniture. If furniture is all he needs, all he has to do is drive to Grandview and he'll find a suite of it and it all matches like suites should and he never wants to see any of it again.

He used to live in Grandview. He and Elise bought a house there. The neighborhood had become a bragfest of trendy restaurants and shops; coffee roaster, sushi bar in the Big Bear grocery; places to find natural elixirs or video-game collectibles or an American acupuncturist who studied in China or a masseuse who would like to study in China et cetera et cetera, not to mention a post office where John and Jenny got him in and out in under sixty seconds no matter what kind of postal difficulty he threw at them. He wishes John and Jenny would come to work for him at the Shredders.

He used to love the neighborhood until Elise left and then he couldn't stand it. He rented out their house, furnished, to a visiting professor and moved back across the Olentangy River and into an apartment clearly intended as OSU student housing. For the moment (only a moment, he thinks), he lives on the second floor of a house off Neil Avenue, the old Professor's Row, the big Victorians now balkanized into tons of semi-liveable units. His second floor dips in the middle as though it once got soggy and reshaped. The wood of the floor is painted a dark brown. He kept the couch that was left behind despite the beer and sperm that had probably soaked into it. He has one kitchen chair from his parents' garage; a telephone-coil table ditched on the street by departing students; and a futon, new, that he bought at Norka around the corner. The people he sees walking the neighborhood all have backpacks slung over their shoulders. Most of them probably have places just like his, decorated with found objects and garage-sale wobblies, although their sparse designs result from financial necessity rather than whittled-down horizons. What always surprises him is how old so many of the students look—graduate students, he surmises—as old or older than him. Many of them are foreign, Asian and Middle Eastern, with worn, tired skin.

Nights and weekends he walks the neighborhood, eats at the over-priced vegetarian restaurant, the underpriced Mexican place with its out-door patio (a favorite of students), drinks espresso at one coffee shop and then house-blend at the next. It's where he wants to be at the moment. Though the students look old to him, he's starting to feel young again. He's only thirty, after all, yet he feels as though he turned thirty-five many years ago, on the day he graduated from college and started work at the Shredders. He married soon after. More than sometimes he regrets what happened to his twenties. His life and career were so settled, his life with Elise, his career at the Shredders. The settledness had become another kind of fog obscuring any future. (He should have admitted to her his own frustration about being middling; instead, he tried to look on the bright side, to stay strong and positive. It ended up middling strong, middling positive, which simply added to the problem. "How bad can sex be if we both have orgasms?" he had asked her. "A lot of people don't have them—they're totally dysfunctional." "Let's be dysfunctional," she said. "At least we'd know we had a problem.")

Now he walks the streets with a bleak, exhilarating freedom. He's young enough to enjoy his own suffering, and sometimes he does.

Tonight he showers quickly and goes out to the Mexican place. Enrique's. It's painted banana-yellow with citrus-green trim and orange doors. Next door is a shoe repair, though at first glance it looks to be a pet shop so many are the geckos and lizards and iguanas that lounge at the window. On the other side is La Rouge, a topless place. The women—a bit ravaged-looking, he's wondering about AIDS—do a tired dance in the window. As he strolls by, they manage to get off their stools, but he's already past.

He could give the money to them. They might not even notice the smell.

Enrique's doesn't quite have a menu—they do have one but it's not representational. They're always out of the special by the time John gets there. They know him well enough that they just give him what they decide to give him. He drinks one beer quickly and doesn't need to order the other—it's there, put down on the table by the girl about twenty with checkerboard black 'n' blond hair and henna tattoos. Amy, her name is. She comes and goes from the restaurant, quits in a fit, comes back a week later, leaves for Texas with a boyfriend, comes back two weeks later. She's on Prozac and then Zoloft and then Mellaril, and sometimes she thinks she's going crazy and sometimes John's afraid she might be right. All this he knows from the time it takes her to set his table, get down on her knees, and take his order. She gets as much in as possible, then relays more information another night.

John knows he's inherited a watered-down version of his father's conventional good looks. He assumes his safe handsomeness has something to do with the ease of Amy's confessions to him. Whenever he sees movie stars and their less handsome sons, he thinks of himself. He's like Michael Douglas, good enough on his own, but put him next to Kirk Douglas and suddenly Michael is beginning to look like an older woman beginning to look like a man. John wouldn't go that far about himself, but he, too, is a little soft around the jawline. There's something there a little pampered, a little second- or third-generation diluted. Yeah he works out, but his muscles are coddled muscles, they haven't been forged on the street. Elise always told him he was good-looking, but it didn't stop his displeasure when he looked in the mirror and saw a fraudulent image of his father. He was good-looking but not *as* good-looking. Like every other comparison with the Senior, just put the words *not as* before the adjective. Good adjectives, bad adjectives. At least the Senior makes his mark in never an average way.

Amy sets down tonight's meal: a burrito, stuffing unknown, and black beans and rice. She kneels down, her chin resting on his table. "Guess what?" she says. Her smile beaming up to him is too wide, too crazed around the edges. "We're back together and I know it's right this time." He can smell Amy's clothes. His nose is hyperactive and paranoid today. Clearly she buys her rayon ribbed shirts from the secondhand places all around and they look vintage hippie and smell of an attic. He can tell she's poor. He makes sure to be a good tipper. Not to ingratiate himself, but because somebody has to be, with all these students eating here.

"I hope it works out," he says.

The Metal Shredders

"We're very happy and I see the road . . . far down the road, you know? Pray for us to always stay this happy."

"Okay, Amy. I will."

"Does that sound insensitive? I know you're divorced."

"It's not insensitive. I want you to be happy."

She squeezes his arm before leaving. He has to admire the limber way she can get up from her knees like Gumby, not a grunt or even a sigh. He's midway through his second beer and he's feeling relaxed. He's sitting outside—*everybody*'s sitting outside, grabbing at the last days of warmth. He wonders if he might see Octavia. He wonders if she strolls. She must—that's what they do in Europe. She moved into the same neighborhood, though on the other side of High Street and far enough south that she doesn't get much of the student population.

It's getting dark now. The tiki lights on the patio are lit.

"This place is totally packed." He hears the voice, it's directed at him, he knows exactly who it belongs to. A pause before John can bring himself to look up. The voice belongs to his downstairs neighbor. Farewell to his peaceful solitude. A pause before he can face this person again, a pause in which he kicks himself for not getting in his truck and driving out of the neighborhood to find somewhere else to eat. Kevin the Neighbor has become one of life's little nuisances writ large.

"Hey," he says lightly to Kevin. Kevin's fingers are poised piano-ready on the table surface. Though they share a yard and park side by side and sort their mixed-up mail, until recently they've had no occasion to converse. Until recently Kevin was a bankerish-looking physicist who simply blinked at him with a nerd's social zero-ness. The only time Kevin bothered to speak to him during those (halcyon) days was to tell him to take off his metal-shredder boots before walking up or down the stairs. It might have been a reasonable request except for the fact that the walls had begun to shake in the middle of the night, two to four A.M. being Kevin's tantrum time.

Kevin says, "I'll go find a chair."

John knows that part of disliking Kevin has to do with disliking himself. Full-steam laterally ahead, that's he and Kevin, two unoriginals who get to feel overly good about themselves, one because he's getting his Ph.D., the other because he gets to pull up to the owner's parking bumper at the gates of John Bonner & Son Metal Shredders (if there were an owner's parking bumper, which there isn't—think of all the winter piss that would ice over that little monument of greatness). His own name, the owner's name, up there in wrought-iron lights. But he hasn't done one original thing to make it happen. His grandfather: eccentric and distasteful. But at least Original. The old man went to his grave hoarding the secret of all pioneers: that it happens only once. The others are just inheritors with egos yearning to make something of their own happen. Which explains the Senior and his white-goods idea, his own stab at originality and his own yearning ego.

Kevin drags back a chair from inside. He waves above the crowd, beckoning in a mighty pantomime for a beer. John experiences some satisfaction that Kevin has to cadge for his drinks. And he probably gets charged for them all, too. Amy sets down a beer for Kevin and a third one for John for whenever he's ready. John knows he won't be charged for that one. Amy drops to her knees again. The smile has left her face.

"I called him," she said.

"Don't do that. Don't make yourself unhappy."

"He wasn't there."

"Amy."

"I can't help it," she says. Her face rests upon his hand as if kissing the papal ring.

"Maybe he's on his way here."

The Metal Shredders

Amy grabs his arm in a hopeful fervor. Mood change. He doesn't like the way she's sweating. The perspiration on her face looks too chemically induced.

"I didn't say he *was*," he feels the need to caution. "He's probably at the grocery store."

"No, you're right," Amy says breathlessly. Now she gently clasps his head and kisses his hair as if *she's* the pope, and then departs.

Kevin has barely registered Amy's presence. His head lowers into the beer and he whines about breaking up with his wife, Cecilia. He doesn't mind losing the specific Cecilia so much (what a loyal guy, John thinks), but he's got to have a girl who looks like Cecilia and there's not many of those. He's got physical requirements they have to meet. And they have to have a graduate degree.

John tries not to hear but some of it seeps through and he's left wondering about himself. Does he have physical requirements for his women? He has tastes, he has preferences. He'd hate to think of them as requirements. He married too young to find out much about himself. Everything was so easy at college. Everybody young and good-looking and just like yourself.

Elise was a petite brunette. He guesses that would be his type if he had to name it. It must be—his gaze lingers on every specimen that fulfills her physical profile. Over the weeks her figure has morphed into perfection by all the offerings he slows down to jog behind (he hopes Elise has been working out in Telluride after what he's been seeing on his runs). The petite ones usually run in sports bras. He's never noticed so many great abs on women before. They greet him when he passes (he doesn't linger too long; it's hard to keep your streamlined form with an erection). There are three or four who have reached a state of nearly unreal physical honing and it depends on which one he sees first that determines who he wants most. He now encounters them at Goodale Park on a regular basis. He wonders if their running schedules are accidentally the same, runners tending toward anal after all, or if they're doing the jogging version of dating. He's almost ready to find out. Ready, but not quite. But before the bad weather sets in, for sure. He's made a promise to himself to stop doing nothing and get back into the action that he was never really into in the first place.

He hears Kevin call too loudly for another round. That means he'll be stuck here for another twenty minutes at least, long enough to hear the Cecilia story repeated. He cares nothing for Kevin's distress. It's awful to admit, but it's true. He just doesn't care. He wants the marriage to be saved only because he wants to stop hearing about it. He wants to stop having to talk to Kevin, and he knows that once Kevin is back in a contented relationship, his neighbor will never think to be friendly to him again. Or speak to him again—that's the best part.

Kevin is just one other reason why John keeps his troubles with Elise to himself. Kevin is just one other reason why John wishes for everyone in the world to be really really happy. Happy people don't come bothering you with their troubles. Happy people don't make you dread seeing them. It's true that John is afraid of his own current unhappiness. But what he's afraid of more is bothering someone else with it. He's afraid of being someone people dread to see coming. Elise has sprung to colorful life inside him, but to everyone else she's gone and forgotten—and at least his reluctance to burden others is something to be proud of.

If it would make Kevin happy, he'd give him all the money under that flagstone rock in the back of his pickup. How much money is there, two or three or five or six thousand? Two or three thousand, he'd like to tell him. Two or three thousand, Kevin, *just to shut up.*

4

Next morning John clears the beer from his head by jogging all the way up to Grandview. He stops in at Caribou. Chalked on the board next to the list of coffee blends is the Question of the Day. You get a dime off your coffee for answering it correctly. Invariably the question is either about Great Works of Literature or the Brady Bunch, which tells John whether Brenda or Kyle is working that day.

If feels good to be back in his old neighborhood where things are scrubbed up and clean. Maybe he's starting to come around. He hasn't thought about Elise until this exact moment, and now this moment is already past and he's not thinking about her. So everything's great. He drinks his Guatemalan Antigua, jogs back, takes a shower, goes down the steps quietly (Kevin was throwing a phone fit at three A.M. so probably no threat of a morning greeting) and makes it into the Shredders a couple of hours overdue. It's the first time he's been late in centuries. It's something he's never dared to do, but now that he's done it, it feels good. And it was so easy. He wonders why he didn't do it before, when Rory and his grandfather were still there, and the Senior, too, before the Senior got distracted with his white-goods project. He could have taken whole days off and nothing would have changed, the place would have gone on running as smoothly as before. Instead of his grandfather, he could have been the one who died. As far as the business of the Shredders, it wouldn't have mattered.

Not so with the current configuration. The family members running the daily operations are down to two, and only one of them knows what to do. There's a bottleneck at the scales when he arrives, the independent scrappers waiting to be weighed and paid out. John is feeling a strange displacement. An axis has shifted. This world isn't his.

An auto flattener with sixteen cars is moving into position for Dooley to mag and stack them. That means somebody has already paid him out. Panicked, he checks the weighmaster's station to see if it's the Senior. It's not. Octavia and Tony are inside. Which further means that Tony, playing corporate leader, is the one who took charge. Checking over what he's done, he sees that Tony has weighed the autos gross, tear, and net, just like you're supposed to, and named the price he'd heard John quote again and again to these guys. With the auto flattener, it's easy—both sides expect seventy dollars per car. Yet John pretends annoyance at the fact that Tony has overstepped his authority.

"I told him he could do it," Octavia tells John. "I didn't think it was a big deal."

Ada gets on the mic, speaks to them through the thick glass. "I haven't paid a soul yet." The weighmaster's cage is her domain, the kachina dolls, the skeet-shooting trophies, the framed certificates and photos on the wall, the shelf of crackers and teas and shortbread, the oversized teacup that announces IF ASSHOLES COULD FLY, THIS PLACE WOULD BE AN AIRPORT.

"Go ahead and pay them out," John tells Ada. Really, it's fine with him, he's thankful actually, but he plays out his annoyance. Tony shouldn't have done it. For his own sake. The Senior would ream him if he found out. And it still might happen: there's no telling what tale Ada might tattle. Her first loyalty is to the Senior, though in the way she constantly chides Tony there lies a deep, hidden affection. In a funny sort of coincidence, Ada used to be Tony's school-bus driver. Tony got suspended in the seventh grade for throwing a can of Pepsi at her head. "An empty can," he reminds her nearly every day.

Octavia doesn't demand where John has been. She doesn't appear to think it's anything out of the ordinary to be two hours late. If anything, he tells himself, it was a good thing because she was forced to learn some new skills.

He needs to be late about once a week so Octavia will think that's his normal schedule. Already he's thinking—and he knows he shouldn't go there—but already he's thinking Tony could act as weighmaster. As long as he knew ahead of time the Senior wasn't going to show up. Tony doesn't have much to do anyway, just repair scams and cracks in the building structures and sometimes the machinery casings. He's used his spare time well. He's mastered the whole operation. He pays attention. He's curious. He knows computers. That should count for something.

But he's not part of the family, and that counts for everything.

John finishes up the weighing. The Welbargers are here with some old fenders and a few radiators John hopes aren't filled with wet sand, a tiresome scam to drive up weight. He doesn't want to get into it with them today. Both Father and Son Welbarger have their eyes on Otty. They track her as she climbs back up to her little house. She's got the Senior's height and Mother's aristocratic bone structure. They're going to start asking questions about her, he's sure, rude questions that will turn polite when they find out she's his sister. He's glad when Worm saunters out and starts up a conversation with them.

Tony continues to hang out in the weighmaster's station. Ada studies him with dramatic suspicion from her glassed-in cage. Above the coin well, she's pasted on her latest bumper sticker: I HAVE A GUN—AND PMS.

Tony lifts up the microphone, says, "Pepsi anyone?" then ceremoniously clicks it off. *Bye-bye,* he waves to Ada. He turns to John. "Whadja do with the money?" he asks softly.

"I got it," John tells him.

"Did you count it?"

"Not yet."

"Me neither." Tony sends a syrupy smile to Ada and mockingly cups his ear. "I'm surprised you weren't here this morning to make sure Greenjeans didn't bust a gut telling everyone."

"What can I possibly do about that?"

"You could do what I did. I got here early and sent him home before anyone else showed up."

"Good for you, Tony. That shows a lot of initiative."

"Maybe saved our butts."

"Maybe."

"So now whatta we do?" Tony asks.

"I don't know."

"Whattaya mean you don't know?"

"I don't know. That's what I mean. I don't know. What do you want to do?"

"Wait till the smell dies down. Then . . . Spend it."

"Sounds like a plan," John agrees.

"The only trouble is Greenjeans."

John says, "Suppose he tells some people? So what? What are they going to do?"

"I don't know," Tony says.

"I'm not going to worry about it," John says. "Why should I worry about it? Are you worried?"

"No," Tony says with a worried look.

"You're worried."

"Okay, I'm worried."

"Why are you worried?"

"I just am. There are plenty reasons to be worried."

"Name me one or two. Maybe I'm wrong not to be worried."

"Suppose they say the money's not ours?"

"Who's they?"

"The police."

"You mean the county attorney's office?" John asks.

"Yeah."

"Okay, the county attorney's office gave us the car so, well, on that account they probably would say that. Maybe it's a legal issue, but it's not a crime. It's not like they'd charge us with a crime. What have we done?"

"So what if Greenjeans runs his big mouth?"

"Who's he gonna tell? Think about his . . . capacity. I mean, Tony, we hit bottom when we hired him. Except for the guy before him, those orgies, and the guy before that."

"Who?"

"Remember the alien sightings? He camcorded them for us."

"Oh shit, yeah. I liked him. Forget his name."

"Too bad he got abducted, but at least they let him use the phone to tell us he couldn't come to work because he was on another planet."

"No shit," Tony says.

"Yeah."

"No shit." Tony laughs. "Yeah, I liked that guy."

"Lookit. Anyway, Joe doesn't know enough to call the county attorney. Maybe he'll blab to his friends, but exactly who are his friends? I've got to believe they're not the smartest folks on earth. Even assuming they believe him they won't know enough to call the county attorney either.

At most all they're gonna do is say 'Hey give me some of that money, too,' and if Joe wants to agree to that, then let him. See what I'm saying? It doesn't really matter who knows as long as the county attorney doesn't know. And even if they know, I doubt that they'd care."

"Who's they?"

"They—the county attorney, they."

"You don't think the county attorney cares?"

John starts to explain again, then thinks better of it. "Not that much," he says.

Tony says, "What if people get mad because we're not sharing and they call the police for spite? Just plain ole maliciousness. It's been known to happen."

"Like who?" John asks.

"Like . . . Miguel and his Mexican pals. Those Cambodian guys."

"Just think about that for a minute," John instructs.

After a few moments of thought, Tony says, "Okay, the Cambodians don't speak English."

"That's one reason," John says.

A few more moments.

John gives him a hint: "They wouldn't want to go to the county attorney, which is a branch of law enforcement, not the same as but similar to another branch of law enforcement know as the INS."

"Yeah okay," Tony says. "But their foreman ain't no illegal. He goes back to the fucking redneck *Mayflower*. And he's a goddam asshole, too. I hate that fucker."

"No really," John says, "tell me what you really think."

"He'd fucking love calling the police."

"Look," John tries to assure him. "If Sherry finds out about it and starts playing some game, then I'm just going to split the money with him and that'll be that."

"Your share of the money, you mean."

"Right. My share of the money."

"You're going to split with that asshole."

"I don't think it will happen."

"I'm keeping my share."

"You're keeping your share."

Tony nods. The worried look doesn't leave his face. Ada's face is pressed against the glass. Tony slams his fist where her nose is. He picks up the microphone, turns it on, and tries on an executive voice: "So that's why we gotta fire Ada. We can't have her giving the Mexicans blow jobs in front of the Cambodians. They're gonna sue us for sex discrimination."

Ada picks up her own mic. It's that kind soldered to its own stand, the kind air traffic controllers use in the movies. She clicks it on to say something back, but when the hefty penile cylinder is up there near her mouth, she and Tony crack up. "Wrong guy," Tony calls over. "That's Marcus." Ada dissolves into hysterics.

"Oh shit," John says. "I forgot about the car. We just left it there last night. Did Joe clean it up at all?"

"No. He slept all night with his goddam radio." Tony starts pacing. "Hey, if you want me to beg I will. Just don't ask me to spend another day on car detail. I can't go near it."

John unlocks the weighmaster's station and heads toward his grandfather's and father's offices. A fish tank built into the adjoining wall allows the offices to view each other. Since they have no doors or windows to the outside, the rooms can risk expensive decoration. No dust and metal spikings collect.

He steps inside his grandfather's office. Plaques of appreciation line the walls. Photos of him shaking President Nixon's hand, Woody Hayes's hand, some Miss Ohio's hand (unbelievably, he was a judge one year). In the coin well of his desk drawer John finds his grandfather's magnet key-chain: WE SCRAP FOR A LIVING it says.

The office is supposed to be John's now. He hasn't begun to use it yet. He still does some of his work up there with Octavia, in the little house on stilts where he's most comfortable. The rest of the time he wanders.

He goes over to the fish tank and peeks through to his father's office. His grandfather had a thing about fish tanks and see-through walls. One time his mother went off to a holistic spa in Arizona for three days and then met the Senior in Sedona for another three, and when they came home the old man had knocked down the wall between living room and dining room and replaced it with a gigantic ant farm. If only John's mother had understood the strong philosophical pull of a metal shredder, the compulsion to keep working through the Möbius verity of *Reduce, Reuse, Recycle*, she would have never left him alone in her house.

Through the fish tank he sees the wavering cherry wood desk (oxygen bubbles seeming to dance upon it), and on the wall, looking like a coat of arms, two antique golf clubs X-ed over each other. It's not an ostentatious office, it's just a very very careful office. There's nothing in it that hasn't been chosen after much consideration. The desk is a functional work of art, hand-crafted by the Amish. The Senior hardly uses his office anymore, what with his new white-goods enterprise.

The neon tetra mistake his nose for fish food and spear the tank glass. Suddenly he remembers something and goes back to his station. He taps on Ada's glass, turns on the mic. "Who's taking care of the fish?" he asks.

Ada smiles proudly.

"Thanks," he says.

She curtsies.

"Find some boxes," John tells Tony. "I'll make a deal with you. You clean out this office—don't just throw the stuff in, label the boxes, somebody's gonna want these photos and crap—and I'll take care of the car."

The Metal Shredders

"What about your dad?"

"Deal or not?"

"I'm on my way," Tony says.

John walks outside to the shredding zone. Dooley is working the crane, finishing up with the auto flattener. John waits until he stacks the last car in the mountain of vehicles awaiting shredding. Dooley climbs out of the Linkbelt. He's an out-of-shape circus strong man, about the Senior's age, but working on a different set of actuarial tables. His big belly of mashed potatoes and gravy and plenty of beer keeps his face strained and red. On more than one summer day John has waited for his heart attack.

John walks over to intercept him. Dooley's eyes are heavy-lidded and because of this he always looks half-asleep and half-menacing. His hooded gaze meets John's. His eyes are empty of clues. Friend or foe: John doesn't know with Dooley.

John points to the LTD sitting alone in the far corner.

"Shred it," he tells Dooley.

The shredder's thirty-four magnesium teeth each weigh 255 pounds. Each tooth hits its target 950 times a minute. What was once a car emerges in mangled droppings and then bobs along the assembly line.

The shredded pieces enter a tower, the air-control system, where the wet scrubber washes it all down and kills the dust and keeps it from sparking into an explosion. A carcinogen, sodium azide, has already been released into the air when the unspent air bag met the shredder teeth.

The wet scrubber forks into two conveyor belts with a magnet making the decision. It pulls the ferrous toward one conveyor belt, with the non-ferrous and trash defaulting to the other. On the ferrous belt, what was once a door and bumper and hood head toward a drop-off chute and bobsled into a bin. The twisted balls of slag, their car colors annealed by shredder friction, are often beautiful. The Senior gives the best away as paperweights.

There's a more interesting ride on the second conveyor belt. The non-magnetic metals as well as the fluff—foam, rubber, plastic, glass—enter a big funnel called the Stafford Slide. The Stafford Slide uses coefficients of friction to separate the metals from the nonmetals. It operates according to the same principle as funnel banks. Kids drop their nickels and dimes and pennies and watch the coins go round and round in descending circles until they finally drop into the hole. A penny will circle slower than a dime or nickel. A penny has copper in it, and copper has a higher coefficient of friction than silver.

The metals that were once part of the LTD shoot along the walls of the Stafford Slide and spew out a side exit. The trash drops straight down into the hole and into a discard bin. Foam, for example, can't slide along the walls. Its coefficient of friction is so high it can't pick up enough speed. Although the Stafford Slide does nothing but sit inertly, passively offering up its funneled shape to the laws of physics, it appears to be a complex motorized engine, mechanically spitting out fluff as prettily as icing rosettes from a cake decorator's tube.

The metals orbit through a side exit of the Stafford Slide and continue along the conveyor belt. Their journey ends in a lean-to where there sits a sorter, in this case Worm, who culls out any trash that piggybacked along. The inspected metals dead-end into another bin. Don Capachi will take these metals and sort them further into his barrels.

So there it is. The LTD is now a little ferrous, a little nonferrous, a little fluff.

A little cancer-causing sodium azide and it's done.

Odor taken care of.

Problem solved.

5

So you turn out like your parents, everyone knows that. But Octavia has this other theory, that in your twenties and early thirties you're given a respite. You get to fool yourself that you're somebody different. It's a way to store up energy to get you through the rest of your life when the bad news hits and you turn into the person you would most hate to become: Mom or Dad. Sometimes both.

Octavia's respite is about over. There's a change coming over her and she knows it's not good: she's about to turn into one of her parents. At thirty-four, she is convinced she's on the cusp of DNA backstabbing. It's inevitable—why fight it. Why not make a choice right now, pick the mom or pick the dad, take the lesser of two evils and surrender to a compromise. She begins a list of her parents' good and bad qualities. She's up in her miniature house on stilts, head down, ignoring the Panavision of scrap metal. She's trying not to hear, trying not to feel the Dolby Surround sound of machine whine and metal agony.

Mom—bad	Dad—bad
snob	pretends not to be a snob
food obsession	money obsession
money obsession	likes to pretend he golfs
superficial	too philosophical
doesn't listen	thinks he knows everything
likes jewelry	likes scrap metal
wears dresses	too much OSU clothing
doesn't like her own friends	doesn't have any real friends
talks too much or	talks too much or
doesn't talk at all	doesn't talk at all

Mom—good	Dad—good
keeps in shape	keeps in shape

The future looks bleak.

But it's not all navel-gazing at her desk. She has spent some quality time trying to get this business straight. It's hard. It remains for good reason a big pile of junk to her. She can't get into it. It's not at all like sinking your teeth into a foreign language. That's Language, after all; it matters. This is scrap. Prepared steel versus alloyed steel—why? Who cares?

It's unhealthy knowledge. It's too much to learn. She can't do it.

Dean's List at Wellesley, she reminds herself. Honor roll, Log of Distinction, whatever, she got it automatically, never gave it a second thought or even learned what it was called—good grades, she was a good-grade machine, she spat them out like a shredder on autopilot. *A* after shiny *A*. What's a ductile pipe compared to that?

The Metal Shredders

John springs up the stairs to his old office. The little house on stilts. It's been his for so long, his own private observatory rising above the scrap like the guard tower some of his employees are used to seeing from their days in stir. He doesn't know if he can really give it up. He can't see how he'll ever get used to being down there in his grandfather's office, the only window a window into a phony blue sea where the fish he doesn't care about are certain to die.

Inside his house—*his house*—Octavia is presumably hard at work. Well, at least she's inside. First things first. Before turning the knob he pauses at the landing and gazes out. The Shredders' farmland of metal has fallen over the land like a nuclear winter, conquered into furrows of the baled, the sheared, the awaiting. Over here the stubbles of slag, tailings, and glass cullet. Over there the fallow bogs of wet scrubber discards: rubber, cork, plastic, and foam.

Beyond the gates is real countryside where things actually grow, real earth, enriched manured soil, flat cornfields now turning late-September crisp, fields of alfalfa, crops of soybean. Between all the fertilized growth sprout wild patches of bromegrass and burdock.

Over the high gates of the scrap yard John spots a bicyclist dawdling along the poorly paved road, backgrounded by the rusty wave of corn stalks. His mountain bike is saddled with front and rear panniers. Rising up like a seat back are the rolls of tent and sleeping bag and ground pad. A child pull-cart wheels along behind.

John Bonner watches as two thousand dollars' worth of Cannondale metal makes a slow turn into the Shredders. A big black Lab springs out of the child pull-cart.

Intrigued, John heads back down the steps. He finds the young man outside the gates, sitting in the dirt, patting his dog's head. He wears a kerchief pirate-style over close-cropped hair that's darkly bearding the nape of his neck. His shiny Lab, big and calm, is necklaced with a red bandana. John can see that the kid is older than he first thought. Graduate school–age maybe. Not from around here. Has a rich look to him despite the grime.

John thinks, Doing one of those backpacking-through-Europe deals except on a bicycle and except in the United States. That's his take, not that it's bad or good. He looks the guy over. He both envies him and doesn't. The bicyclist is taking full advantage of a lull in life's march to do something interesting. So that's good. So maybe it's the lull that John both envies and doesn't envy.

"Morning," John says.

"Is it, still?" the kid says, a bit too laconically for John's taste.

The sweaty kerchief wrapped around the bicyclist's head has some kind of map design on it. John can make out little green pine trees and brown heart-chart lines that must mean a mountain range. He sees a word: *Escalante.*

The bicyclist says, "I backtracked five miles to sell my meal ticket for the day."

"What's that?" John asks.

The bicyclist hoists a big, stiff lasso that's been looped over the child's cart. John recognizes it immediately: it's railroad transmission wire a.k.a. green wire. It's No. 1 copper, which goes by the code word *Barley,* and Barley's selling for ninety-nine cents per pound. They're buying it for ninety-six. Green wire is the heaviest, purest copper there is—often stolen because of this. And because of *that,* none of the John Bonners will buy it. The Welbargers have had to learn this lesson the hard way.

"So where you headed?" John asks.

"Connecticut."

"Parents or . . . ?"

"Yeah. Been pedaling my way across country."

"You're a pedaler," John says without thinking. The sound of the word hits him—*pedaler,* so much like *peddler.* Junk peddler. The way his grandfather started out, on a horse and cart. He peddled his way. He was a peddler, too.

Pretending to check its weight, John lifts the lasso, his eyes glancing at the wire ends, hoping not to find their edges sharp and clean—the indication of newly cut, newly stolen wire. He doesn't want this pedaler to fall in his eyes.

But the ends are worn; the wire's been on the ground for a while. Good. An honest guy. A laconic, honest guy. With his black Lab. Together they walk through the Shredder gates toward the weighmaster station.

John shouldn't, it's against policy. He feels his grandfather looming over his shoulder. He feels his father, too, the one who announced the policy. And he knows exactly what his father would do. The Senior would send this fellow on his way, a nasty warning boxing his ears. Wouldn't care about the two-thousand-dollar bike, wouldn't notice the upper-class upbringing in the choice of bandana and stylish ghetto way he's wigged it over his head. Wouldn't think, *He's not like the others, maybe I should cut the guy a break.* The Senior isn't like that. He doesn't exist to notice or please other people. Other people exist to notice or please him.

Maybe that's exactly the difference between John and his father. If his father were a state, he would be Alaska—big, bountiful, pioneering Alaska. Gorgeous, dangerous, mysterious, and cold as hell Alaska. And if John were a state he could remain standing right where he is because he'd be Ohio—cloudy, vague, remaindered by the East Coast, hicksville Ohio. Nothing to do, the heart of it all friendly Ohio, trying too hard to be liked by the other states. Not there for itself, it's there to please the others. And the result? No personality Ohio.

John says, "I'd say about fifteen pounds." He doesn't bother to throw it on the nonferrous scale. He takes out a twenty and hands it to the bicyclist.

"Thanks," says the kid—the rich Eastern kid, John has decided. "I sure do appreciate it."

The same kind of aw-shucks thing John himself says when he's oiling up some functionary for a minor favor.

"So is this how you've been paying your way?"

"Otherwise I don't eat."

John finds it amusing, the idea of this guy scrapping for his meals when all the green wire in the world couldn't have bought him that Cannondale. Well, everybody's got to create their own survivor story.

"Yeah, I keep my eye out for stuff, you know. Found a radiator one day. But after all that, dragging in thirty pounds, didn't even make fifteen bucks."

John says, "It's not weight, it's grade. Cast iron only pays out fifty cents a pound. You have to search out your pure grades." John holds up the green wire. "Like this. Where'd you learn about it?"

"Friend of mine told me to check around railroad tracks."

"That's true, but you gotta be a little careful. Stuff like this gets ripped off a lot and we don't like to see it coming in. Most places'll turn green wire away. Might even report you." He's wielding his little bit of power for the last time.

"Okay," the bicyclist replies, not even looking at him, probably not listening either. Not being rude exactly. The minor favor's over, he has his twenty bucks in pocket, and John has lost his brief hold; the cool kid on his cool bike has already stopped thinking about him. He's ready to move on. Standing there, John feels like some woman past menopause. He's disappeared. Suddenly he gets it—a little—with his mom, all the weird stuff she does, personal trainers, herbal consultations, facials, massages. She has to pay people to pay attention to her.

All is not lost, however. Something the kid notices is washing the bored remove from his face. John is engaged enough by the change of expression that he delays checking out the guy's line of sight. He finds enough enjoyment simply in the way the arrogant features slacken into a piteous, yearning slush. And the way the kid swallows, just now remembering how thirsty he's been. Octavia must have stepped outside, John thinks. Some men go for her type, he guesses. Her jeans and white sneakers probably suggest good camping partner.

"Oh," the guy says.

Octavia looks around at her new office. It's a little better, but it has a long way to go. She's thrown out the dusty pamphlets warning about chewing tobacco. She's taken down the propaganda posters, yellow and curling from age: SUPPORT YOUR STEEL, IT SUPPORTS YOU! DILUTION IS THE SO-LUTION TO POLLUTION. All the safety booklets—SAFETY GUIDE FOR FORK-LIFT TRUCK OPERATORS, SAFETY GUIDE FOR METAL SORTERS, and so on and so on—she carried down to the weighmaster's station and gave to Ada to pass out. She said something nice about the kachina dolls to get her to take them. Ada makes her nervous. She's quick with the judge and jury sass. Wrap them up in a Kentucky accent and people find the remarks colorful instead of mean. Octavia tries to ingratiate herself to Ada to avoid being one of her targets. She tells Ada how much she likes Loretta Lynn, how fascinating she finds skeet shooting. She finds herself dumbing down, trying to hide who she really is, afraid Ada will put all her Wellesley As in a slingshot and take aim. Her dad doesn't know how good he has it. Ada's like his faithful hunting dog. All he's ever done, she can bet, is bark a few orders. He's never had to work to get her loyalty.

Someone is running up the steps. John pops in, asks her to come down and talk to the railroad rep. She's here making a friendly call, he says. A preliminary talk on these freight costs.

"Okay," Octavia says, glad for the excuse to leave the little house. "Does Ada hate me?" she asks John.

"I don't think so."

"But you're not sure."

"I don't think she does," he says.

"Like me?"

"I don't think she does—not like you. I mean, I'm sure she likes you fine."

"It would be nice if somebody here liked me," Octavia says.

The railroad rep is posed at the bottom of the steps. God, Octavia thinks. God, she moans. It's her. The one who was at the funeral. She has to be reminded of the name, Hayley Badecker, but she remembers everything else, the I got up an hour early to put on my makeup face, the modelesque figure, the Clairol commercial hair. She's slinked into a tight suit. Railroad rep is not what you'd guess. Hollywood realtor, yes.

"Hi! How are you?" Hayley Badecker earnestly greets Octavia. She even sells her simple hellos. Her gaze is strong and enthusiastic. She's a natural smiler. Octavia remembers that from the funeral, too, how the woman had to contort the smile off her face during the sad parts. Octavia checks out the tight jacket, the tight skirt. Professional, but *tight*. A silk scarf patterned in a storm of seagreen sets off the eyes. She has long lashes, made longer by mascara. She's way too beautiful for her own good although all that makeup is not Octavia's style. *Too much makeup*—another thing to add to her mother's **Bad** list.

Octavia's wearing jeans and tennis shoes, and over her shirt hangs a man's tuxedo jacket with the too-long sleeves rolled up.

"Hayley's here to talk about the transport costs," John says.

"Okay," Octavia says.

The Metal Shredders

"They've gone up," Hayley Badecker says.

Octavia glances at John. He nods.

"Yes," Octavia says.

"You're not happy about that," Hayley Badecker says.

Octavia glances at John. He shakes his head.

"No," Octavia says.

"Let's go in my office and talk," John offers.

Octavia doesn't say anything, but she didn't know he had an office, he never told her. She and H. B. follow John inside, behind the weighmaster station and into her grandfather's old office. "Oh," she says. "That makes sense."

"What?"

"Your new office. Here."

Tony is running a rag across her grandfather's desk. The top has been cleared off. A tower of boxes climb the wall.

Hayley Badecker says to John, "I was so sorry to hear about your grandfather. He was such a character."

"He liked you."

"I liked him," Hayley Badecker emphasizes.

John says, "He would have been very pleased you came to his funeral. I'm sorry, I thought Tony was done. Maybe we should talk outside, if that's okay with you."

"As long as that bicyclist is gone."

"Almost there," Tony says.

Hayley Badecker's wide eyes and smile gleam toward John. Hmm, Octavia thinks.

"What bicyclist?" Octavia asks.

"I love the fresh air anyway," Hayley Badecker says.

They return outside, right back to where they were, and the same conversation about freight costs repeats itself. Octavia knows one thing only about this transport issue: that they have traditionally trucked out the nonferrous, and rail-freighted the ferrous. So if it gets more complicated than that, she's going to keep quiet. She starts thinking of other things.

"Your transport costs have been raised," Hayley Badecker begins again.

"Octavia?" John says.

"That's right," Octavia says.

"And you're not happy about it."

"No," Octavia says.

John says, "I think there are a couple of issues here. One: raised fees. But the other: raised fees in light of the fact that you send our cars back unclean. Fact: there's always three or four hundred pounds of scrap left at the bottom. Observation to go along with this fact: it's getting worse, not better. Essential point: I'm paying twice for that scrap to be freighted."

Octavia tries muttering a warning like a ventriloquist: "Weird talking style, John." Flirting, she thinks. Making a fool of himself, she thinks.

"I understand what you're saying," Hayley Badecker says.

"We're thinking of using trucks to haul our ferrous," he says. "Serious consideration."

"Oh don't do that!" Hayley Badecker protests, swaying into John's arm with a laugh. "I wouldn't get to come here anymore."

"I don't want to," John says. "Fact is, I might have to."

Octavia hates to think of her brother as a nerd but right now what choice does she have?

"And business is business," Hayley Badecker adds.

"Right."

Octavia says, "I agree with my brother. I'm new here, but . . ." Actually, she was intending to say, *Fact: I agree with my brother* but just didn't think she could pull it off.

John says, "I'm taking her input seriously. She's got some bold ideas."

The Metal Shredders

"Trucking ferrous is pretty bold," Hayley Badecker says. "You couldn't possibly run a profit doing that."

John shrugs. "We shall see."

Hayley Badecker turns to Octavia. She's being delightfully devilish now. "I'm going to have to talk some sense into your brother!" She trips into his arm again, lets out an *oops!*, sneaks in a clutch of his biceps. "But I understand. You're not happy with our transport costs. That's the bottom line."

John and Hayley Badecker seem pleased. Octavia doesn't know why. The talk has gone around in a circle, twice. Something must have been accomplished because the conversation turns more social. Hayley asks Octavia how she likes working here. She asks John if he's tried any new restaurants.

"I like it fine," Octavia says.

"Not really," John says about the restaurants.

"They're supposed to be good, especially that new fish market."

"Fish market?" Octavia questions.

"They fly it in fresh every day."

"I'm not sure I want to pay extra for transport costs," John says.

Hayley Badecker howls with glee. She goes back to the delicious biceps again, spanking them. She's being saleswoman of the year letting her hair down just this once for her very favorite customer. The fun is over for Octavia: she regards H. B. with a growing distaste.

"We should try it sometime," Hayley Badecker says. "Really." She remembers to turn to Octavia. "The three of us. Fun, don't you think?"

John says, "Okay, great," like he doesn't get that Hayley Badecker is coming on to him.

"So show me around," Hayley Badecker says, surveying the yard.

"Same old, same old," John says.

"I've never really had a tour."

John signals Octavia with a coded dance of eyebrows. "I gotta get back," he says. "Otty, why don't you show her some things?"

"Fine," Octavia says.

H. B. says, "I'm going to give you a call about that restaurant. In lieu of the client golf game, okay?" Laughter. "That's a promise, right?"

"Absolutely," John says.

"And you, too." Hayley Badecker gives a tug on Octavia's jacket. She's being friend to all because you don't know who might start calling the shots. What if John gets shredded? Then it'll be his sister's decision. So be nice to the sister, too.

It's fascinating, really, to watch this woman at work.

John waves and heads back to the weighmaster's station, and when they're left alone, H. B. says, "Your brother is a nice, nice man."

"Yes, he is."

"This is going to be fun. I don't like golf but I love to eat. I love wine, I love the whole thing. You're going to love this restaurant. We'll have some drinks at this great bar right in the center of the room. We'll people-watch. Do you like to people-watch? It's wonderful. You're going to love it."

"Sounds like it," Octavia says.

"So," Hayley Badecker begins, "how do you like your new job?"

"It's fine."

"It's nice to start at the top," Hayley Badeker says. "Have you fixed up your office?"

"No," Octavia says.

"That's number one for getting into the job, feeling, you know, like you're part of it." Hayley Badecker raises both fists and gives the air a dainty, cheerleading jab.

Octavia wonders what exactly John's raised eyebrows were telling her to do. At first she thought it was a warning: *Don't go near the LTD!*—as if she would. *Don't tell her about the money!*—as if she would.

She looks around. The LTD is not there anymore—*as if she cares.*

The eyebrows weren't telling her to float some figures either, given the fact that she doesn't know any figures. What were the eyebrows telling her?

Maybe he simply wants her to make friends with Hayley Badecker. Do some girl talk, get her to be a pal on their side. Obviously she's already on their side, at least John's side—but he's too whatever, lost in his failed marriage, to see it. She wonders if he's still hung up on Elise. She thought it was only herself who stayed hung up more than a week or two. The rest of the world seems to move on so quickly and so easily.

Octavia mentally runs through some girl talk possibilities. Hair, diet, clothes, boys. The usual. None of which she wants to talk about. "I wish you wouldn't leave four hundred pounds of our scrap at the bottom of your railroad cars," is what she finally comes up with.

"We've got to do something about that, don't we?" Hayley Badecker agrees, pulling on Octavia until she falls in with her and they stroll. They pause to look at the mountain of crushed cars stacked on top of each other. Hayley Badecker sighs. "Just think, they all used to be new cars at one time. It boggles your mind, doesn't it?"

"I guess," Octavia says.

"Those cars took Mom and Dad and Sister and Brother to Grandma and Grandpa's house on Thanksgiving, they took Sam to the soccer game, Jennifer to ballet lessons. Dad rode to work in those cars. Mom held on tight to the steering wheel on her way to a mammogram. Lovers kissed and made love in the back seats of those cars. Now look at them."

There's something about Hayley Badecker that's not quite right. Octavia checks out the hair, painted fingernails, expensive suit, expensive shoes, expensive white teeth, bubbly personality, thoroughbred calf muscles. It's not there to be seen but Octavia senses it, a hardscrabble background. She's fighting to hide it. No wonder she wants John. He's not pedigree heaven, but he's good enough to keep her in the upper middle class.

How Octavia knows this she doesn't know. But it's like recognizing the difference between a woman's wallet and a man's wallet. They can look practically the same but you just know which is which. Hayley Badecker is a woman's wallet, sure, but she's imitation natural leather.

Fifteen minutes ago *Snob* was the word she wrote on the list of her mom's negative qualities. Obviously it has caught up with Octavia. She has been given the snob gene from her mother's side. To go along with the scrap gene from her father's.

"You seem upset," Hayley Badecker says.

"I am."

H. B. wraps both arms around her one arm. Octavia's one arm is hanging there, being wrapped around. She doesn't know what to do with it. She starts walking, the arm dragging at her side under H. B.'s tug. Hayley Badecker hangs on and they head toward the crushed cars. Octavia pretends to see something, pushes ahead and frees her arm.

From the middle of the steel mountain emerges that tiny guy they call Worm. He appears to have oozed out of solid steel. As if he could melt and reform.

"What a strange little very good-looking actually tiny man," Hayley Badecker says.

"Everyone except me calls him Worm."

"What do you call him?"

"Nothing."

"That's what I'm going to call him, too," Hayley says. Her hand cups Octavia's elbow, then travels along the back of Octavia's tuxedo jacket and wags the tail. "I love this," she says. "It really accentuates your femininity."

"It's a *man's* jacket."

"I know. I wish I could pull something like this off."

"That's hard to believe," Octavia says.

"No really, think about it. When a woman, a really feminine woman wears men's clothes, it just emphasizes she's a woman."

"Really," Octavia says.

"Just like a man, if he dressed up in my outfit, it would emphasize he's a man." She points out Dooley. "*That* over there would not look good in my suit. He would look even more like a man than he does now." She points out Don Capachi. "*That* over there would not look good in Tommy Hilfiger clothes. It would make him look older, not younger. Do you see what I'm saying?"

"Yes," Octavia says.

"How old is that old man?"

"Old," Octavia says.

"I believe it," Hayley Badecker says.

They wander over to the steel pile of cars. Octavia and Hayley Badecker search for some opening that could explain Worm's magical emergence from within it.

"How did that little man do that?" Hayley Badecker asks. "Quite extraordinary-looking, isn't he?" She pats along the solid steel wall.

"He worms in and out. That's how he got the name." She pulls Hayley's hand away from the steel edges. "You might cut yourself. Look here." Octavia has discovered an interior gap hidden by a front extension. It's a little entranceway. Octavia bends and steps inside. The walls have been hammered smooth. She turns, holding her breath, sucking in her body, and sidesteps. She's suddenly nowhere. Hayley's body at the entrance has shut off the light. She can't see to either side of her. The ceiling of cars is very low. Even with her legs bent low the ceiling pushes her head down. Her chin is tucked to her chest. She can see her belt buckle. That's all. The steel, though hammered smooth, snags on her hair. She sidesteps blindly, picking her way along until her foot feels freedom and open air. The ceiling drops even more. The tunnel shrinks to box size. She contorts herself down to her knees, then maneuvers to her bottom and slides out feet-first.

She is behind the mountain of flattened cars. There is a small sitting area with two bent-up lawn chairs. The lawn chairs look out upon a high wall of graffitied cinder block. Looks like Worm spray-paints in his spare time. The cinder block is a large mural devoted to listing the things he has found in the flattened cars he worms through. Money, rings, necklaces, golf tees, pharmaceuticals, crayons—on and on, and all with hash marks keeping score.

Octavia smells dope. She turns around.

Amazingly, Hayley Badecker has followed her all the way through. She slides out on her back, the tight expensive skirt coated with dirt and twisted up over her hips. She's barefoot. Octavia helps her up and dusts off her back. She lets H. B. pull her own skirt down, but she steals a glance. She had guessed garter belt, but it was plain ol' panty hose. Then Hayley dusts off Octavia's back. "We got dirty," she says.

"Who was that bicyclist you were talking about?" Octavia asks.

"My question exactly. Sometimes your brother can be very mysterious. Oh my. Look at this secret place."

Octavia picks up the wooden cigar box and checks inside. Rolling papers, a roach clip, a pipe, a baggie of weed.

"I'm willing if you are," Hayley Badecker says. She picks up a joint.

"Can't," Octavia says. "I'm being a role model."

Hayley slips off her sea-green scarf and brings it up to Octavia's cheek and cleans it. Octavia trips backward and lands against the scrap wall. A sharpness digs into her back. Not a light sharpness either. She's cut herself, right through the tuxedo jacket. Automatically she starts to twist around to check it out. Then stops herself. It'll get Hayley Badecker's attention. Her enthusiastic attention. Her enthusiastic sympathy. She ignores the cut though her back is growing liquidy. She lifts her head, gaze forward, and Hayley Badecker's face is there in her own and now Octavia flattens harder against the scrap and more things are digging into her back. Hayley Badecker's lips are pressed against hers. They're soft. Soft as the Easter Bunny, Octavia thinks absurdly. I'm going to bleed to death, she also thinks. She smells Hayley Badecker's Pantene shampoo. She wonders what her own hair smells like. She hasn't washed it for a couple of days, just didn't feel like it, too early in the morning. She voted for the extra fifteen minutes of sleep.

She's kissing a woman. She's never done that before, and it's foreign and strange and exciting, and she's thinking with a hopeful thrill—kissing a woman, that's okay, that's good, in fact, she's sure it's not on the list of things her mother has done or plans to do. Which means she's nothing like her mother. Which means when she turns fifty-five she won't do something pathetic to recapture her youth. Octavia was looking at her mom's face at the funeral and it wasn't just the mask of emotion making her look altered (trying not to display her relief that Grandpa was out of her hair), it was a different sort of mask. Plastic surgery. Acid peels, Botox injections—she's had it done. Suddenly Octavia knew it.

She has floated away for a moment to gloat. The kiss is still going on when her mind checks back in. This kiss—what she thought of as simply one woman's gentle offering to another, in its gift already a sweet retreat—has now become a prelude to more. The mouth begins to rearrange itself for deeper kisses, harder ones, and the hands waste no time moving inside her tuxedo jacket and over her breasts. This is no longer like kissing a woman. It's exactly like kissing a man. It's fend-off time. Octavia is deeply disappointed in this bottom-line striving. She tries to wiggle out of it, which poses some difficulties. She can't pull back or she'll impale herself further on the scrap flanges. Flanges that rust. And a piece has already got her good. Rust, roaming inside her. Did Mom and Dad and Sister and Brother on their way to Grandma and Grandpa's house and the soccer game and the ballet lessons ever imagine that their shredded car would be reincarnated as tetanus germs?

She takes her hand and wedges it in between her and Hayley's mouths. She pushes. Hayley Badecker is pried away. Her hand is over Hayley's mouth; Hayley's intent eyes are upon her. Octavia drops her hand away; Hayley's church-social smile beams at her. "You're beautiful," Hayley Badecker says. She gives a best-friend tug on Octavia's jacket.

Octavia sits on the ground and back-crabs into the tunnel head-first. She can feel the hot nest of lockjaw already going to work on her back. Nice rusty steel, she thinks. Before she gets too far in the tunnel she sees Hayley Badecker take the baggie of marijuana and stuff it down her front and into her bra. Then Hayley gets down on her bottom and crawls backward toward Octavia's lap. She wags the tail of Octavia's tuxedo. "I love this," she says.

Octavia is not going there. Hayley Badecker is not getting an answer out of her. Without making it obvious that she's rushing, she wiggles out of the tunnel.

6

I figured out what to do about Greenjeans," Tony tells him.

"What's that?"

John's in the middle of a phone negotiation for new sheet scrap from a metal-stamping plant. He sits on hold at the desk cleared of his grandfather's stuff and restocked with new. He's broken down and accepted the office as his own. He went to Target and bought desk supplies, chrome steel baskets for ingoing and outgoing mail, a Krups coffeemaker, a couple of plain ceramic mugs with no cute sayings (he's so sick of everybody's idea of cute), and a new, cheaper desk chair with plastic arms. His grandfather's luxurious leather one (still smelling of him) can be for clients. It's too comfortable to do any work in. In the doorway hangs a wind chime Marcus's daughter made from brass punchings.

Tony sits down in the leather chair.

John palms the receiver and tells him, "I might have to cut you off. Is this a long story?"

"Long and short of it," Tony explains, "I should spend the money right away. That way if Greenjeans blabs and the county attorney wants it back, I can honestly say I don't have it."

"Better to say you never had it," John says.

"You got it. There you go. I never had it. By then Greenjeans'll be"—Tony's finger twirls the crazy sign—"he'll have them so confused they won't know what the story is."

"That'll work," John says.

"Have you counted it?"

"Not yet."

Tony says, "That's the only thing standing in my way. I can't spend it till it stops smelling. Has yours stopped smelling?"

"Not yet," John says. The guy at the metal-stamping plant gets back on the line.

"It's been over a week."

John holds up a finger.

Tony sighs. "How long does it take for money to stop smelling?" He wings out his shoulders to stretch them, presses himself into the soft leather. He's dressed in khaki pants and a smoothly ironed blue jean shirt with a dress collar. He's stopped with the T-shirts. John looks down at himself: cargo pants and a ratty old Lands' End shirt. But that's the point: he doesn't even think about what he wears. The cargo pants cost seventy-five dollars at Galyans and he lets them get ripped and dirty without a second thought. The ratty old Lands' End shirt probably went for forty. If Tony shelled out that kind of money, he'd take ultra care not to soil it.

John suddenly thinks of the bicyclist and his two-thousand-dollar Cannondale. He wonders if he uses his ATM card when he can't find enough scrap.

Ada's announcement on the PA echoes through the yard: "Welbargers!" A few moments later she struts in, hand on hip. "You didn't hear me?" she says.

The Metal Shredders

Don't have time for this, he mouths to her over the phone.

Tony bounces up. "I'll do it," he offers.

John nods okay both to Tony and to Ada. He shouldn't let Tony do this, family members only after all, but what choice does he have. He can't waste his whole day doing weighmaster duty. That's what cousin Rory was for.

"The one of 'em hasn't cut his hair in about three years," Ada says to John in her Kentucky lilt. She pauses, looks over her shoulder. "It's about down to his butt."

He's got to get Octavia up to speed soon. But he can't have her doing weighmaster duty all day either. Stuck with haulers and Ada all day, she'll be AWOL by Christmas.

He finishes the details of the shipping. The metal-stamping plant is just down the road. They make car-door frames. It's a thriving business, now with the Marysville Honda plant. John buys their leftovers as No. 1 baling material and sells it as No. 1 steel.

Still got tons to do.

Outside Tony's yelling at the Welbargers, asking them what do they think he is, a total idiot? The father and son smile their crafty, low-IQ smiles at Tony. Both have matching chips in their front teeth. Chained to the back of their pickup is an old Nova.

"Found it in a cornfield," the elder Welbarger brags.

"Looking good," John says, hurrying past. He takes a glimpse at the ferrous scale. A Nova should weigh about twenty-five hundred pounds. This one's coming in a thousand pounds higher.

He keeps walking. He doesn't even want to know.

Marcus has seated himself on the porch near the nonferrous scale, both to keep tabs on the Welbargers and to put in his glaucoma drops. He leans his head back and aims the philocarpine into a pried-open eye. Last year in the Kroger's parking lot John saw the Babe Zacharias mammogram truck, free screenings, and called their number and one thing led to another and he got a truck out to the Shredders checking cholesterol and blood pressure, and screening for glaucoma. Not surprisingly, Dooley's blood pressure was through the roof. About sixty percent of his workforce had high cholesterol. The surprise was Marcus's glaucoma. But Marcus is faithful about his eyedrops. John suspects Dooley ignores his medication, but he doesn't ask—not with that glint from Dooley's shuttered eyes. The Senior is the only one who can handle him.

Marcus blinks over at him, his eyes pricked wide.

"Flu shots this afternoon," John reminds him.

Marcus gives him a hand up and John jumps onto the porch and takes a look around for Don Capachi. He's over at the alligator shear. "Don!" he calls to the old man, waving both hands to get his attention. Don Capachi scrapes over. As always, he's carefully dressed for safe shredding, to the point that the aged body nearly disappears under all its protection. Hard hat, safety glasses with wire-mesh side shields, metal-toed boots, gauntlet work gloves, and leather cassock. A white collar peeks out from coveralls, adding a priestly note.

John raises his voice and enunciates carefully. "A nurse is coming over to give everyone flu shots. You're going to get yours, right?"

Don Capachi moves over to the Birch barrel, No. 2 copper, and drops in a piece of the copper gutter he's cutting up. His much-delayed nod, pointing to some kind of ongoing sadness, is disturbing to John. It's been almost a month since the funeral. Don Capachi is starting to get that mortally doomed turtle look.

"Good man," John says to Don Capachi, trying for enthusiasm. He continues into the warehouse. Past the carom-bumper placement of barrels filled with turnings and borings bought directly from industrial plants and shipped to foundries. Past forklifts parked wherever they happened to stop. Past Dumpsters of heavy brass gears and bushings. Past the shiny half-ton of new brass punchings bought from a watch factory. The sparkling discards are wafer-thin and as pretty as Christmas decorations. It's with these that Marcus's daughter makes wind chimes. She's a fourth grader at Duxberry, the arts-impact school, and Marcus is always taking over interesting scrap he thinks the teachers might find creative use for.

Now John is deep inside the warehouse. He sidesteps past the pig iron waiting to go to market, the batches neatly crosshatched, and finally arrives at the bales of new sheet scrap piled high across the long flank of the warehouse. "If Hephaestus were Zeus, we would be kings of the earth." His grandfather, taking this same tour through the metallic phlegm the working world coughed up, could always be depended on to repeat one of his favorite original sayings.

Though the warehouse proper ends here, it's still not over. A large garage door opens out into a three-quarter open space where a portable, hydraulic basketball system is set up. Beyond that, a shotgun addition. Inside is the ferrous grading area where the Hispanics and Cambodians work. They've got their own little universe back here, and it's run by Evert Sheraton. Sherry believes his duty as foreman is to stay on the sidelines and send in orders. Nobody can understand him, and nobody can hear him anyway. The thunderclap of clanging metal effectively nullifies the language barrier.

And so Sherry has the easiest job at the Shredders. The Cambodians and Hispanics work so hard he can sit at his desk and drink vodka. That's where John finds him, rushing a bottle into a drawer when he glimpses John. On the dirty wall behind his desk, Sherry has taped a photocopied sheet that reads, EVERY DAY ADDS TO THE NUMBER OF PEOPLE WHO SHOULD KISS MY ASS.

What is it, John thinks. Everybody's got a cute saying. Everybody.

What is it with that? John yells, "I got a county nurse coming out to give everyone flu shots over lunch hour. Make sure all of them get their flu shots."

Sherry gives him the thumbs-up. Big smile. He's always real friendly to John.

"Tomorrow I got a shipment of new sheet scrap coming in."

"We'll be ready," Sherry says. Another thumbs-up.

John steps over to watch the graders. It's fairly recent that the Shredders has started to purchase new sheet scrap. By sorting out the good stuff from the contaminated, basically the noncoated from the coated, they can brick it alloy by alloy and sell it back to the steel mills for a tidy profit. It was the Senior's idea. But its success was dependent on coming up with a group of men who would work long and hard for crappy wages. But crappy wages paid in cash climb up a rung to not-so-bad. And not-so-bad wages paid to a group used to Third-World wages climb even higher to pretty damn good. The Senior was awfully proud of himself when he found this group. Then he promptly deserted them for his white-goods project.

The graders are sorting out the galvanized and throwing it on the toothed conveyor belt that carries the scrap uphill then drops it into a hopper. A hydraulic arm drives in the hopper wall and the scrap is tamped into neat boxes. John is happy to see that everybody's got their ear guards on. And of course their gloves—without strong leather gloves reinforced with metal stapling, they'd be without fingers by midmorning.

Without ear guards for himself, John can stand to watch for only a minute or two. The clanging of the sheet scrap, like metal laundry flapping in the wind, is nearly unbearable. None of the Cambodians has looked up at him. They keep their heads down, some kind of cultural deference, he assumes. The Hispanics one by one give him a tight smile of acknowledgment.

The Metal Shredders

Safety check completed, John gives them a wave and is about to leave when he notices a wet spot on the floor right where the graders are working. If one of them slips against the sheet scrap, he'll slice his thigh wide open. Workman's comp for an illegal is not exactly what they need right now. John spots a hole in the corrugated roof. He feels some irritation with Tony. Tony's supposed to find these things before they happen. And Sherry, fuck him, is supposed to report it.

After throwing some burlap over the wet spot and motioning to Miguel to be careful, he marches back out, through the sunless maze of scrap varieties, and finds Tony still giving hell to the Welbargers.

"There's a roof leak needs patching over at the ferrous grading area."

"Got it covered," Tony says. "Spotted it this morning."

"Someone's going to get hurt," John says. He takes in the Welbargers, their boot toes innocently kicking the dirt. He doesn't want to ask, but he does. "What's the problem?"

"Check this out." Tony goes over and lifts the Nova's trunk. The trunk is packed solid with bricks. Next Tony demonstrates the Nova's muffler, pouring out of it a muddy stream of stones.

"What else?" John asks the Welbargers.

"Nothing," the elder one says with a sort-of laugh.

"I've give you seventy bucks for the car minus a twenty-dollar processing fee."

"How much is that?" the son asks. His three-year growth of hair charges out of his Columbus Clippers ball cap.

"Fifty."

Dad Welbarger nods toward the bricks. "Sell 'em to you for ten bucks," he says.

John produces his wallet and pulls out a five. Judging from the way it's grabbed out of his hand, they eagerly accept. "Okay good-bye," John tells them. And then to Tony: "Get on it."

He's got one more thing to do before lunch: drive over to Joe Greenslade and pick him up and make sure he gets his flu shot.

My job, he thinks. It's been reduced to playing nursemaid.

The phone rings. Octavia picks it up, feeling pretty pleased with herself. She's just learned about coated and alloyed steel. "Hi," Hayley Badecker says. "What's going on?"

Oh, Christ. It's her. She knew it would be eventually. What to do about this creature. A guy, a kiss, you move on. Even a quick overnight mistake, you move on. You both agree to forget about it.

But . . . A girl, a kiss . . .

It happened and Octavia doesn't care and she doesn't want to get in a long drawn-out involved girl drama about it, she wants to move on. She doesn't want to play Barbie dolls over it, nothing happening but they keep changing outfits and going over the same thing.

She gives Hayley the Star Wars approach—shoot, kill, no blood spilled, next scene. She says, "I was going over this problem with getting our rail cars back dirty. If you bring us back four hundred pounds of coated steel and we put it in a new load of differently sorted scrap, that's going to cause annealing problems at the foundry and then they're going to blame us." Which is another way of saying I'm being a grown-up with a job, and I'm being a grown-up about you because it happened, it's over, we're moving on without blood or victims, here's the start of our new chapter.

"Is it always four hundred pounds, Octavia?"

"As far as I know," Octavia says flatly, not liking the sexy way Hayley coos the words.

"Did you dream about me last night?"

The Metal Shredders

Octavia sighs. She says, "You see what I'm saying, right, Hayley? The foundries get all screwed up and then they blame us."

"For those four hundred pounds. It's always four hundred pounds?" Something about the way she says *four hundred pounds,* like it's the G-spot.

"Sometimes it's less, sometimes it's more."

"I keep thinking about what it was like to hold you."

"I don't remember you holding me. I remember you pushing me against sharp pieces of metal."

"I held you, I didn't push you."

"My back says you pushed."

"What's wrong with your back?"

"Nothing a tetanus shot won't fix."

"When are we getting together again?" Hayley asks.

"That's between you and John."

Now as Octavia listens to Hayley's voice the cuts in her back begin to throb. It's been three days since the kiss and the cuts on her back are still hurting. She opens and slams the bathroom door, calls "I'll be with you in a second," and tells Hayley Badecker she's got to go. She hopes she didn't hear correctly when a pair of lips smack good-bye.

She takes a stool into the bathroom, lifts up her shirt and uses the mirror to get a glimpse of the wounds. The lighting is too dull to see well. Down off the stool, a search for a flashlight. Back to stool with flashlight in hand. The highlighted cuts keep sliding out of the flashlight's beam whenever she cocks her head enough to view the damage. Down off the stool, search for a second mirror. She gets the cosmetic one out of her handbag, a tad small but it'll have to do. Back on stool, one hand holding the flashlight, the other the mirror. Now no hand available to hold up her shirt. She loops the shirt over her shoulder and secures it in her teeth.

Finally, using two mirrors and a flashlight, she sees the marks. Very impressive. In the nest of scratches tinged in black and blue, she spies a modest-looking wound that is probably causing the trouble. A deep poke mark. It hadn't bled so she hadn't thought to check it. But now she sees it's pretty deep. And she realizes it hurts, now that she's thinking about it.

A deep poke mark that didn't bleed. Which means an anaerobic wound. Which means an anaerobic wound brought on by scrap metal. Which means rust boring inside her. Which means tetanus.

She sits down at her desk to think this through. Counts one finger after another, backing up one year after the next to her last tetanus booster. Forget it, it's been well over ten years. The last one probably goes back to elementary school. She moves her jaw around. Still nice and loose. She's not dead yet. She gets out the medical dictionary John keeps in the filing cabinet, looks up *Tetanus,* and reads,

> **Tetanus** (lockjaw), causative bacteria Clostridium tetani, is probably
> the most devastating lethal microorganism that afflicts man, causing
> as well Gas gangrene and Botulism . . .

Botulism too, she thinks. Great. And gas gangrene. Who could ask for more?

> Any deep though minor-appearing injury, such as stepping on a nail
> or tack . . .

or leaning into scrap metal while being kissed

> which can seal itself, thus making the wound airless, provides this
> organism with the proper environment to multiply and produce its
> toxins.

The Metal Shredders

She's seen it in the mirror. Definitely sealed. Definitely airless.

> Onset usually begins with headache, low-grade fever, irritability,
> apprehension, and restlessness.

Apprehension? Oh my god, she's been apprehensive all morning. And restless. So restless! Can't concentrate on this annealing, casting thing problem. And irritable! She was downright irritable with Hayley Badecker on the phone, low grade feverishly irritable, cutting her off and telling her she'd call back later when she had absolutely no intention of calling her back. A lie! Lying! Is lying on the list?

> Tetanus today appears only as the result of gross neglect. It must be
> blamed on the ignorance of adults to provide proper immunization
> for their children and themselves.

No, lying is not on the list. Just stupidity and gross neglect. She's in for a lecture on her stupidity when she goes to the doctor.

What doctor? She has no doctor. Hasn't been to the doctor in years. She'll hear about that, too. No health insurance until a month ago, lecture lecture (except for the catastrophic her parents bought her every year— *for your major car accident, dear, Merry Christmas*). If she goes to a doctor, they won't do what she asks, just a simple shot, in and out. They'll want to weigh her, give her a Pap smear, weigh her, check her breasts, weigh her; it'll snowball into a big ordeal and she'll get some harangue on birth control and STDs, and maybe, *maybe*, if she kneels before them properly chastened, maybe at the very end they'll reluctantly deign to give her the tetanus shot that will save her life, the disgust with her stupidity and gross neglect written all over their faces.

Clearly she's better off dead.

She changes into sweatpants and jogging bra and T-shirt, pounds down the metal steps, and begins her Last Run. Not toward Jefferson this time, though that gives her a mileage check and she likes to keep track of that sort of thing. But she's sick of that puny town. Everybody from the Shredders heads there for lunch and they're always honking. No, this time she turns left out the gate. Out into the country. She wants to get lost among the cornfields.

Isn't that her head hurting, by the way? Headache is one of the signs. The very fact that she's worried about a headache points to her symptomatic Apprehension.

So make this final run count, she tells herself. Make it a good one. She takes off through the gates.

"Hey!" A voice from the sky. A trickle of a shout is all that's left when the air reaches her. "Hey!"

She keeps going. She checks out the seed crop signs, PIONEER 3474, PIONEER 3421, COMPETITION CHECK 4544, still staked along the harvested furrows of corn.

"Octavia!" Well, it is her name, so she twists around, jogs backward. There on a rooftop stands Tony, face shield thrown back, welder wand hanging from his hand like a rifle. He's waving her back in. She purposely misinterprets, waves back, and renews her strides.

"Dogs!" His shouted warning is nothing but a bubble in the air.

Talk about paranoia. Tony and his dogs. The dogs no one has ever seen. The bogus reason they can't dump Joe Greenslade or at least get him a guard dog. Supposedly the dogs are like members of a gang, constantly recruiting and corrupting others. She is not apprehensive about the dogs, not in the least. No apprehension there. Which means she's still asymptomatic. Still plenty of time to get her tetanus booster before the jaw starts locking up. There's got to be a doctor around who doesn't want to bother with all that other checkup crap. She knows she should get a Pap smear, do the whole female rigamarole. Because, for example, breast cancer. She's not too young to get breast cancer. Ovarian cancer—what if she has that? A Pap smear's not going to do her any good as far as early detection. Half the time they read the lab smears wrong. The other half they read the mammograms wrong. If you do have breast cancer they miss it. If you don't have breast cancer they tell you you do. And Pap smears—even worse! The Pap smear labs are on commission. She read about someone who did ten thousand slides in a week. You can't do ten thousand slides in a week unless you gather them up in your arms like a load of laundry and throw them into the *Unremarkable* bin. Those labs are like those Nike sweatshops in Thailand, they might as well hire seven-year-olds to read the slides.

Ranting and raving. Is that on the list of symptoms? This is a good topic, though. It's got her going. She must have run half a mile already and not even noticed it. She's running alongside a wild vine fence; she takes the same turn the fence does and follows a gravel road. Soon she's sandwiched between two high cornfields. The cornfield on her right looks strangely carved up. She hears in the distance the guttering roar of a thresher. She checks out the cornfield as she runs along it. It appears to be cut up in a sort of maze. Then she comes to a cleared apron in the middle of a cornfield. Not a sort of maze. An actual maze. HALLOWEEN MAZE!!! ONLY $6.00!!! a big sign reads. OPEN FRIDAY'S THROUGH SUNDAY. There's a long deserted banquet table, the kind they set up in gymnasiums. She jogs past, then backtracks and checks it out again. The thresher has carved a straight swath a hundred yards into the cornfield. Perfect for wind sprints.

She decides to do it. The farmer won't mind if he catches her. This is Ohio. Everybody's friendly.

She takes off as fast as she can, up and back. Then once more, kicking her knees high. That one's a killer. She's bent over when she finishes but she struggles forward, flop jogging, until her breath comes back. She lines up at the swath again, lets it all out. This time she stops at the end and does ten pushups. She feels her head swell and burst. She sprints back to the banquet table, does ten more pushups, girl style.

A misty emergence of sunlight rewards her effort. She does it again. Back and forth down the swath, ten pushups each way. She knows who's watching her. She knows who's impressed. *He's* watching her, *he's* impressed. The married one, Byron, the one who turned her against herself. He's wearing his city-issue rec-center shorts. He wears them no matter what the weather. They're fashionably long, and even a thousand miles away she can still see, just above the knee, the almost penile surge of thigh muscle. Around his neck a whistle hangs from a lanyard, something for him to finger while he talks. His smile is pleased and friendly, a beacon without irony or guardedness. His desk is messy. Hand weights on top of stacks of paper. Monthly reports under Ping-Pong paddles. Half the time the picture of his wife and daughter was hidden under a baseball glove, not that he ever purposely hid it. He was perfectly at ease showing her the photo of his wife and child, and just as comfortable kissing her. They sat on the empty bleachers in the gym, a snowstorm raging outside but him still in his city-issue shorts, and the kiss seemed as normal as the basketball he twirled in his hands. It didn't leave him confused or feeling guilty. It simply took him to the next logical step.

One more time. She pushes off from the banquet table. Her sprint this time has thickened to a trot. She can't make it through the pushups. The rubber hoses her arms have become deposit her on the ground. She counts out thirty seconds to let the strength return, then finishes out the ten pushups in a series of phony snakings up and down. But today they count; nobody is here to tell her they don't. Arms to rubber again; she plops on her chest. Angry people are inside her head, pounding down the door of her temples. She tries for two more pushups. Real ones this time, all the way down. Byron's watching, and she's always trying to impress him, even now. He uses his niceness to demand more. He uses his niceness to tell her stories about his daughter. He uses his niceness to submit some of her own seriously intended artwork to the Museum of Dad Art and when it gets accepted he comes and tells her with that sociopathic niceness and unguarded smile, so that she has no choice but to act thrilled. Thrilled that her stuff is such a joke. Quite thrilled. She's lying in the dirt of the cornfield. She smells dry dirt and the way it smells different from soil. She inhales the weedy smell of dried cornstalk. It's nice not to smell oil and metal and bearing grease. Even the weeds breathe needed life into the air.

Now she hears the crispy rustling of cornstalks. The thresher slicing in the distance cuts off, and now all that's left is some kind of aftershock in the air. It's quiet but she can hear something, as if the quiet is a motor itself and hasn't settled down. Something's out there. But what she hears are her own breaths sniffing loudly against the ground. It's her hatred for her own self riding the wind. She wishes she were a kid. Lying here in the dirt, smelling the start of autumn, proud of the sweat that's dropped from her forehead and turned an ellipsis of dirt into mud, she remembers how it was, in childhood, when all the pain and all the beauty of the world was due to the mistakes of others.

It was just another temporary job after she got back from Spain. She did the art program at a city rec center. Then she became program director. Byron ran the athletic side, and she was technically his boss, but it was all like a big gym class, everybody having fun. He was good with kids. He had on his city-issue shorts and T-shirts. She couldn't imagine what he looked like with anything else on. He gave that beautiful smile to everyone, and he seemed like someone who taught his daughter's Sunday school (which he did, she found out later), so for a while she didn't know. For what seemed like a long time she was happy being his friend, then happy being his good friend. And then unhappy that they were friends at all. Her own feelings had moved forward without her permission. Even after the affair started, his Sunday-school smile remained unabashed and he never seemed embarrassed by the family photo somewhere on his desk. That's when she first had an inkling he was a sociopath—a sociopath of niceness. It allowed him to hurt others and be nice about it. He was just as nice to her before, during, and after the affair, and he hugged his wife and kid unfazed when they came to visit the rec center. She'd first met his wife a few weeks after the affair started. The wife was on her way back from the doctor's appointment to give Byron the good news, that she was ten-percent effaced. He ran to tell Octavia and introduce them.

It's a bad dream and why do the bad ones have to be on rewind? The same images keep popping up and she's face-down in the dirt, smelling the dry cornstalks, trying to dream it away. She's hidden here in her cornstalk tomb. She hears a car pass, brakes squealing, the jerk in the motor housing as the car reverses. The pounding feet rushing toward her before she can decide what her reaction should be. No danger, she decides. She hears then sees them next to her nose—steel-toed workboots.

Decibel and octave are both so high in Tony's voice that she can't help it. The laugh curls her into herself. Tony turns her over, panicked, yelling, "Where'd they get you, where'd they get you!"

"I'm doing pushups," she says.

"I thought they got you."

She decides not to make fun of him.

"I'm taking you back," Tony says.

"I'm running back."

"Too dangerous."

The Metal Shredders

"Good-bye," she says and takes off.

Exactly as she would have predicted, Tony follows her in his car. She's tired. She makes herself go faster because he's watching. She's worried about her butt bouncing. She's worried what she looks like from behind. She waits for some smart remarks. When they pass the wild vine fence and turn onto the main road, he passes her and waits up ahead, almost as if he has sense enough to understand how she's feeling.

Joe Greenslade is his usual addled, agreeable self, and John has no problem getting him to ride out to the Shredders for a flu shot. He lives just a few miles away, in a flat-roofed Lego-sized house for him and his wife, with an old school-bus on the side for their daughter. The house and bus sit alone off a graveled road, next to a culvert that has probably stirred toxins into their gene pool for a good many years. When he pulls into their dirt drive, Greenslade's wife comes out to greet him and John can't help noticing that the wife is a reshuffled version of Greenslade. Her face appears boneless except for the same kind of witch's jaw that Greenslade has. Perhaps it's simply in her collapse that she resembles her husband: she's aged beyond her years.

John is startled when the daughter comes out of the school bus, so much younger than he would have guessed. But then he realizes, Greenslade is barely seventy, his wife probably younger. Their daughter is maybe around thirty, his own age, although she could pass for forty or twenty. He knows she's the daughter; she could pass for the son. She's huge, vertically and horizontally. Key chains and other kinds of chains are hooked onto her pants and belt loops. A pocketknife in a small leather pouch is snapped over the belt. Her face, including jaw, is large, boneless; a Down's syndrome roundness adds a tender note. She wears her hair in a man's cut, combed straight back in the front and hanging in a thin oily sheet in the back.

John doesn't know quite what to make of it. He doesn't quite know what she is, but he sort of likes her anyway, there's something about her. She stands silently next to her mother with a lack of expression that she has probably carried all through her school days, but he has this feeling, that if he smiled at her she'd smile back. She has to wait for the other person to go first.

John says, "Nice to meet you." He smiles and holds out his hand. And see, she smiles right back. Their hands squeeze together, hers soft, surprisingly small—a girl's hand.

He and Joe ride back to the Shredders. He asks Greenslade about the money, shouting over the truck motor. Greenslade zippers his mouth and gives him a proud, sealed-tight smile. John tries to get him to understand that he and Tony would like to know what he's planning to do with it, but Greenslade simply agrees with the question, however it's posed, and after awhile John gives up. Why should he go to this trouble. Why should he care what Greenslade does with it. He's a little surprised Greenslade's wife didn't say something, at least some kind of coded friendly remark: "I sure do appreciate all you've done for my Joe" or some such thing. Maybe Greenslade's slyer than he thinks. Maybe he's got that money stashed away for his own little getaway. Joe in Las Vegas. Joe in Cancún. Joe on a Carnival Cruise.

The sun is out, sharp enough to throw puddles of tree shade on the road. He keeps thinking his tires will splash.

He hits the brakes to avoid a dog jumping out of one of the dark hollows. He honks the horn. The dog trots lightly down the middle of the road, impervious. It's a garbage hound of scraped buckskin color, its rib cage abrupt and mean. John tailgates it, but it doesn't move away. He doesn't have enough room to pass on either side. He's about to nudge its rear end when the dog flicks away, its valentine of tight balls the last thing John sees.

Greenslade turns to him with another smile. "Dog," he explains.

At the gate of the Shredders stand Tony and Octavia kicking at the ground near the fencing. Octavia's in sweatpants and sweatshirt. "They're back!" Tony calls to him before he's even out of the car. He stands pointing to the ground. He shows John the doghole in progress. So far it's just a pawed depression, but with a little more work the animal will be able to squeeze under the fence. In case John isn't convinced, Tony points out a rusty twist of tailpipe, except it isn't tailpipe, it's dog poop from a poorly nourished hound.

"The dogs," Tony says. "I told you they'd come. That car brought 'em back. See? You believe me now?"

John doesn't say, "That's ridiculous" even though he knows perfectly well it's not the LTD that brought them back. It's his own pickup, parked right here day after day with the money still in the garbage bag, still under the flagstone rock. There is nothing he can do with it but leave it outside, and there's no outside to leave it in except the open air of his pickup bed. The backyard isn't his; it would surely attract Kevin's attention, not to mention squirrels, raccoons, cats, and maybe more dogs.

Octavia has pulled her arms out of the sweatshirt sleeves and is hugging herself inside the fleece to keep warm.

Tony says, "I say get some rat poison and throw them some hamburger."

"If you think it'll work," John says.

"It'll work."

"I'm going to go get changed," Octavia says. She starts to move away but pauses at the sound of a car.

"Here comes the nurse." John gives the car a wave. "You going to get a flu shot?" he asks Octavia.

"That's not the nurse," Octavia says. "That's Dad."

He looks again. The car moves into the sunlight. Gunmetal gray. A sports-utility vehicle. The OSU tire cover for the college football season.

He's here. Checking up on things, the LTD among them. At least John will be able to tell him the odor problem has been eliminated, along with the rest of the car.

7

Evening. John walks fast, his newly sociable neighbor an unwanted companion. He's heading south, to a restaurant in the Short North, there to have dinner with his father, his probably very angry father, although it's hard to tell. John increases his pace, using the full length of his stride. His neighbor Kevin, at five-foot-six or five-foot-seven, has accelerated into cartoon motorlegs to keep up.

John's favorite route is up the one-way streets; he never drives them so he doesn't get a chance to see them otherwise. He's trying to think as he walks, what to do in general, what to do about the Shredders, what to do about Elise, what to do about the money, what in particular to do about ridding it of its smell. He's got to come up with a plan, but he can't. He can't think of anything.

Kevin hurries beside John, hugging John's strides, head cocked so he can focus solely on John while he chatters and gulps air. John can't stand it that Kevin won't look anywhere else, at a tree or a house, at the sidewalk or sky. Just at him, at John's determined-to-stay-a-profile profile.

"Look over there," John says. He pauses. He makes an obvious gesture of checking out a new FOR SALE sign. The windows are boarded up and much of the brick is crumbling, but it'll sell. The refurbished Victorians, announcing themselves with tricolored porches, are starting to outnumber the dilapidated ones. It's boomer territory now; the Appalachians are steadily being dozed out. The students who live around here are few enough that their influence isn't felt at all. Three streets beyond his apartment, and OSU suddenly seems to end, its higher educational culture completely unfelt in the rest of the city where nothing but the school's football team seems to matter. The streets here are cleaner, too, without the morass of flyers, ragged tapestries of Kinko printouts staple-gunned to telephone poles and specially constructed information cages.

"I wonder what they're asking," John says, prodding the FOR SALE sign with his foot, but his attempt to change the subject doesn't work.

Kevin's in pain over the latest Latest Development. He gets to the new episode with his wife via the old episode. The story is repeated up to the last Latest Development that John had to hear about at the Mexican place. He tries not to listen but he's hearing it anyway. Through the noise of his neighbor's voice he tries to break through to his own thoughts. Another day piddled away at the Shredders, he thinks. He's having this feeling, that things are falling apart. He's having this other feeling, a ghostly message, that he's being set up for it. It doesn't help that his usual reaction is to find a way to do nothing. He has such a vague sense of himself—or a sense of himself as vague. That's the trouble with someone like him. He can't even pinpoint what went wrong with his marriage. The Senior would have no trouble pinpointing, if ever John dared to ask. The Senior would know exactly what went wrong. *She flirted with other men. She never washed the kitchen floor. You didn't get her pregnant.*

He cuts around Doctor's Hospital, an osteopathic hospital he hopes never to land in, and heads toward Goodale Park. Follow the park up to

The Metal Shredders

High Street and the gallery district where the restaurant is and he'll be home free, at least free of Kevin. Kevin is still maintaining his half-jog to keep up. The end is almost in sight. He tells Kevin he's late, but his neighbor doesn't mind. Why should he? Kevin's not the one who's late, it doesn't concern him. As soon as John got home from the Shredders and cruised the street for a parking spot, a hassle since his vintage V-8 needed a longer space, his heart dropped at the sight of Kevin's bicycle on the porch. That meant he was home. As John parallel-parked, which took precious moments, he imagined Kevin lifting a blade of the venetian blinds. He jumped out of the truck and rushed across the lawn and up the stairs. No Kevin so far. Maybe his neighbor was in the backyard or ranting on the phone. He ran straight to the shower and turned it on—in case Kevin was following him, the noise would turn him away. He stood listening for a minute. Nothing.

Safe.

A hot shower later he was forgetting about Kevin. He got a beer and stood in the kitchen in his towel. Went over the day in which he seemed to accomplish nothing beyond rounding up people for flu shots and royally pissing off his dad by shredding the LTD. After all that, when the nurse came, no one lined up for their shots and he had to go round them up again.

He'd been having several bad feelings lately where work was concerned, and one of those bad feelings was about Joe Greenslade, which was maybe one reason he was so crazy to get him a flu shot. As if this could postpone the inevitable. Greenslade was currently without transportation, but that was the least of it. "The car's in the shop," he said although John didn't know what that meant. It certainly didn't mean the car was actually in a bona fide shop somewhere, being fixed. It was probably at some shade-tree mechanic's, up on concrete blocks in a backyard, the engine swinging from a dying hackberry limb. In addition,

Greenslade now performed his night-watchman duties lying down. When John left him he practically had to tuck him in. He got out Greenslade's pillow, afghan, and ancient transistor radio from the filing cabinet while Greenslade headed straight for the couch. John handed him the radio— the old man liked fingering the dial and holding on to the 9-volt battery that dangled out the back. John made one request of Greenslade: keep an ear out for any dogs. But then he realized one more thing: Joe's ears were shot, too. He got out Joe's coffee mug, another cute saying—OLD JAZZMEN NEVER DIE THEY JUST DECOMPOSE—poured him the rest of the coffee, about half a cup, then turned the machine off so the place wouldn't burn down (that'll be next). Joe used his chest as a tray. John watched the coffee mug tremble against Joe's clogged breathing, and with a sense of doom left him lying there and drove back home and then scrammed upstairs to avoid his neighbor.

Probably the flu shot'll give Greenslade the flu, that's the kind of luck they've been having. And it's a respiratory strain this year. Danger of pneumonia, they say, particularly high for the elderly. Standing in his kitchen, half-naked and drinking a beer, John relived the coffee mug bumping up and down on Greenslade's chest, riding the unsteady inhales and exhales. Not good.

He finished the beer, put on slacks, shirt. Then a jacket and tie because his mother would be at the restaurant, too. He considered giving Tony a quick call, telling him to get there early in the morning to check on Greenslade and the dogs. Tony was an early bird, and if he was going to be passing out poisoned hamburger, he should be doing it without anyone knowing, without alarming anyone. But he dismissed the idea—it was his problem, not Tony's—and hurried down the stairs. Off to the restaurant and his pissed-off father.

On the porch at the bottom of the steps was Kevin. Bending over his bike, but really waiting for him. Bending over his bike, John thought, like the social idiot he was, butt in the air, pretending to adjust a pedal strap while he waited.

John kept moving. A quick wave to Kevin's butt—*how you doing.* Kevin quickly straightened, said, "Hey, I was just going for a walk, too," and fell in with John. "I'm not going for a walk," John answered. "I'm meeting someone and I'm already late." Kevin started talking.

So now he's stuck with him. As they head down Dennison, past Hubbard Elementary which John has recently learned is the school where they bus all the kids from homeless shelters, Kevin has now reached the very latest Latest Development with his wife whose name, John is reminded again, is Cecilia. After thinking about sleeping with the guy in her study group, she went ahead and did it. "I knew she would," Kevin says. John crosses the street to the ceremonial corbel arch through which no one ever enters Goodale Park, voted in one of the alternative papers as the best place to have sex after dark. Gay sex, that meant. Not sex for him, not for him and Elise. John wonders how true it is. He jogs it all the time and one loop around is nine-tenths of a mile. It hardly seems big enough—and there are no hidden, interesting topographical pockets that could turn it into a sex arcade after dark. Maybe this subject could be the conversational opener when he draws shoulder to shoulder with one of the petite brunettes he "runs with." Instead of a nod and a great-day! hello he needs to slow down for more in-depth conversation. Slow down for two of them, that is. There are now four that he has his eye on. The two he passes are Elise perfected—on earth. The other two are Elise perfected in outer space. These two he can't believe. They motor right past him, a half-naked pair of physical phenomena who make him want to move to Florida for the year-round summer parade. They must be full-time exercisers. Last time they passed him they were wearing lycra cat-burglar outfits, all black, tighter than skin, and although every inch of flesh except hands and head were covered, it was a sight in some ways more provocative than the exposed shoulders, abs, and upper legs that had kept him going through the long summer days (and nights).

Just two more blocks and he'll be at the restaurant. It's too bad about Cecilia and the study-group guy. He was really hoping for a happy resolution to this marriage so that Kevin and Cecilia could get back together and leave him alone. But now that Cecilia has slept with the guy, Kevin will need to chew and gnaw that much more. Longer chewing. Longer gnawing. Longer and longer monologues as the story develops into one Latest Development after another. It's not that Kevin is a bad guy. He's just a block of uninterestingness. He probably has that new form of autism, John thinks, where the people are really smart but have no social skills whatsoever.

But it doesn't matter how many times John tells himself that Kevin is not such a bad guy. Because he's driving him crazy. John doesn't know if he can stand much more. He's got to do something. Maybe move out. It's not as if he's financially stuck with a crummy upstairs apartment with a brown painted floor. It's just that its crumminess fits his current mood. Yet there's nothing at all preventing him from moving someplace nice.

On High Street (almost there!) he passes a fleet of newspaper boxes—the free weeklies, the real estate booklets, the coin-operated box for the *Columbus Dispatch.* He won't find what he's looking for in the real estate booklets—their ads for suburban townhouse rentals with fitness center and one-month's free rent are pretty pictures of existential despair. He'll be out in the wetlands somewhere looking over the highway while he rides a LifeCycle with the left pedal strap missing. He grabs a *Columbus Alive,* the alternative weekly that always carries a listing of neighborhood rentals. He decides it right then and there: he's moving. The long winter nights are just ahead. Long long nights for Kevin's long long visits.

He finds it funny that he's starting to look forward to this Kevin-free dinner. Especially because he knows the dinner is meant to torture him.

The Metal Shredders

When the Senior showed up at the Shredders and found the LTD gone, more than gone, shredded, he issued his ultimate punishment: a dinner invitation. But now here's John in jacket and tie, his dress shirt buttoned all the way to the top, standing across the street from Enigma's restaurant, salivating for cuisine volatile.

Across the street John spots his parents walking with Octavia. They're heading into one of the shops, killing time before their reservation.

"There they are, gotta meet my folks. Hey!" John calls showily across the street but not loudly enough for them to hear. He cuts away and jay-walks over before Kevin can answer. Then he ducks down the alley, adjusts his tie again, and enters Enigma's from the back. He checks in with the maître d', an oversized portrait of whom unaccountably hangs as one of the pieces of art, then half-stands, half-straddles a stool in the bar area and orders a beer. He checks the rentals in *Columbus Alive* while he waits, reads the "Dishing the Dirt in Cowtown" gossip column about Columbus celebs, except there are no Columbus celebs. The writer of the column seems to choose which one of his personal friends had the most interesting week. John reads about an exquisite dinner of Chinese cuisine prepared by a "nationally known painter in his beautiful northwest Columbus home." The things John misses by being at work all day. And he doesn't mean that nastily. Somebody's No. 1 dim sum is another person's No. 1 copper. Every day that he's at the Shredders, life goes on and he's missing it. Important things are happening to other people; they're not important to him but maybe some of them should be. He doesn't know, for example, who that nationally known painter is, he has no idea (although the rest of the nation must). His trouble is that he picked one hydrant and one hydrant only to piss on, and now he wants to widen his territory. But it's hard. His hydrant is his home, has been for a long time. It's hard to go elsewhere.

But he's only thirty, he tells himself. That's like being fifteen these days. So what that he staidly acts twice his age, two times fifteen means he's still only thirty. There's time yet to make a change.

He puts the paper aside. The ink has already smeared his palms black. He asks for a paper napkin but they don't have any. He goes into the restroom to wash. Maybe, he thinks, dispensing soap on his hands, the answer to the money problem is as simple as washing it. He realizes now that he has to do something. If he lived on a farm, he'd burn it. Nowhere to burn it here. He can't stash it in the backyard. He can't bring it inside because of the smell. He's going to have to take measures. He squirts out more liquid soap. Wash the money. Of course. Just wash it, stupid.

For some reason he assumed that his own measured disinterest in the money would act as another type of Stafford Slide. He could stand still and do nothing while the laws of physics miraculously enacted themselves upon the money. The problem would take care of itself. The odor would dissipate, Tony and Greenslade would enjoy a tidy festival of spending, and for himself, he'd spend or not spend his share, or maybe give it away. In fact, that's what he's been thinking of. He's been seriously considering giving the money away. To whom is the question—a question like that opens the page to a brand-new world—children, minorities, abuse victims, elderly—discovering that world and sorting it out will probably be more complicated than this current problem of deodorizing the money. If he tries to do something good with the money, his choice of recipient—those homeless kids, for example, who are bused to a school right in his own neighborhood; now that seems like a logical choice— even that will be open to recriminations. If you choose kids, you haven't chosen the elderly dying in the winter because they can't pay their heating bills. If you choose the elderly, you haven't chosen minorities trying to start up their own businesses. If you choose minorities, you haven't chosen foreigners struggling to learn English and better themselves. If you choose foreigners, you haven't chosen American women who are hiding in shelters from their American husbands. If you choose women, you haven't chosen men. And if you choose men, you haven't chosen children and you're back where you started from.

On the other hand, if you just spend the money on yourself, no one will have a problem with that. That would be fine.

As with almost everything, it's simply easier to be selfish.

When he comes out of the restroom, his parents and Octavia and the maître d' are waiting for him. He says hi and kisses his mother on the cheek. Through a crack in her hair he spies the real-life maître d' looking at him and behind him the oversized portrait of the maître d' also looking at him.

"This way," the maître d' says.

Octavia's father taps the salad fork against the cloth napkin. In others it would be a sign he's thinking something out, using the fork like a metronome to tap out his thoughts. In the Senior's case it's the fork itself that he's thinking about. The WE SCRAP FOR A LIVING magnet slips out of his pocket and he clicks it against the utensil. "Look at this," he murmurs.

Octavia checks out John's reaction, but his face is mild and content, his usual expression. He takes things so calmly, she thinks. Just goes along, digs in, never complains. She wishes she could be like him, or at least talk to him, really talk to him to find out what he's like so she could decide if she wants to be like him. But at least she'd prefer to have his contentment. At least she'd prefer to stop torturing herself over Byron. Like now. If she goes one step farther in this direction, she'll start talking to herself, which is another form of talking to Byron. Right in front of her parents who will see her mumbling. Her glance moves from table to table, from diner to diner, wondering if Byron is eating here tonight. Maybe he's here on a trip from Boston and has chosen this restaurant. It's supposedly the best one, so therefore it would be the one he would choose. In her mind it's possible. *It could happen*, as some lady comedian is always saying on TV. It's so possible that whenever she sees a car with Massachusetts plates, she has to speed up and pass it on the road to make sure he's not inside.

"It's very strange," her father says, tapping the magnet to the salad fork.

"A slight pull?" John asks mildly.

"Slight," her father says.

"Oh John," her mother says. Their wine orders come and Octavia's looking forward to taking a big gulp to help her get through the evening. The wine is served in huge goblets but they're filled only about an eighth of the way. Octavia wants it all the way to the top. All the way. In ordering their wine her mother had put up a fuss about a certain label. Now, as a different label is set before her, the waitress assures her that it's on the house.

"Our maître d' has recommended this wine," she says. "It has many of the grassy qualities you mentioned."

She waits while Octavia's mother takes a sip, raises her chin to queen level, and sucks it around her palate. The best part of the whole show is that her mother knows absolutely nothing about wine except that sometimes it's red and sometimes it's white and sometimes it's even pink. She's just real pleased with herself. She found out about some Chardonnay from the Russian River Valley ten minutes ago when they walked into Europia, the wine-and-gourmet-food shop a few doors down. They were just killing time, but the owner, a lively attractive woman wearing a BAD HAIR DAY baseball cap, started schmoozing her mother right away and the next thing you knew her mother, usually so chilly and flatline, was laughing and doing her version of social flirting, a painful-to-watch extravaganza of arm-sweeping and cackling. The owner grabbed her mother like they were best buddies and said, "Come here, I want you to taste this," and the two of them went in the back to share a glass of the Russian River vintage. The owner was about Octavia's age and lived in the neighborhood—Octavia had seen her working in her yard—and Octavia would have liked a friend, especially a friend who owned the best wine store in Columbus, but no matter. She heard her mother's hypergirlish giggle from the back room. She busied herself with checking through the gourmet mustards and jams and the do-it-yourself sushi kits while the Senior played the distracted husband, checking the wine, trying to look busy. His deep breaths gave him away. When they left the store, her mother offered the owner a wide embrace—her mother who usually hugged like she was passing out mason jars of formaldehyde. Octavia couldn't exactly say she was jealous, but she couldn't exactly say she wasn't.

"How is it?" the waitress asks her mother.

Her mother says carefully, "I would say that takes some of the disappointment out of not being able to enjoy the DeLoach."

"I'm glad," the waitress says gamely.

Her mother's not actively trying to be pretentious when she says this. It's just a natural gift of hers, utter pretentiousness.

As usual, her father ignores her mother with such complete success that it's no longer an act of rudeness. Through long practice and discipline he has stopped receiving the sensory messages that would inform him of her presence. She doesn't anger him, she doesn't embarrass him, she doesn't please him. He simply doesn't register her. In this way, she's even less than the air he breathes, which might, due to its pollution or pollen count, cause a reaction.

"Do you think I should go with fish tonight?" her mother says.

"I think I'm going to go with fish tonight," her mother says.

"Now this," he says, still tapping the fork in question, "could be a magnetic stainless, or it could be a chrome steel."

Octavia is caught between her mother and father, neither one of whom she wants to listen to, but both of whom she tries to, out of politeness.

"It's a strange business with flatware," he continues. "You have something one-hundred-percent magnetic—steel—and you put seven-percent nickel in it and it becomes nonmagnetic."

"This is such a fabulous place."

"I'm surprised they'd stock this kind of flatware. I'm surprised it stuck to my magnet this easily. Look at this. There's about a five-percent pull."

"Where have I heard that before," Octavia says.

"Very good, darling," her mother tells her.

"Mm-hmm," John says to their father.

"Anything where food is going to be touched, you don't want it to rust."

"It's stainless, John, for god's sake," her mother interrupts. "Henry the Eighth didn't have cutlery as good as this."

"Stainless, Janet, if it's magnetic stainless, only has very little pull, but look at the pull on this."

"Maybe we'd better ask for chopsticks," her mother says.

"That's funny," Octavia says, surprised, shocked, awestruck that her mother could say something even remotely humorous.

"This is what we call 301 stainless," her father decides. "It's got about six and a half percent nickel in it."

Octavia's mother raises her hand for the waitress. "My husband will be needing chopsticks. Your fork isn't good enough for him."

"Janet," the Senior corrects.

Octavia's mother ignores him by retreating to a hazily pleasant nowhere land. She smacks at the wine. Her hair is rigid, looped under each ear so that together the style forms a closed set of quotation marks. Octavia checks out the plastic surgery she's sure her mother has had. Those creases that used to be in her forehead are gone, from Botox injections no doubt. Botox, the same bacteria that causes botulism, the same bacteria she needs a tetanus shot to avoid. While she's trying to get rid of it, her mother's injecting herself with it. The nurse who gave her the flu shot checked out her back and cleaned the wounds and told her yep, better go to Med-Ohio for a booster. And if she didn't? One soaring invasion of Botox. At least she would die with lovely skin.

Thanks to Elise, John now puts a metaphorical spin on everything. He has to. She'll never come back if he doesn't learn to view the world poetically. And the poetic translation he's giving to the Senior's disquisition on silverware requires no dictionary, it's that obvious. The LTD is gone, nothing to remember the old man by, no farewell gesture to the horse-and-cart days when the metal-shredding sphere was the whole backside of the world. Without the LTD there's nothing to do in homage but for his father to metamorphose into his grandfather. And that's what has happened. The Senior is impersonating his grandfather. This silverware analysis, it was another one of his grandfather's favorite stunts. The day his grandfather denounced his mother's silverplate utensils in Trillia pattern as nothing but common 301 dung, he had her in tears. That won't happen again. His mother, he sees, has clocked out.

John can't say it's bad, he can't criticize a marriage that has lasted six times longer than his own, but at least he and Elise didn't ignore each other. At least they fought, or tried to fight. He wasn't much of a fighter and though she bragged about how much she liked a good battle, neither was she. When it came time to step into the ring, she turned tail and ran away to her sister's.

Now Octavia, he muses, looking over at his sister gulping down the wine, her expression stuck between shock and amusement at his mother's call for chopsticks, Octavia'd put on the boxing gloves and have it out with you. She's all extrovert, and that's good, he supposes, she gets it all out so there's nothing inside to gnaw at her. Elise wasn't like that; she let things fester inside. She got down on herself. She had that self-hatred stuff so many women seem to have. He wishes she were more like Octavia in that way, Octavia who appears to love herself. He wishes he hadn't said no to counseling. Maybe they could take a kickboxing class together when she comes back.

He's logged on now. Elise dot com. There's no going back. He's deep in the chat room, surfing through the message threads. He knew he was headed here as soon as Kevin started up. It's another reason he doesn't like to hear his neighbor's marital troubles: it takes him to Elise. Kevin's story serves to add an extra worry: Elise with another man. He's got a search engine looking up all those possibilities. Out of the 249,000 matches Google comes up with, the one that seems most likely is this: a man she'll meet substitute teaching in Telluride. An English teacher, sensitive, literary, *caring*. He *cares* about his students, especially the ones from broken homes.

But Elise! John wants to shout. I care, too! After all, I'm giving the money away to the homeless kids bused to Hubbard Elementary.

Caring about kids, he wants to warn her. Does he brag about all his caring? Caring is just another man's hustle. If he's so caring, he'd stay away from a married woman, separated or not. He's going to care her right into bed, like that study-group fellow who got what he wanted from Kevin's wife.

He needs to talk to her. He needs to warn her. He wonders if she has e-mail yet.

Earlier that day:

"Honey, everyone is happier when they know their place."

Octavia knew this was the opening line of a lecture. Her father had followed her up to her little house on stilts, the place she was trying without success to turn into her own office with her own personal stamp. She had a framed Jasper Johns poster up now, but it still didn't feel right. The whole place was so dirty and Goodwillish. Her desk was metal, not wood; it made her feel like a lowly civil servant working in the cellar of some World War II government office that had yet to discover alphabetical order, much less the computer.

"Okay," she said, moving into the bathroom. She shut the door and stripped off her sweats and began a sponge bath while he talked.

"One thing my own father taught me and it was one of his most valuable lessons: these people are not your friends. Can you hear me okay?"

"I don't want them to be my friends," she called through the door.

"You may think it sounds unfair, but inequality is the way the world works."

"Okay," she said, a little more forcefully. She turned up the water. But he didn't stop.

He gave the door a knock. "Look at scrap, the best and the worst. You've got pure grade, and you've got pure, excuse the term, shit. What happens if you mix them? Shit happens. The shit doesn't turn into pure grade, but the pure grade sure turns into shit. So you keep them separate. The same with people."

The problem was he'd driven up in his Trooper and there she was in her jogging sweats, standing with Tony and Joe Greenslade and John and checking out the dog holes and dog poop, and right when he caught her she was laughing. She was actually looking as if she were enjoying Tony's and Greenslade's company, which was ridiculous of course, but he didn't know that. Of course he didn't know that because he had never taken the time to know her at all. Had he asked her question one about Spain? Six years she was there. No questions. Saving his questions for the seventh year? He never even suggested that she pose as translator for the Hispanic graders—probably didn't realize she could speak Spanish after six years in

Spain. He'd married young and had kids young and lived his life and it hadn't included Spain, so there was no point bringing it up. Maybe that was ungenerous of her, but that's what she thought. It was a little frustrating being around family members who not only didn't understand you but didn't seem at all interested in understanding you. If not them, then who? Maybe that's why Byron was so appealing. He seemed so interested in her. His curiosity burned through her.

Asshole.

At any rate, the point is she didn't feel a camaraderie with Tony or Greenslade or any of those others, and if he knew her the least little bit he would have known that and not bothered with this lecture, which she was trying without success to drown out with the faucet. She turned off the water long enough to say, "I might not know anything about scrap, but I know a little bit about life." She rammed the faucet back on. She pulled on her jeans and white sweater. White—stupid color to wear in this place.

Her father played his palm on the door. "Steel rusts whether it's in a scrap yard or a palace. Copper doesn't. You use steel for your pipes, see what happens. You're going to have trouble below."

"Okay!" she yelled. "Enough already!" She put on SPF 15 moisturizer and lip gloss and brushed her hair.

"The fact is, human beings come in different alloys—what can you do about it? By the time they're adults their alloy has a specific gravity of this and maybe a tensile strength of that and it's not going to change."

She opened the bathroom door and stepped out. "I have to go get my flu shot now," she told him.

The Senior is in the middle of talking about white goods and he doesn't pause while the waitress slides in his plate of prime rib. The city is starting to give him problems, he tells John. He's tested out at ninety decibels, and they want him to build four soundproof walls around the yard.

"That'll run a few pennies," John says.

Otty has ordered the grilled salmon with chive oil, his mother (after all her fish talk) the duck breast with picholine olive and thyme sauce. John went for the Enigma's meat special. Despite the lemongrass-and-leeks sauce, it's pretty unmysterious chicken, about as undaring as the Senior's plain prime rib. He wishes he'd ordered something more adventurous.

The Senior says, "With start-up costs at half a million, that's an expense I don't need."

John nods his agreement. This is a conversation he can do in his sleep. It doesn't interfere with the surfing going on inside his head. He's adding a message to an old topic thread: the first time Elise met his parents. They'd made love before going over, a spur of the moment thing that left them late and rushing. Breathless, faces flushed, their insides tumbling, they sat stiffly far apart from each other in the living room with the other two still lifes. Mom, this is Elise; Dad, this is Elise. It was before his grandfather had come to live with them. There was no ant farm axed into the wall; the carpet woof flashed golden as a breeze-blown hay field. For long excruciating moments between gambits of dialogue, the only sound was the tinkle of ice cubes in their gin 'n' tonics and John imagined the sound as arising within a hay field. He saw little Beatrix Potter mice having tea. When he looked over at Elise, he saw another little creature on her foot, the molted skin of snake atop her shoe, clinging there through the grace of static electricity: the condom they had just used.

His glances at Elise burned like heat-seeking missiles, drawn uncontrollably to her feet. He tried not to stare at the condom, but the more he tried the more ridiculous his conversational posture became. He feigned rivetedness on the opposite side of the room, the vase of lilies, the book-bound *National Geographics*, the framed golf ball autographed by Jack Nicklaus, the painting of the Eiffel Tower, the scarlet OSU logo carved into a garden boulder. He craned toward the window as if at a car accident. He checked out the ceiling's plastering job, fake-mesmerized by the half-moon sweeps. But always after these brief contortions he swung back to Elise and watched horror-struck as the condom on her foot enlarged into an eye-catching carbuncle. When he looked again, the carbuncle had bloomed into a bridge troll screaming *look at me look at me!* He quickly twisted away and aimed his stare at his empty gin 'n' tonic glass bleeding water drops upon its coaster. He bore down, straight ahead, fighting the urge to look once more at her foot, until the commanding pull of his neck muscles swung him back around and he came face to face with a snorting rhino, its horn sheathed in pleasure-giving Trojan. It was pawing Elise's toes and getting ready to charge the room. How could they not see it?

At any moment he expected his father to reach over and sock him in the jaw.

But the scene from hell never materialized. No one ever noticed it, not even Elise. As they all left to go out to eat, John reached down and swept the condom from her shoe without Elise's being any the wiser. He had nowhere to put it except his pocket, and during dinner he reached inside and felt his own sperm squishing inside the casing. What was beautiful one minute was gross the next, his life force turned into scrap goods. While his fingers examined inside his pocket, his eyes inspected outside. He considered his parents, who now and then had locked themselves into the same embrace. He looked at Elise, cheeks tingling with wine blush, her face suffused with vulnerability. He felt the urge to throw the condom on his warmed dinner plate, next to the veal medallions, his golden coin, his declaration to the world.

He didn't, of course. People might have taken it the wrong way.

Ohio,
The Heart
of It All

 Part Two

8

Med-Ohio is in a lousy part of the city, but the nurse at the Shredders recommended it and Octavia needs her tetanus shot. The waiting room reminds Octavia of a marriage license bureau, the manila walls, the linoleum floor patterned to match a spoiled potato. Everyone in the waiting area is quiet, the way you are when you're entering into a big mistake. The patients, stymied and irritated by their fill-in sheets, are so downtrodden and unsightly that at first Octavia thinks it's a joke, something intentional in the spirit of Halloween, tooths crayoned out, skin afflictions pasted on, sewn-in fright hair under the John Deere caps. Welcome to the primary care–less crowd. She's one of them. No personal physician to write down on her fill-out sheet. Octavia slumps in the orange plastic bench and stares down at the dark spoils in the linoleum.

It's not that these people were destined to look this way, not judging by the prettiness of the little girl skipping toward her. It's just that they've taken their package of natural gifts and stomped all over them. In a remarkable way they've made the very least of what they have. Octavia jerks to attention when she hears a mother snap, "Get over here so I can spank you." Of course she's going to come now, Octavia wants to respond to the woman. It's beyond her what the little girl has done. Something, must have been something, in the split second Octavia spaced out. The girl refuses to march toward her spanking and now she's in for it. Octavia keeps her head down, her heart beginning to thump. The mother probably senses Octavia as a disapproving interloper; she might take it out further on her kid if they make eye contact.

Once again she's back standing in line at a 7-Eleven in Framingham, idly thinking to herself, *I think I'm the only one here who hasn't been recently deinstitutionalized.* She remembers how she even glanced outside for the bus and the reintegration counselor. Everyone in line had forty-ouncers or cigarettes, they coughed up precancer phlegm when they talked, their flamboyantly filthy hands and nails fished for change in each one of their dirty pockets. Then a man walked into the store, a gun was produced, and Octavia thought, *He's going to choose me, the normal one, sticking out like a sore thumb.* Did he choose her, or did she imagine that he chose her? Was the gun at her head? She stood there not believing what had happened. Only seconds afterwards, the lady next in line pushed her Colt 45 to the register as if nothing had occurred. "You're gonna have to wait a fucking minute," the counter guy told her. Their untreated cavities snarled at each other. "Aren't we brave now, asshole," a thin and corroded man called out in a friendly sort of way, but the counter guy didn't like it, and that started it, a shouting match and threats to knock some teeth out. And then the lady tried to leave without paying for her Colt 45 and the counter guy grabbed her and they were on the floor. Soon everyone was on the floor, although Octavia doesn't think she was on the floor. There was still a gun pointed at her head, just hovering there.

From there it was almost a beeline to Byron's bed—despite the wife she knew about (she didn't know about the pregnancy, although that would explain Byron's increasing albeit absolutely *nice* urgency).

In her moments of inner truth-telling, Octavia knows she upped the ante on the traumatic effect of the robbery even though the robber was perfectly civil—except for the pistol to her head, which she may or may not have imagined. She knows she was just looking for an excuse to be with Byron. Being temporarily detained with those other customers while she waited to give her statement to the police (which diverged so remarkably from what others were saying that she almost believed she might be delusional; what she witnessed was *gun, gun at my head, give me money, thank you, have a good day, good-bye everyone*). What she witnessed of her fellow human beings there in the 7-Eleven made Byron a god among men. But then again she was Miss America compared to them—and Madame Curie and also Jackie Joyner Kersee.

The swat is over—well, two swats and a rather forceful tug on the shoulder—and the little girl is crying. "She's gotta learn," the mother says. Octavia is repulsed by the mother's showoffy pride, and the way a woman across from her murmurs "hmm-mmm" as if to a powerful preaching. Octavia watches the floor in misery. She can feel it in the air, the little girl's stubbornness; as soon as the crying dies down she's going to do something else. She wants to telegraph her a message: *Don't do it. It's not worth it. It's a bicycle against a car.*

But the sun is shining when she finally escapes outside, and she's received her tetanus shot, and her left arm is already sore, and life is great again or at least passably good. She can keep on living. That's the main thing. She feels the full heat of an Indian summer. The good-bad throbbing of life.

Next to the Med-Ohio is a discount card shop. She strides inside and finds a once-expensive foam costume of a red M&M reduced to $8. She saw the same M&M costume somewhere else for $29.99.

She's excited about Halloween. She's already gathered some cornstalks across the road from the Shredders and bundled them together to make an autumn decoration for her front porch. Around her neighborhood the houses have started to come alive with preparations: trash-bag pumpkins swollen big and round with leaves, spider-web ropes curtaining porches, plastic skeletons frozen in mid-dance. This is great, she thinks. She makes two trips to the grocery before she decides on what candy to buy: miniature boxes of Nerds, miniature Snickers, miniature Three Musketeers, and full-size bubble-gum Pops. She can't wait to see, she has to admit, what Ohio has to offer for Halloween. The heartland, after all.

She can't believe that John isn't letting everyone at the Shredders off early. Trick-or-Treat is from five to seven. She can't believe the world isn't tingling with anticipation.

John doesn't even know it's Trick-or-Treat. Good thing he's now living with her—the kids would be soaping his windows and trashing his front yard. Out of the blue he asked if he could stay with her until he found a new place. She didn't mind, she has a big house to herself, and John was partly responsible for how she lucked into it. He was the one who helped her find a place, driving her through all the neighborhoods he thought she'd like, Grandview, German Village, Bexley, Clintonville, the Short North. There was some interesting stuff going on once you got outside the staid 'burbs of Upper Arlington where her parents live. They parked the car and walked the streets of the Short North; she could see the buildings of downtown not a mile away. The neighborhood was bustling. A lot of good-looking guys were out, although most were walking with other good-looking guys. Everyone was strolling the sidewalks, enjoying the day, getting ready to pick out their restaurant. The places with outdoor seating were already jammed. The weather was brilliant, with a touch, just a touch, of early autumn sadness: the light fading that much more quickly, the heat and sunshine like a final hug at the airport. On a whim they walked into a realtor's office and the lady there took them down the street to two apartments above the High Street shops. She was expecting something cramped and Bostony, but the roomy apartments bloomed out like one huge mushroom after another. The floor-to-ceiling window and the blond wood added an intoxicating sunshine to the place and she was ready to say okay on the spot but John had stationed himself behind the realtor and was flopping his head to and fro—no, no, no. Let me take a day or two to think about it, Octavia demurred. John led her down the side streets and they walked some more. That place was *perfect!* she told him. Why did you do that? John just shook his head.

On one of the corners sat a brick house, so new the porch and its pillars were still wrapped in plastic, awaiting their coat of paint. The house was funky and high-tech but styled to fit in with the older brick houses. In the small front yard a woman with spiked blond hair unloaded rhododendron bushes from a Toyota truck. She surged with friendliness and energy and told them about the house, how she had designed and built it—one of several houses she had done, in fact. "Isn't it fun!" she said about the house. She offered to show them inside and they introduced themselves in between enthusing about her house, her sense of style, her great bathrooms, her open-air designs. The woman said she was buying this house herself she loved it so much.

Her name was Connie and she took them to another house she had built down the street. The owners were professors, going abroad for a year, and their rental deal long struck with a visiting professor from Wellesley had just fallen through when the woman was abruptly diagnosed with leukemia. That's where I went to school, Octavia wanted to say, but it quickly seemed out of place. The couple was leaving in a week, leaving it for Connie to rent after they departed.

Octavia took it immediately. It had three bedrooms upstairs with three full baths, and the open-air feel of Connie's other house. Her grandfather would have liked the glass-block kitchen counter; he could have perhaps started an alligator farm in there. The rent was $950 a month, a price she'd be lucky to score for a studio in Boston. Octavia remembered how things like this had routinely happened to her in Spain. It was the way most things had come about in Spain, walking around, happening into things, the next place to live, the next job, the next set of friends. Plus, she would just be *staying* there, housesitting for the couple, and the psychological factor was addictive, she was not *living* there, she could leave any time. For her friends back in Boston who kept feigning ignorance about Ohio (was it a state? where was it exactly? did people or just cows live there? did the abacus work as fast as the cash register?) she could now apply these words: *housesitting, temporary, doing someone a favor.* Only doing that, until it was time to go back to New England.

Her house (she quickly liked it enough to start using the possessive) had a master bedroom far from the other two. Guests could stay at the house and she wouldn't even know they were there, so when John asked a few weeks later if he could stay there for a while, she could hardly say no. She had seen the place he was living in. She knew he had a house somewhere else but he hadn't offered to show it to her. Perhaps because he would then feel obliged to follow it up with a conversation about Elise. She understood what he was doing, creating a deliberate limbo so he wouldn't have to make a choice. His second-floor apartment was a gloomy tube of bedrooms recarved into living room and kitchen. It was never meant to be the apartment it was trying to be but that, she supposed, was why it suited John.

That kind of apartment meant you were free of obligations, free of rudimentary social awareness. It was no wonder John had no idea when Trick-or-Treat was. That was okay, she's been happy in fact to take care of it, leaving work early to make sure to be at her station at five o'clock, arm wrapped around a big bowl of candy, waiting for the throng of Trick-or-

The Metal Shredders

Treaters. She has on her red M&M outfit. The weather is an autumn bless-
ing, warm enough for T-shirts. She stands outside on her porch and sees
that her other neighbors have done the same. Down the street she can see
them; like her, all of them are costumed, some elaborately. She hears
spooky organ music coming from one porch. What will be the big costume among the kids this year? she wonders. Pokemon, Harry Potter,
Scooby Doo? What will be the original costumes, the ones the kids have
thought up and created themselves, robots made out of boxes, tunics their
mothers have helped to sew. She likes those best. She stands ready.

John can barely see the eyes within the chocolaty chewy inside of the
M&M. He stoops down and draws closer to the two eyeholes. The rapid
blinking he manages to see he interprets as surprise. He's pretty sure he
mentioned this in advance, but Octavia's red arms flex their irritation.
He's reminded of marriage and the negotiation that goes into all acts that
otherwise wouldn't be given a second thought. He's happy not to have
Kevin in his hair, but now in living with Octavia all his free will is subject
to a second opinion. Not that this particular activity qualifies as something negligible. It is Octavia's washer after all (or rather the people she's
housesitting for's washer), and as far as the double date with Tony and
Hayley Badecker, he guesses that's not exactly negligible either. Maybe he
should have mentioned both items. In advance. But that Hayley Badecker
comes on so strong. Since Tony was already going to be here . . . One
night, two birds.

"Sorry. Thought I mentioned it," John says.

"No you didn't think you mentioned it." Octavia sounds truly irritated. He scoots away so he won't hear the next sentence. It probably will
have the world *wife* in it.

Out of habit he goes upstairs and prepares to shower, then remembers what he's about to do. He doesn't need to be clean for this. He puts on a pair of yellow Playtex gloves. He looks up when he hears stomping, but it's Halloween beggars. He's sitting on the couch looking at his yellow hands when he hears Tony's voice go "Trick or treat!" Tony is zipped up to his neck in his blue jumpsuit. In his hand is his own Hefty bag of money.

John ties a grease-reeking bandana around his face and leads the way. Spread on the floor of the basement are disposable pie tins growing cultures since last night. A few bills are in each pie tin and on top of these are ladled different liquids whose odor-removing properties will now be tested. Last night Octavia got into the swing of it, searching through her cosmetics for perfume samples, nail-polish remover, hair spray, et cetera. They searched the house for weird chemicals the owners might have on hand.

As they clomp down the basement stairs, John imagines that he can smell it, the fumes of putrefaction rising higher and stronger than the other smells that assault his senses: the Go-Jo and grease from his bandana meets cheap perfume meets mothballs meets garlic meets ammonia cleanser.

First he checks the washer. The load he put in this morning has cycled through. The damp bills cling to the tub sides like paint splotches. He pulls off a freshly laundered twenty, brings it to his nose and pulls down the bandana. Ah . . . yuck.

"Your turn," he sputters to Tony.

Tony moves to the first tin, a U. S. Grant sprayed with shaving cream.

"No, right?" John asks.

"No is right," Tony says.

"Wishful thinking."

In the next tin a twenty is buried in a bog of chewing tobacco and cooking brandy. Another twenty is drowning in Jovan Musk John found in the clearance bin at CVS. "Yo!" Tony shouts out. "Smells like two dead dogs checked into a cheap motel."

"No, huh?"

"No is correct," Tony says. "Who will be next?" he asks, strolling down the aisle like a county fair judge. Strawberry potpourri, cider vinegar, lime tile cleaner, English Leather (another clearance-bin item), rug cleaner, cat pee deodorizer, Lestoil, Chinese fish oil (possibly more rancid than the bills), and Korean chili paste that dyes the bill a garlicky, suppurating red.

Tony gasps, "Lestoil's the best so far." He runs up the basement steps for air.

At the stroke of five, a battalion of Trick-or-Treaters briefly scattered in attack formation. One, two, three, four groups, one right after the other. It was only 5:05 and Octavia was panicking that she'd run out of candy. She started to ration it—instead of four items, one of each type, she cut it down to two.

Then, suddenly, after the initial flurry it stopped. She stood on her empty porch. All was quiet. She heard the detonations of a monster's laugh beating from the house across the street. There were some outstanding costumes—good thing Octavia remembered her camera. The witch gave her an evil grin—neon-green face makeup, greener lips, a wart on the nose, a shiny witch's hat and cape. She snapped Dracula in full regalia: red cape, teeth dripping in bloody canines, an exaggerated widow's peak shoe-polished into his slicked-back hair. The Bride of Frankenstein had wrapped her own long hair around a cage made from a plastic flowerpot.

Excellent.

There was just one problem. All the outfits were worn by the adults passing out the candy. The kids didn't bother with costumes. They wore their street clothes. They didn't bother to say "trick or treat." They moved quickly but with blank expressions, like marathoners at a water station, zapped into a type of fervent nothingness.

"What are you?" Octavia asked one of them.

"I'm a pirate," said a kid in T-shirt and jeans.

"No you aren't," Octavia said.

He took his candy and moved on.

Now it's 5:30 and there is not a soul in sight. Against the unseasonable warmth the thickening darkness feels good. Octavia feels a summer-night loneliness, the kind of loneliness you don't take seriously, the kind that fills you with possibilities. The homeowners in their costumes have moved from their porches to the sidewalk. Everyone starts to gather, and the talk is the same: we're the only ones who dressed up, it's so different than when I was a kid, I spent weeks working on my costume, our neighbor made homemade brownies and wrapped them—ooh, can't do that now. Octavia moves down the street, still carrying her bowl of candy— she has an overflow of the stuff, same as everyone else.

On the corner she finds Connie and a group of her friends celebrating Halloween in high style. An electric piano has been dragged onto her long wraparound porch (the pillars still wrapped in plastic), and a man dressed as the Phantom of the Opera pretends to play as the Broadway album blasts from a speaker. Connie herself has gelled her already spiked hair into thicker spikes and sprayed them and her face silver. She's going for the medieval mallet look.

On the porch sits a bowl as big as a sink filled with candy. "Take some! Take lots!" Connie encourages Octavia. "Isn't this fun! How are you enjoying the house? Isn't it great?"

Octavia heads back down the street to her own house. Tony is outside. He's huddled on the front porch, curled over the railing like a seasick man lurching his vomit into the ocean. He explains the problem. Well, she knew it wasn't going to work, the money will stop smelling when it stops smelling. John with his ideas. She watched him march down to the basement with an armload of stuff, squirt a shaving cream snowman on top of U. S. Grant—what was he thinking? Contact lens cleaner? That is not going to do anything. Moth crystals? They'll keep away the moths. Chili paste? It'll make it spicy. Still, it was sort of fun and she got into it. They went hunting through the house and garage and dug up some interestingly foul liquids with potential deodorizing capabilities. In bed she thought of more things—lime juice, Alka-Seltzer, rubbing alcohol. She half-dreamed them, then fell asleep.

Now Tony tells her they're going to run a load of wash using Lestoil.

"You're not putting Lestoil in the washing machine," Octavia informs him. "You're not putting Lestoil in the washing machine," she repeats to John who's just come out. His bandit's bandana and yellow Playtex gloves work pretty well as a costume—a hell of a lot better than anything she's seen on the kids.

"It says you can put it in the washing machine," John reads from the label.

"You are not putting Lestoil in the washing machine."

"He already ran a load of money in it."

"You did *what!*"

"It's an experiment," Tony explains.

"How could you?"

"Regular detergent," John says. "No harm done."

"This is my house. You are not putting Lestoil in the washing machine."

Tony says, "All I want is money that doesn't stink when I take it into a store and spend it."

"Do you think Lestoil doesn't stink?" Octavia shouts.

John removes a glove and sinks his hand into the bowl of candy. "Let's get back," he says to Tony.

"You are not putting Lestoil in the washing machine."

"Do you want me not to put Lestoil in the washing machine, Otty?"

Octavia marches angrily away from them, to the sidewalk and then down the street and all the way to the corner and then back and around an alley. She has to muster smiles for the drifts of stranded adults, and the smiles actually help to soothe her and she heads home and goes inside and drops her red M&M costume to the floor. John doesn't even know it's Halloween and he doesn't care, it's not on his blip screen, but she knows and she cares and it makes her mad. Oh yeah, and the stupid kids, they want the candy bad enough but none of the ceremony that goes with it.

She plops down on the couch and clicks on the TV. She switches to a cable access show, because that's her mood. A storefront church service is going on, camcorded in bad light. She checks out the home-shopping channels to see if Marie Osmond is talking up her doll collection or Susan Lucci her cosmetics or Richard Simmons his Deal-a-Meal. You'd think that on Halloween Joan Rivers would be on—selling on the Home Shopping Club is the only time she's seen Joan Rivers act nice to people, and it is scary, Halloween scary, she seems even more perverse trying to be sweet. Octavia checks all three shopping clubs. Nobody pathetically famous is shilling tonight.

She switches back to the church service. The lighting is so dingy and cheap-looking. As if light itself, when you're poor, comes in a remaindered spectrum.

She can't believe that John did any of the things he did today, from start to finish. If that was the way he lived his married days, no wonder Elise left him.

On the cable access station the camcorder's wide-screen shot wobbles to a close-up of the pastor, a mountain of a black woman dwarfing her podium, knocking it around like a broom handle. Her parishioners sit in metal fold-up chairs. They're both black and white, it's a healthy mix, and

The Metal Shredders

Octavia is always curious about this, when she sees poor blacks and poor whites together—what is it that connects them? The pastor pushes out from her podium, which bangs to the floor. She prepares to heal. The clank of metal chairs as the people line up.

The doorbell rings. Octavia grabs her bowl and runs. A pair of preteen girls dressed in street clothes, one black, one white, lovely as only preteens can be, stand mutely on her porch. Octavia meets their silence with her own, pretending she has no idea why they're here. They smile. They're too cute. Octavia gives in. "What do you say?" Octavia prompts.

"Trick or treat."

"So what are you dressed as?" she asks.

"I'm a cheerleader," says the one with long, shiny blond hair.

"You are not," Octavia says.

The girl points to her sweater and skirt.

"Where are your pom-poms?"

"What are those?" the girl asks.

"What's your name?"

"Sarah."

"Sarah, you are not a cheerleader."

"I think I am."

"How old are you?"

"Twelve."

"Can't you think of something else besides cheerleader? Or princess?"

"I was a princess last year," Sarah says.

"You know what, if you keep dressing up as princesses and cheerleaders you're just going to be dressing up as a housewife pretty soon except it won't be Halloween. What are you?" she asks the other girl.

"A rap singer."

"No, you're not. What's your name?"

"Jamelle."

"What are you really, Jamelle?"

"Pocahontas," the girl says.

"No, you're not. Where are your pigtails?"

"I don't like pigtails. They don't look good on me."

"Well, the Indians wore pigtails."

Jamelle looks at her; she seems to be wondering whether she should smile.

"So what are you really?"

"A Powderpuff Girl."

"No you're not."

"She's Hermione Granger," Sarah says.

"Who's that?"

"Harry Potter's friend. But she won't say 'cause somebody ragged on her about Hermione Granger is white."

"And she's got buck teeth," Jamelle adds.

"Yeah but she gets those fixed," Sarah said.

"Does Hermione Granger wear Old Navy T-shirts?" Octavia asks.

The two girls stare at her.

"Hermione Granger is British, isn't she?"

"I don't know."

"If she's Harry Potter's friend, she must be British."

The two girls look at her.

"So what exactly is so Hermione Granger about your T-shirt and pants?" Octavia asks. She watches them try to make eye contact with each other without moving their heads. "Is Old Navy a British company?" They don't answer. She holds out the bowl. "Take as much as you want."

"We can come back and visit you sometime," Sarah says.

"Sure," Octavia says.

The healing is in full throttle when she returns to the TV. Two bulky strong men, too muscular to fit nicely into their suits, help to catch the healed. They're young and black-pride bald. They seem intensely conscious of themselves, their own role-model professionalism. Octavia has never had to be anyone but herself, she's been no one's role model. There's plenty more where she came from. Plenty more educated white girls sprawled on a couch, currently hungry for take-out sushi.

The next person up in the healing is large and white, a woman, Octavia believes, with a man's Brillcreamed haircut. She takes her healing hard on the forehead and tumbles back with a vulgar groan. She sprawls backward over metal chairs, crash-folding them on top of herself and the two assistants, and bringing down to the floor with her a domino row of the faithful. The screen goes black, fuzzes, then returns to an image of the poorly lit next person getting healed.

Octavia turns off the TV. She's suddenly had her own vision of healing: baking soda and vinegar. That's the thing that'll do it. That will fix the money right up.

She halts as soon as she starts down the stairs. Ooh . . . Parfum de Cadavre, still going strong. She backs up, finds a wool muffler in the closet, bandages it around her face and tries again. In the basement John has collapsed onto his haunches, his back against the chilly basement wall. Now Tony is working with Didi Seven, a miracle cleaner that comes in a tube like toothpaste. Octavia found it in one of the cupboards. He complains that chili paste has turned one of the bills red. A hundred-dollar bill. He wants to clean it.

In an empty tin can Octavia spreads out a twenty. She sprinkles a mound of baking soda on top, then pours on the vinegar. A hissing foam gobbles the bills.

"Ow!" Tony yelps.

As the bubbles fizz to a flat cream, Octavia watches the face of Alexander Hamilton ebb from sight. Tony squats beside her. He holds out the hundred rubbed with Didi Seven and demonstrates. Benjamin Franklin's face smears between his thumb and forefinger into a greenish red finger-paint.

Octavia looks at her twenty, then at Tony's hundred. She looks over at John, still collapsed. He looks up.

"You put Lestoil in my washing machine for nothing. It's all counterfeit."

9

Sucked in. Now that the money is counterfeit, she's totally into it. How pathetic is that? Already schemes are traipsing about in her imagination. Just once, just one time, she wants to spend fifty or a hundred dollars of counterfeit money and get away with it. She imagines pulling back her hair, lowering on a Reds baseball cap, and with heavy lipstick and eye shadow and lots of zirconia around her neck to trick the camera's reflection, walking into a 7-Eleven—except probably a United Dairy Farmer around here—and passing on a counterfeit bill. She'd never go back to the store again. They'd never *make* her—isn't that what they say? She'd buy a forty-ouncer of Colt 45 like everybody else and they'd never figure her for who she was no matter how many times they looked at their security camera. It's not so much the money as the revenge fantasy it allows her to have. The robbery wasn't that bad, but it could have been a disaster. She's a victim of a tragedy that might have been.

John goes upstairs to call Hayley Badecker and cancel the dinner date. They're too roiled up to do anything tonight but attend to this problem.

He leaves a message on Hayley's machine. It's rude to cancel at the last minute, but in a moment they forget all about her. The counterfeit problem has pushed another problem to the surface: Greenslade, what to do about.

She sees that by the time this is over Greenslade will be a new entry in all their lexicons: Greenslade: 1. (n) an affliction; 2. (n) a crisis characterized by defective personnel or equipment.

John goes up to take a shower and Octavia follows Tony outside where he unzips himself out of his jumpsuit. Considerately, he stands on the sidewalk and throws the uniform into his trunk. He's not so bad, Octavia thinks. He's a little bit thoughtful, a little bit honest, and you need somebody like that for your partner in crime.

It's not yet seven o'clock. Although Trick-or-Treat is still ongoing, technically, the street is dead. All the adults have given up and gone inside and stripped off their costumes with her selfsame dejection. The sadness revisits. Come on, she tells herself, it's such a stupid holiday. It's Halloween. It's not Christmas or Thanksgiving or Passover or even the Fourth of July. It's meaningless. And orange.

She blows out the jack-o'-lantern she carved while sitting on the steps, hoping kids would wander by and sit with her (they didn't). She throws her cornstalks to the ground. No, it's not, she decides. Halloween is not totally meaningless. The words *breach of contract* pop into her head. Children have a contract with the world, too; they're not without responsibilities. *They have a contract with their own childhood.* And nobody tonight fulfilled their childhood duties.

It makes Octavia feel older to worry about children; she's always been a child, a daughter: that's her identity. She's not sure she wants to move up a notch into the next generation. She picks up the cornstalks, stands them back upon the porch.

A half-slip of a whistle pivots her around. Tony catches her attention, shakes his head over thataway. A Mercedes is parking across the street.

138

"No," Octavia whisper-moans. "She's here."

Tony shrugs. He moves in closer to her. "I can go out to Greenjeans myself and you two can go with her."

"I'd rather go to Greenslade's, believe me," she says.

"Well, come on then." His hand reaches out and almost pulls her by the waist. He stops himself so abruptly neither can pretend it was a casual gesture. "Come with me then," he says.

But now it means something to go with him, so for that reason she can't go. Across the street Hayley Badecker waves to them. The pool of light from a street lamp has blackened her into a trim silhouette. She bends inside her Mercedes to retrieve something, and when she does Tony's hand finds the small of Octavia's back. The hand blocks Octavia's retreat when he leans in and kisses her. Then both hands briefly rise up to caress her waist but quickly, fearfully drop away. He's afraid to touch her, she senses; he's afraid even to press his lips too hard. His kiss to her has been a girl's kiss, and Tony's face when he pulls away is a girl's face, embarrassed and tormented.

Hayley, her insouciant man's kiss ready to unleash itself again, is heading their way.

"I shouldn't have done that," Tony says.

"Oh well."

"Should I have done it?"

"Hello!" Hayley Badecker calls. "Thought I'd spare you a pickup."

"You didn't get your message," Tony says. Octavia notices how he clears his throat, trying to sound normal.

"What message? I came straight from work."

Octavia says, "We called you a little while ago. To cancel. Unfortunately, something's come up."

Hayley Badecker's smile doesn't falter. She charges ahead, brimming with confidence. Octavia realizes that she's a little afraid of this chronically upbeat woman. She realizes something else: Hayley Badecker knows right where she lives.

"What's come up?" she asks. Hayley's beautifully white teeth aim their grin from one to the other until they are compelled to answer.

"A big problem with our night watchman," Octavia says.

"That strange little man?"

"One of them."

"Oh dear. That's not good."

"No, it's not. Unfortunately."

"You haven't been robbed, have you?"

"I don't think so," says Octavia. *And she knows about the 7-Eleven,* she thinks. *She knows all my secrets.*

"Actually, we don't know that yet," Tony adds.

"He's not hurt, is he? Fighting off the criminals?"

Octavia shrugs.

"Let's do this," Hayley Badecker suggests in her aerobics instructor's voice, cheerful, hortatory, invincible, unrefusable. "I'll go inside and use your powder room and then we can figure this out and still have a nice dinner. It's Friday. Time to party, boys and girls."

Octavia shoots a glance to Tony, Tony shoots one to her. It doesn't go unnoticed by Hayley Badecker. Octavia watches Hayley register their furtiveness. It doesn't flatten her smile or scorch the enthusiasm. Actually it seems to encourage her. "Okay!" she says.

Octavia was hoping Tony was a better liar than he was. She was counting on his forcefulness. But as Hayley Badecker strides through the door with the two of them dragging behind, she understands she's not getting out of this. An abysmal smell has exploded in her house. The individual odors have fought through the basement. Octavia retreats, unable to take a full breath until she's back outside.

Hayley Badecker asks, "Do you have roaches, is that it? You're doing the right thing, bombing them. This'll kill them. We need to go out to eat because you certainly can't stay here."

"We have a problem," is all Octavia can manage to say.

John drives them all to Greenslade's house. He wonders if it's his fault Greenslade is bedridden. Was it the flu shot or was it coming on anyway? The Shredders has been passing its nights unattended, and each night John has taken about forty thousand dollars home with him and slept with it in one of Octavia's bedrooms. He hasn't told Octavia yet. He doesn't know if this would make her nervous. He assumes it wouldn't, but he has no confidence in any of his character assumptions these days.

Hayley Badecker rides beside him in the front seat. Octavia and Tony sit silently in the back. He has to check the rearview mirror to make sure they're there. Sometimes he sees his own eyes when he angles his head up. Hayley's doing a lot of talking, but that's no surprise. Elise liked to talk, too, but it wasn't so noticeable. Maybe because he liked listening to what she had to say. He's not sure how smart Hayley is, though it strikes him that she could be very successful running her own company or even running for office. The company would have to involve the marketing of some product no one wanted—because Hayley would make them want it. She's got that kind of talent—talent to get you to do the things you don't want to do. Like right now, for example. None of them wants to do this except Hayley. Suddenly Hayley Badecker is fully involved in their strategy sessions. Suddenly she's in there with them making plans. (Well, he doesn't care, really, not if she can solve it. If she can come up with something to get them out of this fiasco, he'll be happy.) First thing, Hayley says, biting her lip fiercely, the wheels turning, first thing is to get the money out of that strange old man's hands. Because he'll be committing a crime if he spends it—and here she leans intimately into John's shoulder as they drive in the dark, she and he in their own front-seat shell of darkness and twosomeness, the silent duo in back almost not there—and who cares if he commits a crime, she adds, but it'll come back to you, John. And will you have committed a crime? Will you be an accomplice, is that what it'll mean?

Until now John hasn't much cared what Tony or Joe Greenslade would do with the money. But now he is starting to cringe. If Greenslade screws up, and with Greenslade that's pretty much a given, they might all be in trouble. John can't trust Greenslade to get rid of the money. John has to get the money himself, he has to have the money in his own hands, he has to watch the money burn up in smoke before he can relax. He imagines the smoke skywriting its good-bye in the air. On the wings of that smoke will drift the last remnants of a husband and wife, two doomed Smalltown, Ohio, schemers. *And that's not a metaphor.* He directs this thought to Elise. Not a metaphor. A fact. Those counterfeit bills are stained with the DNA of a would-be Bonnie and Clyde. People thinking of going into a life of crime should have their genes tested, to make sure they have the Bonnie-and-Clyde gene. Those two didn't; they were genetically coded for disaster.

The porch light shines on Joe Greenslade's unit-sized house. Four or five pumpkins, stair-stepped in size, still flicker their ghoulish faces. Mrs. Greenslade meets them at the door, holding a jumbo pack of miniature Tootsies.

"Mrs. Greenslade, it's John Bonner."

"Who?" she barks out.

"John Bonner. Your husband works for me."

"Thought you was some more Trick-or-Treaters. Well, come on in. I guess that's what you're here for."

"We came to see Joe."

"He's in bed."

"We need to talk to him, Mrs. Greenslade."

"We was supposed to went to Dayton to buy a car, but he's too sick. He's real sick."

"Why do you have to go to Dayton to buy a car?" Octavia asks.

"You give him that flu shot and he got kicked in the stomach with the flu."

"Aren't there cars in Columbus?" Octavia says.

John gives her a look: drop it.

"I know you meant well though, but what's done is done." Mrs. Greenslade removes a tissue from inside her sleeve and puts her mouth to it.

"Has he been to the doctor?"

"What did she just put into that Kleenex?" Hayley Badecker is holding fearfully on to Octavia, whispering too loudly into her ear. John motions the two women to follow him. When they are several steps away, he says, "Stay here until I call you, please."

"Doctor says he's got the walking pneumonia," Mrs. Greenslade says.

John says, "Mrs. Greenslade, I don't know how to tell you this, but if you were going to buy a car with that money Joe, you know, found . . ."

"It's not real money," Tony says.

"What? Is this Tony? Are you Tony? Joe talks about you. Now you are someone he likes."

From several steps away come Octavia chuckles.

"Look at this here." Tony takes out a fresh twenty, squirts some Didi Seven on it and smears Alexander Hamilton's face into mush. "See? It's not real money."

"Who're these other two?" Mrs. Greenslade asks, suddenly noticing the women's huddled shadow.

"Can we come over now, John?" Octavia asks.

John introduces Octavia and Hayley Badecker.

"Y'all look like Trick-or-Treaters. That's what I thought you was." Mrs.

Greenslade turns to Hayley. "Why're you dressed like that if you're not Trick-or-Treating?"

"Oh, you are a darling, you really are," Hayley Badecker says.

"That's her work costume," Octavia says.

A delighted Hayley Badecker plunks her head on Octavia's shoulder and leaves it there. John watches Octavia's jostle, but the head stays put.

"It's late to be working," Mrs. Greenslade says. "Unless you got the night shift."

"I wish," John hears Hayley reply, her head still on Octavia's shoulder, and then he feels a meaningful squeeze of his biceps. He guesses he should be flattered. She's the type to have fun with—fun with a capital F. Everything they did would be fun. Hayley Badecker has the fun gene.

"Can we see that husband of yours?" Tony asks.

"You mean Joe?"

"Yes," Tony says. "You know, me and him are buddies. I need to see that old buzzard."

Mrs. Greenslade starts laughing. "Now you he likes," she says. "You're one of the ones he likes. Well. Well, come on in and talk to him. You're Tony, right? He likes you. Joe!" she calls. "He's in bed," she says.

John follows her past the living room into the squat of a hallway. There are two small bedrooms, one of them used for storage from what John can see. In the other lies Joe. The famous portrait of Jesus hangs at the entrance. This version of Jesus, the movie-star handsome version, is so popular he never thinks twice about it, but tonight it gives him a queer sensation, as though he's entering this dark chamber to administer last rites.

"Joe!" John hails him in an overly loud and cheerful voice.

Greenslade grins and thumbs the air victoriously.

"Look at this," Tony says and holds up the smeared bill in the dimness.

"You're confusing him," John tells Tony. "Step by step. Joe," he says, "Can I turn on the light?"

"Sure," Greenslade croaks.

"How're you feeling?"

"Great." The raspy assurance is hacked out without irony. He gives them the high sign again.

"You remember that money we found?" Tony asks.

Greenslade grins.

"It's counterfeit."

Greenslade laughs happily.

"You understand what I'm saying?" Tony turns to John. "Does he understand what we're saying?"

"I don't know," John says.

John leaves to find the interpreter and Mrs. Greenslade is in the living room talking about the pieces on her mantel to Octavia and Hayley. The living room is surrounded by exposed wallboard. The wallpaper has been steamed off, leaving yellowish glue patches. Pringles potato chip cans line the other end of the mantel like votive candles. Hayley Badecker is explaining to Mrs. Greenslade that she should put her collection of Camel cigarette lighters on an online auction.

"What do you need, honey?" Mrs. Greenslade asks John.

"We need help in here," he tells her.

"What's he doing now, is he dying or anything?"

"No, he's just having trouble . . ."

"Breathing? Nothing to worry about."

"No no, he's fine."

"Then what is it?" Mrs. Greenslade does a finger twirl at her temple, and her raised eyebrows complete the question.

"Something like that," John agrees.

"I know how to talk to him," Mrs. Greenslade assures them. Like a shopkeeper delighted to be overburdened with so many customers, she directs Octavia and Hayley to another collection, on the TV hutch, and then attends to John.

"Can you ask him where the money is? We're having trouble getting through to him."

Mrs. Greenslade moves to the bedside and puts her hands on her hips. "Joe, now you tell them where the money is and stop fooling around. These people are busy and I got one of them going to help me with an auction so I don't have time for this. Joe, are you listening to me?"

He looks up at her.

"Tell them where the money is. Right now."

"The money!" Tony yips.

"The money you come back with in that trash bag I said don't bring in here 'cause it smells worse than a skunk. That money. You know what I'm talking about."

Joe chuckles to himself.

"Don't play stupid with me, old man. Stop your foolishness and answer them."

Joe holds up a finger, his throat hitching several times.

Mrs. Greenslade shakes her head. "Don't know why I bothered to marry him. I'm sorry, boys. Joe!" She leans down and shakes his shoulders. "I thought these boys was Trick-or-Treaters!"

Greenslade's stutter finds its way into a sentence: "I put it in the storage shed."

"Why'd you put it in there?" Mrs. Greenslade asks.

"Where's the storage shed?" John asks.

"Why'd you put it in there? I got things in there I don't want stunk up. I told you not to put it in anywhere where my stuff is going to be impounded by it. I explained it to you how bad it was. Says he has something for me, I'm supposed to be happy because he's happy about something he got from you boys at work. Well excuse me, I've seen what comes out of that place. And I'm not having that in my home."

"Right," Tony says. "You're absolutely right, Mrs. Greenslade."

"How'd it come to get stunk up so bad?"

"You don't want to know."

"Just sitting around that dirty job site too long," John says. "It can be a rather greasy place. So—is the storage shed back here in the yard?"

"Go out the kitchen door, honey. You need to clean up your Shredders, John Junior, take some pride in your work. You need a porch light on?"

The well of light reveals on its far perimeter a storage shed designed like a minibarn. The door is trimmed in white with a white diagonal slash across its top half. It's every bit of craft-cute and cozy that Greenslade's house is not. Mrs. Greenslade goes to fetch the key, but drawing closer, John sees that the hasp hangs loose. He unhooks the lock from the door and opens it. He doesn't smell anything. Instantly he's worried. "Bring a flashlight," he calls to Tony. When he turns around, he sees the light in the bus go off, the bus that sits in the garden. He sees the curtain draw back. It's black where a face would be, but he knows the daughter is watching him.

When they scope the inside with a weak flashlight, they find a battery lantern. The three of them, John, Tony, and Mrs. Greenslade—Otty and Hayley hang back on the porch—search the shed. The odor is there but not strongly. It was there briefly. John knows the bag is gone.

"Who might have taken it?" he asks.

"Nobody would've tooken it." Mrs. Greenslade is still looking. "I can smell it," she says. "It's here."

"No, it's gone," John tells her. "Trust me. If it were here, we'd know."

"I smell it pretty good," Mrs. Greenslade says. "I told him not to bring it in here. I said I don't want no more roadkill in my house. I'm tired of that."

"Who might have taken it?"

"Well who would take it?" Mrs. Greenslade says.

"Who would?"

"Who would want it all stunk up like that?"

"Is your daughter here?"

"Sylvia? Sylvia wouldn't want it. She keeps her place too nice and neat to bring in something like that."

"Can I talk with her?" John asks.

"You're gonna have to talk to her about it," Mrs. Greenslade says. "She's got a neat place, you'll see. She wouldn't want that in her place."

"Is she here?"

"Sure, she's here. She's not off running around if that's what you mean."

"I remember meeting her. I'd like to speak with her," John says.

"You want me to go get her?"

"Thank you, yes," John says.

"Hold on then," Mrs. Greenslade says. She shuffles back into the lighted perimeter toward the back porch where Octavia and Hayley continue their silent, rather dumbfounded watch. "Well, all right," she says, moving past them to the side of the house. "She can be difficult. She's got her own side to her."

John follows but he lingers several steps behind so as not to appear too pushy. But really he's ready to push. He's ready to push them all off a cliff. He wants the bag of money and he wants to leave. Monday, he starts looking for a new night watchman. He wants Greenslade out of his life, yes he does. He's startled by the anger he's about to spit up. This was stupid. How did he get involved in something so stupid?

"You're talking to yourself," Octavia whispers as he passes.

"I'm about to solve this thing. Don't say anything to her."

"To who?"

"The daughter."

"There's a daughter? Where is she?" Octavia whispers.

"She lives in the bus," John answers. "I'm warning you. When you see her . . . Don't say anything."

"This is getting better and better," Octavia says.

"You're not the one going to jail over this," John says.

"You're right," Octavia says.

Mrs. Greenslade knocks on the door of her daughter's abode. The bus is still a bright yellow. It hasn't rusted into the ground yet. It's a school bus, and when the double doors suck inward to open, a stop sign juts out and nearly swipes John on the jaw. When he trips back, he feels something squish under his foot. He puts his foot down again and something else squishes. The flashlight reveals dead goldfish on patterned stepping-stones. He quickly switches off the light. He doesn't want to give Mrs. Greenslade any excuse to veer off the topic. "Hi Sylvia," John says. "We met a few days ago."

Mrs. Greenslade says, "Sylvia, this here's that John Bonner Daddy works for and this here's Tony who Daddy's always talking about. Now I want you to be nice to them. Daddy likes Tony a lot." She turns to Tony. "It'd be nice if you two could be friends."

"I hope we can be friends," Tony says.

"Did you hear that, Sylvia? Tony wants to be your friend."

John says, "Hi, Sylvia, we met, remember? Sure hope you're not getting the flu your daddy's got." He doesn't know why he's talking like this, as if the girl is fifteen years old and he's their good ol' neighbor farmboy. He reaches out his hand but she doesn't shake it this time. Her stomach swings over her belt. Her hair is slicked back. And all the while, all the things he's noticing about her make him worry about Octavia and Hayley. He just knows one of them is going to say something.

"You gonna invite your new friends inside?" Mrs. Greenslade asks her.

"Maybe."

"Maybe yes," Mrs. Greenslade says. "Maybe yes you'd better show your manners, missy. Come on," she tells the boys. As they step up into her bus, as if for a ride to school, she adds, "I taught her better'n that. But she's got Joe on the other end."

John scrapes his shoes against the step to wipe off the goldfish. The yellow bus: sense memory of elementary school, chilly mornings, groups of kids, a knapsack on his back. Another memory as he steps inside: his teacher reading *Arabian Nights.* For entering Sylvia's bus is like entering a sheik's tent that expands magically, genie-like, into an immense oasis of lush riches and fruits. Inside, the bus is gold. Gold.

Gold everywhere.

Gold draperies pad the windows. Gold valances swim above them like fairy-tale mermaids. In place of bus seats is a living-room suite: sofa and two easy chairs extraordinarily vinyled in shining, molten gold.

A huge, gilt-framed painting of white horses in golden bridles covers the bus's rear window, where the children once turned to make faces at the car behind them. On a faux-marble table is a bowl of candy and golden apples.

The only thing not gold is Sylvia herself. Head hanging, shoulders slumped, she stands looking at the floor, Sylvia with her Brillcreamed hair, her work pants sliding under her belly. This room is the woman Sylvia cannot be. The bus is telling all her secrets. It's as bad as if he invaded her underwear drawer.

Her mother says, "This here's that Tony your daddy's always talking about. He didn't say Tony was so good-looking. Did he, Sylvia? What do you say to Tony?"

Sylvia hangs her head.

"That's all right," Tony says. "I'm shy, too."

The Metal Shredders

Suddenly the bus rocks, and then rocks again.

"What was that?"

"Sylvia," Mrs. Greenslade warns.

John feels bad for Sylvia, but he doesn't have time tonight for any walk a mile in my shoes stuff. He needs to get down to business. He decides to come right out and ask her. *Do you know anything about the money your father found at work?* Something like that. Direct, yet not too confrontational. Instead he hears, "All right, Sylvie, where is it and don't lie." Mrs. Greenslade has beaten him to it.

Sylvia's head keeps hanging. Her muteness is one loud decibel of pain.

"Answer me now."

Sylvia mumbles.

"What? Look at me! Did I raise you like this!"

"Gone," she mumbles.

"You know what I'm talking about then, right?"

Sylvia nods, still eyeing the floor.

Tony steps down on the bus steps. "What happens now?" he whispers.

John follows him out. "It's just never easy," he says.

Ever since the waiting room at Med-Ohio Octavia has been burdened with the illusion that everyone is in their Halloween costumes, everyone of course but the very children who should be in them, and now she is traveling in the back seat of a car, pressed next to the most confusing costume of all: a person going to the party as a Neither. For it's neither man nor woman next to her. Sylvia, the name is, a hyperfeminine name. Greenslade's daughter. John has invited her out to eat—"to eat," a new form of the infinitive "to interrogate, to torture, to elicit a confession." Maybe Sylvia *has* spent the money. Maybe she was telling the truth. Maybe they should leave her alone.

Sitting beside her in the darkened car, Octavia sees only the thighs and big kneecaps protruding through the pants. She uses the passing headlights to check for hair—sideburn hair, the buzzed hair on the neck and above the ears. Her morbid fascination is fueled by physical hunger. Abruptly, as they left the Greenslades she was hit by hunger, and now she pictures the bag of Tootsies Mrs. Greenslade held in her hand and she wishes she had dived in and taken a handful. She wishes she had filled her pockets with her own candy—Snickers, Three Musketeers—every year she buys candy she doesn't like so she won't eat it. Every year she eats it anyway.

This half of the ride finds Tony in the front with John. So that means Hayley Badecker is in the back with her and Sylvia, and H. B. is really enjoying herself. Octavia can feel H. B.'s mockery of Sylvia in the way her hands are boldly and recklessly attempting to roam Octavia's body. Octavia pins one hand down and then the other as they engage in an increasingly fearsome patty-cake. She tries sitting on Hayley Badecker's hands but that doesn't work for obvious reasons, and she lets out a yelp that sends John's eyes to the rearview mirror. Thank god for that mirror, or a pair of lips would be on a relentless foraging mission. Whatever happened in the bus between John and Sylvia she has no idea because Hayley Badecker led her to the other side of the bus (why did she follow, did she think there was another door?) and then she found herself pushed once more against scrap metal (she's starting to glean an m.o. here) and so strongly held there she was shoving and flailing while trying to keep absolutely quiet. They nearly knocked the bus off its support blocks, and she nearly chipped a tooth.

Now they are inside a Mexican restaurant and Octavia keeps touching her lip to check for bleeding. Of course Hayley Badecker is staring lovestruck at Octavia but she refuses to look her way and instead renews her inspection of Sylvia. Compared to the darkness of the car, the dim light of the restaurant is like a searchlight. Sylvia's skin is pimpleless and clear, yet the pores are so big and deep her whole face appears dimpled like a golf ball. The face is featureless, no bone structure in sight, as if God in His Irony threw a ball of oatmeal and called it Woman. Yet she isn't ugly, Octavia finally decides, not at all, not really. Stare enough and there's something sweet in the effect as a whole. A sweetness shines out of her. Suddenly she likes Sylvia, and just as suddenly comes her worry that everyone else is about to ridicule her. When Sylvia leaves to go to the little girls' room, there is total silence at the table.

"I'm so hungry," Octavia finally says.

"Me, too, darling," says Hayley Badecker, who has been slowed by hunger to a sultry pace. Now every sentence addressed to Octavia has a smoky "darling" attached to it.

"I wonder what she did with the money," John says.

"She's not getting back to her house until she tells us," Tony says.

"Stop right there, Tony," Octavia says.

Tony holds up his hands. "I'm only interested in the money."

"She's got it hidden somewhere."

"Order her an extra-strong margarita," Hayley says.

Just as she says this, a waitress dressed up as a cat brings them a tray of unordered Dos Equis. When Octavia finds herself introduced as John's sister, the waitress drops to her knees and puts her chin on the table, the penciled whiskers twitching up at Octavia. The black kitten ears of her headband perk up. Octavia doesn't know how to react. Meow? The waitress is wearing a forearm's length of costume jewelry on each arm. Her sleeveless shirt reveals henna tattoos of mythical creatures. The young woman says dreamily how much she has been wanting to meet Octavia.

"This is my friend Amy," John says.

"And I'll be your waitress tonight." Amy laughs, her eyes still riveted on Octavia.

"We're going to need a round of margaritas, too," Hayley orders. "Yoohoo, over here."

Amy's little whiskers crinkle in her direction. "Okay," she says agreeably. She pulls her chin off the table to register Sylvia politely standing behind her. She scoots out of the way, still on her knees, to let Sylvia in. "Hi," she says with such conviction that Sylvia answers back.

"Hi," says Sylvia, and her colorless face is quickly aflame.

Amy writes A-M-Y on the paper placemat and shows it to Sylvia. "I'm going to be your waitress. That's my name."

"This is Sylvia," John says.

"Hi, Sylvia. I'm so happy to meet you." Then Amy on her knees addresses the group, chin back on the table, the lilt in her voice turning her comments into questions. "I just want to tell everyone that I'm multitasking tonight? I'm waiting tables, I'm breaking up with my boyfriend, I'm trying to get into college, and I'm on two medications?"

"Just do your best," John tells her.

Hayley holds up the beers. "You're making a good start. Margaritas, too, okay?"

"Okay, I just wanted everyone to know." She smiles extra at Sylvia and pats her forearm. "I'm a little distracted tonight? I'm filling out a college application? Oh!" she exclaims. "What a beautiful bracelet, Sylvia!" She gets on her feet for this, leans over the table and fingers Sylvia's bracelet, a gold band with an oval of turquoise.

"It's Navajo." Sylvia has mustered the courage to speak. Her nervous smile at Amy makes Octavia's heart begin to crack.

"I love it so much, Sylvia. Was it expensive?" Amy asks.

"Five hundred and fifty dollars," Sylvia says.

"What!" Hayley Badecker screams, banging across the table to grab Sylvia's wrist.

"No, no, no," Amy admonishes gently, putting her hand over the bracelet. "This belongs to Sylvia."

"I just want to see," Hayley Badecker says. "I just want to see and shriek. My god, honey, I've got a bridge to sell you!"

Octavia sneaks a glance at the bracelet, and what she sees of it is not five hundred and fifty dollars' worth of bauble. She says, "I guess we're ready to order, aren't we?"

"What are your specials?" Tony asks.

"Oh I don't know," Amy says.

"Try," Tony encourages.

"We have a Halloween special."

"Which is?" Tony throws up his hands. "Somebody tonight get with it."

"Oh frighten us, darling," Hayley Badecker purrs.

Octavia says, "We don't need the specials, we can order off the menu, come on, everybody ready to go?" Tony throws her a hound-dog look. "I just want to get some food." Tony eyes her for an extra beat, but she won't acknowledge him.

After they give their orders, Hayley suggests a pinball game to everyone, but her eyes are on Octavia. Octavia stands to get everyone else to stand, and then she sits down. Tony and Sylvia and Hayley Badecker take their drinks and squeeze toward the game corner. "I think she likes pinball," Hayley Badecker, great big conspiratorial smile on her face, theatrically whispers to Octavia as she departs.

"This dinner is not going to work," John tells Octavia when it's the two of them. "I thought maybe if I got her alone."

"What? That you could work your charms? Because she's so ugly she would melt at the sound of a man's compliment?"

"I didn't say she was ugly."

"You did, basically."

"How?" John demands. "How did I basically do that? You're assuming that I think she's ugly. You're the one who thinks she's ugly."

"No I don't," Octavia says.

"Yes you do. You women are worse than any man."

"Forget it," Octavia says. She remembers a transgendered man who used to come to the Framingham rec center. He was in all the classes, the Raku pottery class, the macrame class, the cartooning class, and the women's aerobics class. Then he began using the women's restroom. He was undergoing hormone therapy and was required to live as a woman for a year before any further steps would be taken. Octavia overheard the other women deciding whether the man was a he or a she or an it. They wondered what to call him. They decided on a word combining *she* and *it*: *shit*. She has to admit, she never heard the men utter a single remark.

"I'll have to think of something else," John says.

"Get Amy to ask her."

"Did you see how she volunteered a sentence to her?"

"What's her story anyway? Is she for real?"

"Amy? Yeah. It's hard to say. Troubled. Hard to say."

"The kneeling on the floor stuff. Is that because she's a cat?"

"No."

"She always does that?"

"Mm-hmm."

Octavia says abruptly, "Do you think Dad has ever been unfaithful to Mom?"

"Why are you asking me that?"

"I've been thinking about it."

"Why?"

"Well, do you?"

"No."

"He's so predictable. What about Mom?'

He pauses. "Harder to say."

Octavia feels the same way.

"Too conventional," he decides.

"Aren't conventional ones the ones that do it?"

"I don't know. I'm conventional and I don't."

"And I'm unconventional, and I do."

"You've got to be married first."

"One of you has to be," she says, giving him a brief but piercing look.

John heads quickly to his beer. He gets half a bottle down, then says, "Am I cramping your lifestyle by staying with you?"

"No. It was a singular event."

"It's over now?"

"Duh."

"You're better now?"

"Duh."

"I don't have to stay with you."

"What does that have to do with anything?"

"I can go. If you need your privacy, I can find another place."

"What?"

"I can go."

"It was in Boston, John. So far I have no need for privacy here."

"Okay, so *duh* means Boston. Just let me in on your vocabulary from time to time."

Octavia shakes her head.

"I can go," he says.

"*Duh* means Boston, John. Shut up already. I like you there even though you're starting to take over."

"Take over?"

"Lestoil. Number one. You're arranging my evenings for me. Number two. Don't do that. Don't arrange any more double dates with Hayley. God, please. First it's tetanus, then it's dental work."

"You know, Octavia, you talk in circles and you think it's really cute when I don't understand."

"No Lestoil in my washing machine. Does that sound like a circle?"

"What's the tetanus shit about?"

"She threw me up against some scrap metal. I cut myself. It's not going to end."

"You're . . . So . . . What you're saying is that she wants attention."

"Yeah . . ."

"I thought so," John says. "All right, I'll take her out from now on. You don't have to worry about her."

"It's not you she's after."

"It's certainly not Tony."

Octavia sinks back in her chair, rolling her eyes.

"You?" John asks incredulously.

"Duh."

His eyes widen, then narrow in an attempt to control his amusement. He checks her margarita to see how much she's drunk.

"Pay attention, John. The woman's practically raped me. I had to get a tetanus shot because of that tart. I actually went to Med-Ohio and got a tetanus shot this afternoon. My left arm is killing me and you're laughing at me."

"I'm laughing at the word *tart*."

"Why are you laughing? Because lesbians can only look like Sylvia?"

"I didn't say Sylvia was a lesbian."

"Neither did I."

"As a matter of fact I don't think she is."

"Neither do I."

"You just told me she tried to kiss you."

"The vampire! The vampire tried to kiss me. The one you think is flirting with you."

"She's a vampire now."

"You didn't notice we practically pushed the bus over. That was us."

Now Octavia's the one who gets to laugh as she watches him carefully tuck his expression into neutral.

"Yeah. Her idea of a romantic overture. Attack! Look at my lip. And I'm sure my ass has a giant bruise on it."

"Why don't you just go for it?" he asks. "She has a great body."

"Because I don't like her."

"You don't like her because she's a lesbian?"

"I don't like her because I don't like her. She's a weirdo. Did I say she was a lesbian? I didn't say that. I have no idea whether she's a lesbian. She's just a whatever-bian."

"She's after me, too," John says.

"No she's not."

"Yes she is. If she's omnivorous, she wants me, too."

"No she doesn't."

"Why? Does it make you feel less special?"

"Just forget it, John."

He shrugs.

Octavia leans back and howls. "That was such a Dad shrug," she says. "Total Dad shrug. Just watch," she says. "Just watch her."

10

Saturday afternoon and Tony and John are at the Short North Tavern for lunch. John has asked Tony to wear sweats so he'll look like a personal trainer. Except for the sweatshirt picturing Wynonna at the Ohio State Fair, he could easily pass. He's buff, John thinks, looking him over. He seems to be naturally buff, hard-work buff. John wonders if he augments with weights.

"So you said you had a plan," Tony says.

"I do."

"Why am I a personal trainer?"

"This is awkward," John says.

Tony doesn't help him out.

"You know I'm divorced, right?"

"You're divorced divorced? I didn't know that."

John shrugs.

"Forget it," Tony says. "I've never been married, never been divorced.

Forget it." He looks around. "Where's Octavia?" he finally asks. "You told me we were meeting about the money."

"I never told you that. We're meeting so you can act like a personal trainer. You added the rest in your own mind."

"That's why I'm acting like a personal trainer, right? It has something to do with the money."

"No."

"Then why?"

"I'm meeting this girl. I want you to be a personal trainer."

"I don't want to be a personal trainer."

"Just be one." John goes back to his beer. "Just be one for one minute and then leave."

"What about the money? What about Greenjeans? We gotta get it back. This could cause problems."

"We will."

"How?" When John doesn't answer, Tony makes as if to leave. "No personal trainer."

"All right, I have a plan."

"And?"

"I'm going back out there to talk sense to them."

"That won't work."

"Well, Tony, they seem to like *you* an awful lot. You go out there. Sweet-talk Joe's wife."

Tony shakes his head. "No. Hell fucking no."

John pushes a beer at him. "No thanks," Tony says. Then he says, "Actually I'm going back out there this afternoon. I promised to fix their goddam carport roof."

"Great. See what you can do." John downs the rest of his beer. He eats from the basket of free nachos.

Tony says, "It's that girl the one who has it."

They check each other out. No one will go first.

"She's that one, that uh—"

"Lives in the bus."

"The daughter."

"Right."

"Yeah, I agree, she's the one. She's got the money. And a big crush on you."

Tony says, "The *mother* has a crush on me. Not the daughter. Octavia should be here. We need everybody's input." Tony gets up from their booth and wanders. He keeps glancing around. He's got it for Octavia, that's clear. It's good she's not here, not with his Wynonna Judd sweatshirt. Way too hillbilly for Otty. John recognizes the horny energy in Tony's pacing as he skitters up and down the bar, grabbing a handful of peanuts. John checks out himself and understands that his tapping foot is more than a foot tapping. His glances at the tavern door are not just glances at a door.

Her name is Crystal. She usually runs with another petite brunette. The two triathletes of Goodale Park, both of them in unearthly shape. Two days ago John spotted her alone. She was way ahead of him. He shortcutted through the park to catch up. He'd been running for a while. His endorphins had kicked in, he had broken a nice sweat and was getting hot enough to wish he'd donned a T instead of a sweatshirt. He was buzzed by a conceivably false confidence but it was real enough to make him do it. He ran up beside her. He really had to haul ass to keep up, and then he barely had enough left for conversation.

The weather was chilly and the wind was blowing. Crystal's skin was beaten red as if someone had slapped her. She still wore a jogging halter and lycra shorts despite the sunless cold. Her hair was longish short and tied back like Paul Revere's. The too-short bangs stood up like a brush cut.

"Getting cold!" he blew out.

"I hate to see it end," she called over.

"What end?"

"Good weather!"

"Do you keep running through winter?"

"Yeah of course," she called over.

"I mean, what do you do about the snow and ice?" He paused. He didn't want to sound out of breath. Or wimpy. "I'm too worried about another ACL injury." He made that point—*another.*

"There's always the treadmill," Crystal shouted over her shoulder. She had speeded up to take the sharp turn around the corner and he coasted back to negotiate it wide and slow and keep the pressure off his knee. Then the hill started. Though it didn't look like much of a hill until you had to run it. She was already ten feet in front. He added a lunge to his pace but he was falling farther back. She was doing some kind of wind sprint up the hill. He settled in behind and when they turned again by the pond and the ground leveled out, he galloped harder until he was shoulder to shoulder. Her bare skin flared with fierce poinsettia blossoms. No sweat on her except her neck. The cold blotted the moisture as soon as it started.

"Just a few days off and you feel it," he heaved.

"I *thought* I missed you."

"You did. Work." The word burst out of his lungs like vomit.

She had enough breath to laugh. "What do you do?"

"Own a business. Scrap processing."

"Wow," she said. "What's that?"

"Third-generation." Huff huff. "Industry. We buy scrap, like. Maybe leftovers from the Honda plant. Like that. Sell it to a foundry. For a profit."

"Much of a profit?"

"With volume, yeah."

"Great!" she said.

"We're like rare-book dealers."

"Oh," she said.

"But more. Like the stock market."

"Oh!" she said.

"What do you do?" he asked.

"Sales," she yelled. "Restaurant supplies. One more?"

"Whatever you want." When they got to the downhill, John pulled ahead because of his longer legs. His pace dawdled until she caught up. "Hard on my knee," he explained.

"What do you do about a real hill?" she said.

"This is real enough for me." He added, "My buddy's a personal trainer. He takes me on during the winter when I can't run. He says it's not good to do the same thing all the time."

"That's true," she agreed.

"You have to vary your routine."

She said, "I use a personal trainer. I do some personal training myself. What's your friend's name?"

"Tony. You wouldn't know him. He does these small towns. You know. Farmer wives. Even. Nursing homes. Get people started. Not athletes. Health."

John had no idea why he was saying all this. Oxygen deprivation to the brain. But then it became clear when he added, "But he'll kill you if he thinks you're in shape. Nobody can keep up with him."

"Sounds good," she said.

"I don't know, maybe he could give you and your running partner. Trial run. At least it'd keep your workout varied."

"Yeah maybe."

"We could meet somewhere. I could introduce you. He's either too nice or too mean."

The Metal Shredders

"I don't know about this guy."

"Workout-wise, I mean. I mean, he could go a little harder on the farmers' wives, and a little easier on people like you."

"I like it hard."

"Okay," he said. He waited for her to correct the implication, but she didn't. "Gotta stop." His lungs spat out the words. They didn't seem to come from him. He hung down and grabbed the fleece of his sweatpants.

Now in the Short North Tavern he checks his watch. Tony has gone off to a pay phone when she shows up. Over her shoulder swings a leather handbag, big as a workout sack. She struts right to his table, swinging her bag. "I was afraid I wouldn't recognize you," she said.

"I recognize you."

"People who wear hats and all that shit. I never know them in street clothes. People say hi to me and I'm like . . . okay . . ."

John laughs agreeably. Crystal's hair is still Paul Revere so it's not just an exercise convenience. The bangs start way back and end as soon as her hairline begins. Her tan is still dark from all her summer running. Maybe she helps it along.

"Tony, the workout guy? He's on the phone. He'll be here." He waves, trying to get Tony's attention.

"You know, I was thinking about it. I'm not sure I need a second personal trainer. And my friend's still on a business trip. So I don't know if she wants it. I could ask her when she gets back. How much does he charge? I don't know, maybe she'll want . . ."

"That's all right."

"I didn't want to sound like I was promising . . ."

"It's okay, I got him a couple of other gigs right around the corner."

"Wow, I'd like to have a friend like you."

"I think he's even getting too booked up. He needs to see how this works out first."

"Good, 'cause I don't want to—uh . . . You know."

John says, "That's fine. Really. Can I get you something to drink?"

He's not surprised she turns down beer. Beer turns to fat. Apparently vodka does not. She orders it straight. He goes up to the bar to place the order, then moves to the pay phone between the two restrooms. Tony is hanging up, sliding the quarter out, dialing again.

"You can leave," John tells him.

"She's not there."

"Who?"

"Your sister."

"Better go find her. She never answers her phone. Now just tell this girl you'll give her your card if she changes her mind."

"I don't have a card."

"Fish for it, then say, 'oh shit.' And then leave." He pushes Tony toward the door, almost feeling bad. He's the one who forced him here. They detour to his booth. "This is Tony," he tells Crystal.

"Hi, Tony."

"Hi."

"If you change your mind . . ." Tony pats his pocketless sweats.

"You told him?" Crystal asks.

"Yeah."

"The first session is free if you change your mind."

"I might do that," Crystal says. "I didn't mean to back out . . ."

"If you don't have your card, I can get her the information." John makes a show of looking at the clock. "Don't forget. You've got the address, right?"

"On my way," Tony says. "Satisfied?"

"Nice meeting you," Crystal says.

"I got my sister and her girlfriends to sign up and then he nearly forgets." John shakes his head.

"Does he like the Judds or something?" she asks.

"Who?"

She pokes at her chest.

"Oh that sweatshirt? Present from one of the farmers' wives."

"Lays potato chips. Eat just one."

"What?"

"Wynonna Judd," Crystal says. "Lays potato chips. Eat just one."

"Yeah," John laughs. He's not quite sure at what.

"The mother's okay, though. And the sister."

"Yeah," John says.

"Poison," she says. "We are so addicted to junk food, our society."

"You don't look like someone addicted to junk food."

"No, *I'm* not, but society is."

He watches her pour the vodka into the temple undefiled by junk food, where collarbones punch out of the shirt and the delicate neck is tough and corded and the jawline sweeps tight with bursting health. But the conversation moves like his muscles, not hers. Thick, too poorly defined. Luckily she goes for a second vodka. He's got himself a party girl. A party workout girl. He waits for the second vodka to ransack the temple. "How do you get your abs like that?" he says straight out.

"You want me to show you?"

"Yeah."

They get up from the booth. He does a movie thing where you jam your hand into your pocket and pull out too much money and throw it on the table without caring for the change. He's sure he's going back to her apartment but he finds himself following her to Goodale Park instead. His hopes swing low. He might actually have to date her now. They're right across the street from Goodale Park where they both do their running, and he's preparing himself to feign enthusiasm over the public demo she'll be giving under the trees, like the Tai Chi club that moves across the green like a slowly spreading stain, when she turns in a different direction. His hopes swing high. He follows her to one of the new townhouses overlooking the park. She fishes in her large bag for a key. They walk inside an apartment whose living room and kitchen have been zapped by a neatness gun, it's as sleek and shipshape and scary otherworldly as her body, and he asks again how she gets her abs like that and she shows him, taking out weights hidden in a home entertainment center. She lies down on her back and asks him to stand by her head. She grabs his ankles and brings her legs straight up. "Push them down," she says. He stands over her and drives her legs down. They spring back up. "Push them sideways," she says. "Push. Push!" He forces them down again and again. Feeling-good grunts intensify into no-pain-no-gain grunts. "Fifty!" she exclaims. "Wow," he says. "Okay, so now I know the secret."

She acts baffled and disbelieving and scrunches her face. "You're kidding, right?"

"Of course," he says.

"That's just the start."

She pulls herself halfway into a sitting position and holds it, then rocks in a crescent that barely twinkles an inch up, an inch down. "Doesn't look like much," she says, "does it? Try it." John obediently contorts according to her directions. He manages to last the duration. "Now this way," she instructs. She lifts one stiff leg in the air and holds the other straight out a few inches from the floor. "Come on," she says. Just the leg pose is hard enough. She raises herself for those one-inch isometric rockings. He knows right away he won't be able to reach the finish line on this one. "Hard, isn't it?" she preens. "Men can't do it." He craps out after thirty seconds, feeling like he's popped a hernia.

"That one gets you right there," he says.

"I know. Feel that right here."

The Metal Shredders

He touches her stomach through her shirt and encounters stony ridges. Her prideful gaze lies in wait. At his amazed appreciation she chuckles her assent. She does crunches with one leg up and the other leg down, then both legs up.

"I'd like to become a professional one day," she gasps.

"A professional what?" He catches himself. "I thought you already were."

"No, I sell kitchen supplies, remember?"

"I just meant, you could have fooled me."

"You're sweet," she says.

She asks him for the ten-pound weight. She lays it on her chest and starts in with typical crunches. He keeps his hand over her shirt to feel the squirming of muscle. He begins to roll the shirt up. He affects a detached, clinical manner as he does this. He stops rolling at her diaphragm. He takes his hands away. He leans over on his fists studying her torso as if it's a bathtub and he's checking the plug. She's gasping now with the effort. Her short bangs flop up and down. His hand hovers over her naked stomach. He lowers it lightly until palm meets skin and the fingers spider out in their search. He listens to another heave expel from deep within her. He begins to move his fingers in and out of the six-pack muscle, admiring, feeling. Sweat has gathered in the ridges. Her tanned stomach shines. He bends down and begins to lick the sweat and his tongue sucks upon the new terrain. Each ab muscle becomes a small breast in his mouth. She's about to moan and his hand is about to move lower when she raises herself up and says she's going to shower and he says okay. She shuts the bathroom door but it doesn't click. Door meets jamb but they don't lock together and the air soon begins to crack it open. He walks into her bedroom and opens the closet and a queue of headless people are hanging there to greet him: all her workout outfits arranged on hangers. Each hanger has a number that matches the number she has written inside the lycra halter or pants. There are twenty-five outfits standing at attention, all in a row, in numerical order.

Good, he thinks. She won't want me to stay too long. He goes back toward the bathroom. The shower turns off.

The air has blown the door a peek wider. He pushes it open. She's coming out of the shower and she sees him and keeps coming. He takes a towel and wraps it around her shoulders and begins to wipe her, drying some spots and leaving the others wet for him.

11

The statue Sylvia could win is just like some of the ones in ancient Greece. It's a goddess leaning back to accept a proffer of ambrosia, her long tresses splashing. Made of gleaming marble, or a material just like it.

Finally Sylvia Greenslade is going to be a winner.

Hearing her friend Nikki describe the statue over the phone ("ambrosia, the food of the gods") is better than any catalogue photograph. Already Sylvia has grown so excited she interrupts the description with a torrent of redecorating ideas. It will only take a little rearranging to make room for the statue. It would look great in the bus. It could fit in the back, next to the big painting of the horses. What's that called when all the pieces of furniture bounce off each other in the right way? The lady in the furniture store explained it to her. *Dialogue.* Sylvia remembers it now. Good furniture dialogue.

Or she could really do it right, take the painting down and in its place erect Grecian columns. Two Grecian columns, one on each side of the statue. Sylvia asks Nikki about buying something like that to go along with the statue she might win, and Nikki says Grecian columns? You mean like a Doric pillar on a marble-like pedestal? Nikki promises that if she can't locate genuine Doric pillars she's going to go straight to the president of the company and see what he can do about it.

Now how about the Navajo bracelet? Nikki asks.

Sylvia says how her friend Amy just loves it!

And don't forget about the Chevrolet Astro Van, Nikki adds.

She's got a future now thanks to Nikki, a future she looks forward to. But right now is the present and she's got to get that straightened out. Yes, her bus would look nice with an ancient statue of a goddess in it. Yes, it would look great with Doric pillars. But first things first and when push comes shoving her back to her senses, she knows she needs a brand-new twenty-five-thousand-dollar Chevrolet Astro Van that looks just as nice as a coupe but does all the hard work of a truck. And she also knows she's almost there. She's almost in line for the top prize.

Almost.

But she's not dumb either, and as Nikki has told her, *almost* doesn't count except in horseshoes (and especially not in sex, Nikki laughed, or girl, she'd have *almost* been in trouble so many times—you know what she's saying, right? Oh, don't I! Sylvia burped back). The twenty-five hundred dollars Sylvia has already sent in so far will be no better than somebody else's measly three hundred dollars, 'cause they'll both go into the general drawing. The chances then are not good at all that she'll win the van. She might not even win the statue at that point. She might win the home-care products, and even though they are excellent products, they represent the lowest rung of prizes.

In a weak moment Nikki confessed that as it stands now, all things being equal, without sending in any more money, Sylvia would probably get the home-care products. Not even the statue at this point. Nikki was just trying to help her out. I'm telling you this on the Q.T., Nikki said. She lowered her voice to a whisper. Look, Sylvie, the odds are not good if you stay in the midrange of product purchase. I'm not supposed to tell you this, I'd get in trouble if they knew I was giving away company secrets, but I want to see you get the van. Because, like you, the Chevrolet Astro Van plays to win. You're both winners. It's got standard seating for up to eight with plenty of cargo space. It's got all the room you need, Sylvia, and with its versatility it's the undisputed champ—just like you'll be the undisputed champ when you receive your prize. Sylvie, you two deserve each other, you know that as well as I do. You're almost there, Sylvie. Another forty-five hundred dollars of product purchase from our catalogues should do it. Another forty-five hundred and you'll be in line to win the top prize.

Three hours they've been talking and Sylvia is so happy to hear from her again. She doesn't feel hunger or time passing or miss her soap when it comes and goes. She only feels Nikki there beside her. She feels the electricity of her own life, of someone also named Sylvia Greenslade, yes it's herself and she's living a different life, not moment-to-moment living but something way beyond that. She's skydiving, that's what it's like. Nikki makes that happen. Nikki makes her life—her real life—happen. Nikki puts her future in gear. They're old pals by now. Nikki even calls her by a nickname, Sylvie, and Sylvia keeps trying to think up a nickname for Nikki but Nikki already sounds like a nickname.

One time on an earlier call they talked for hours and Sylvia had to go to the bathroom so bad she didn't know what to do. She didn't want to have to hang up. She opened the bus door and threw out her goldfish which landed squirming on a daffodil-patterned stepping-stone (a previous purchase), and peed into the emptied bowl. But now she's so certain of Nikki's friendship she can come right out and confess it and not be ashamed. She clears her throat and says matter-of-factly, she says, Nikki, I need to go to the bathroom.

What Nikki answers back surprises her. Nikki says, So do I, honey, but I was afraid you'd hang up on me if I took a break.

Imagine Nikki being worried that Sylvia wouldn't wait for her! That Sylvia doesn't care enough about her to tolerate being put on hold!

Then she bump-runs out of the bus and into her parents' house. Her mom is scissoring something at the kitchen table, the overhead light on against the afternoon dimness. Seeing her mother's ugly mouth pruning in and out, and the light fixture above her like an upside-down cake, Sylvia is thrust out of that electrical abandon that floats her own life high above her. Her tether to Nikki is snapped, and now she is surrounded by the muddy walls of herself and she can't get out. She has to go to the bathroom, bad, and she's hungry and her stomach rumbles like a freighter. She hasn't even eaten lunch. Nikki made her forget all about it. She opens the bread drawer and finds a frosted angel food cake. She takes it with her to the bathroom. She thuds down the hallway, sees her dad still in bed. "Why aren't you at work?" her mother calls. She closes the door. There's a red tag stuck on the plastic wrapping of the cake, *buy one get one free*, so that means she can have this one and her mother can have the other. She's not paying her mother back because she's eating the free one. She tears off a piece; she likes the way angel food cake tears in your hand; she imagines clouds that way.

Sometimes she wonders what Nikki looks like. She doesn't even know if Nikki is white or black. She does know, her imagination is so strong on this point she just knows this for sure, that Nikki's got manicured hands, real long fingernails painted a different color every week, probably with little jewel studs in them. She's got style and she's the type who'd be really creative. Even if she had to wear the same shirt two days in a row she'd wear it with a scarf so that no one could tell. When she thinks about Nikki's hair—a long auburn mane she styles differently each day, up in a French twist, down in a cascade, braided, ponytailed—she pictures a white woman, someone like Dr. Quinn, Medicine Woman. But when she thinks about Nikki's hands, she imagines the elegant shiny hands of a beautiful black woman.

Okay, I'm back. Sylvia exhales breathlessly into the receiver and pushes herself into the driver's seat of her bus. I hope you didn't mind waiting, Nikki.

Of course not, darling. You wait for me.

I waited all week for your call. I figured you forgot about me.

Oh, honey. I had to go back to Mississippi to bury my daddy. That's why I haven't call you for a while. I thought maybe you didn't notice because you were at work.

I'm sort of laid off. I guess I didn't tell you that.

Oh no, Sylvie, you've been laid off? Not that road crew job. What happened, girl?

It wasn't my fault.

I know it wasn't. What'd they do to you? Cause if they did something, they're going to have to answer to me. That's when I get involved. I don't stand around and look the other way when my friends are being mistreated.

They just haven't called, Sylvia says. It's not exactly laid off. They call me when they need me and they haven't called.

The road crew? They haven't called you? It's not because of that time you put the GOD in their STOP-GO sign, is it? Because I thought that was really sweet. Who else would think to draw a D after GO except you, girl? I know at least one person in those passing cars got witnessed to that day. You know what?

What?

I was glad you felt close enough to me to confide about changing that GO sign to GOD. It made me feel closer to you. I felt our relationship moved up a notch after that.

I felt that way, too, Sylvia tells her.

Until then, girl, I sensed you had a spiritual side, but I didn't want to ask—you know? I'm born again, too, but I don't go there unless I'm invited.

Why not? I don't mind what you say to me.

Religion and politics. A lot of people have that fence there.

Oh, Sylvia says.

Why? Nikki asks.

I thought maybe you didn't ask me because you thought . . . 'cause . . .

Why, Sylvia? What are you thinking? That I thought you were an atheist?

An atheist! Sylvia exclaims. I'm not an atheist!

I know you're not.

Did you think I was an atheist?

Of course not, honey. I didn't think you were an atheist.

Even for a minute?

Not even for a minute.

Sylvia says, I bet you thought I was a party girl or something.

Why do you say that?

Because we're always talking about having fun together. Like maybe you think that's the only thing I do.

Good heavens, Nikki says. I have really failed if that's the impression I've been giving. I like you because you're Sylvia and the Sylvia I know is special and sincere. You're not just out for yourself.

I'm not, Sylvia agrees.

I know you're not. You really care about people and you go out of your way to show it. You're a winner, Sylvia, and so's the Astro Van. Like you, it plays to win. Sylvia, you're both the undisputed champs in your fields. Okay? You understand what I'm telling you?

I don't know.

The Metal Shredders

I don't know. Sylvia hears how Nikki repeats her words, *I don't know,* with an exasperated cough.

What? Sylvia asks, afraid for a moment that she's annoyed her.

I don't know. Nikki clips out the words. *Translation: No.* You're telling me *No, Nikki, I'm just a little nobody, I could never ever win anything not even a little ol' bitty mousetrap. Oh no, not me, not this huddled-up zero.* Wow! Do you hear what you're saying about yourself, Sylvia? You don't think you're somebody, you don't think you're a winner in life, do you? Sylvie, why don't you feel good about yourself? Why? You got so much going for you. Get some self-esteem, girl! You've got to take the heart's minimum wage and give it a raise! I want to help you, Sylvie, I want to make you feel good about yourself. You know what, I'm going to have you laughing all the way to the bank. No, I am. Yes. You silly girl, you're gonna be laughing yourself silly all the way to the bank. Forget about those bozos at your job, and those skanky work shirts and work pants you got to wear to protect yourself against all that gravel and hot asphalt. No way, girl, you're going to be in high heels and a red dress laughing all the way to the bank.

Me in a red dress and high heels? Oh no, Nikki, no no.

You put on that red dress and strut on by all those coworkers—ex-coworkers. Go on, picture yourself now. They'll be working all day in hot asphalt and you'll be retired. Drive by in your new Astro Van and listen to the whistles. They'll never even suspect it's you! Girl, those cast-aluminum wheels be shining so bright in their eyes they won't be able to see a thing!

When Sylvia lifts up from her tittering, the poor reflection in the windshield is of somebody else. That ugly image. It's not her. She's somebody else now.

And when wintertime comes in your new van, you'll have a heater with a windshield defroster and front side-window defoggers and rear-area heat ducts. Okay? No matter how hard Ol' Mister North Wind blows, you're never going to get cold. And on those boiling summer days—oh, girl, if Mississippi is anything like Ohio you're going to need that luxurious air-conditioning with CFC-free refrigerant. And God forbid you're in an accident, Sylvie, but if you are your driver's-side air bag will protect you. Does your car have an air bag now?

No.

When Sylvia falls silent, Nikki asks her, You don't think you're worth an air bag? Do you think that poorly of yourself, Sylvia Greenslade? You're willing to risk your own life? Sylvie? Tell me I'm not hearing you correctly.

Who would care if I died?

Sylvia! Sylvia Sylvia Sylvia! I am not even going to dignify that with a response.

My mom wouldn't care. My mom doesn't like me. She makes me pay half of the groceries. She won't even share any of her food if I don't pay for it.

Sylvie, like you told me so yourself, life is full of terrible trials. Isn't this trial telling you something? Isn't this trial telling you it's time to make a change?

Yes.

Then make a change. Get out of there, girl, and get into life, capital L-I-F-E. You gotta get out there and live. You are depriving others by not letting them get to know you. That's nothing but being selfish. You need to share *yourself*. Let others see who you are.

You've said that before.

And I'm saying it again.

Sylvia hears her and her heart clutches. For a long time they've been beating around this bush, and it's now or never that Sylvia came out and confessed it. Because she knows Nikki's got the wrong idea about her. The complete wrong idea. Sylvia steels herself before looking directly into it, the windshield. The reflection it gives back is at least partly true. Sylvia knows it is. She knows the mirror isn't lying completely. She knows she looks at least somewhat like the ugly portrait in the glass. It's not fair to Nikki to keep this from her.

I'm not beautiful, Sylvia tells her.

There, it's out. It wasn't so hard to say. Didn't even come out like some embarrassing confession. It came out matter of factly, but the release Sylvia feels is anything but matter of fact. Instantly she feels lighter, an ecstasy of floating. Such a weight lifted from her. She didn't realize how heavy it had become. There. The truth. The last thing that stands between her and Nikki.

You're beautiful on the inside, Nikki says.

Sylvia says, Don't say that. Please, Nikki. That's what everyone says. I'm not beautiful and that's all that counts.

All right, Sylvie, let's deal with that. Being beautiful counts. I won't disagree with you. Being beautiful counts, and you're not beautiful. Tell me why not.

I'm fat, Sylvia says.

You're fat, Nikki says. You mean you're overweight.

Yeah.

You mean you've got a weight problem.

Yeah.

A weight problem. That's different from being fat, isn't it? That's a lot different. A *problem* is something we can handle, Sylvia, can't we? A *problem* is something we can solve. But *fat*, honey, *fat*—that's a no-no mindset. We can't do anything about that until you throw that mind-set away.

But I'm fat.

Don't give me that *F* word. Throw it away! Right now! Throw that word away, I don't ever want to hear it. From now on that word is as bad as taking the Lord's name in vain! Don't you ever say that word to me unless you want to insult the Bible blood ministering through my veins. Do we understand each other? You have a weight problem, Sylvia. Repeat that after me.

I have a weight problem.

I don't want to hear the *F* word, you understand? I'm gonna get angry if I hear it.

I have a weight problem, Sylvia says. She can feel it in herself as she says it, she can feel that this problem isn't as bad as being fat, this problem has a solution. She loves Nikki's righteous anger, her determination to solve this problem. She's excited, that's what Sylvia is. The last piece in her future's puzzle is being fitted into place.

Okay, Nikki continues, now what are you going to do about it? What are you going to do about this problem? Let me ask you this, say you got a MasterCard bill and maybe there's been some overspending going on, a lot of overspending you know, and now it's out of control. What are you going to do about this MasterCard bill problem? You gonna give up and keep on overspending, let it get *more* out of control? Don't stop me now, girl, 'cause I'm on a roll—

—You are! Sylvia almost shouts but claps her mouth.

No! You're going to pay off a little bit this month, then a little bit next month, and little by little, step by step, you're going to solve that problem. And soon enough you'll go down from Overspending Size to Budget Size. Can I get a witness to that, young lady?

Amen! Sylvia wants to cry out.

So little by little, here's what you're going to do, you're going to cut down on your eating, and little by little you're going to add exercise to your daily routine. Now the first week, maybe you cut out dessert with lunch, and you walk up and down your street once a day for exercise. And then the second week, you cut out a second thing from your eating, and you walk a little farther and then add a few arm twirls and leg lifts, you can do those lying in your bed before you go to sleep.

The rush of joy, oh the happiness running through her just thinking about it. She is so lucky to have a problem she can mark out and identify and cut into tiny doable sections and little by little but in no time at all, solve.

Okay, so that's your weight problem, Nikki concludes. You got any other problems that's making you think you're not beautiful?

The way I look, Sylvia tells her.

The way you look. All right, Sylvia, I'm going to ask you some questions, you answer them honestly.

Sylvia loves the way Nikki has become all business. It's not Sylvie now, it's Sylvia. Okay, Sylvia says, ablaze with delight. She loves the way Nikki can take charge, oh she loves it. She can't wait for the questions.

Do you wear makeup, Sylvia?

No.

Nail polish?

No.

Control-top panty hose?

No.

Demi-cup bra?

No.

Underwire?

No.

When's the last time you wore a dress?

I don't know, Sylvia says.

What about your hair?

It's short, Sylvia says.

Is it styled nice, you know, like funky or dyed or anything?

No.

How do you wear it?

It's just short.

You don't put anything on it?

I got to cream it down because it's curly.

You got a lot of body, in other words, Nikki says. Okay, listen here. Think about the beautiful women you know. Pick out one of them. The one you really admire. You got the picture in your head?

Yes, Nikki, I do.

Does that woman wear makeup, does she have these nice long eyelashes and full shining lips, does she wear her hair like a sexy woman should and have her nails done up nice? Hmm? Does she?

Yes.

And doesn't she have herself decked out in some kind of sweet dress?

Yeah, Sylvia says. Except sometimes Dr. Quinn wears buckskin.

When she wants to look pretty, though, she puts on a dress, don't she?

Yes.

Yes. Yes, she does. Now keep looking at the picture. Are you still looking at that picture? Now I want you to do something to that picture. First off, I want you to take out your magic eraser and wipe off all that makeup. Wipe off that blush and take away her cheekbones. Then take out your scissors and cut off all her hair. Go ahead. Make it real short. Now what's she look like? She don't look too good, does she? Would you say she's beautiful now?

No, Sylvia says.

No, she's not beautiful. But she can become beautiful again real quick, can't she?

Yes.

By doing the right things to herself. By thinking that she's worth doing the right things to. Now you hold up another picture, Sylvia. This time the picture's of you. You have in your hands a picture of Sylvia Greenslade. Now I want you to do the same thing to that picture except in reverse. I want you to add that makeup, add that long hair. I want you to put on some blush and lipstick, I want you to bring out those eyes, girl, make those lashes long and beautiful. Sylvie, you are beautiful. Girl, look at those beautiful blue eyes. The men are going to stop and stare. They are going to be memorized by them blue eyes you got.

How'd you know I got blue eyes?

Sylvie, I just know what you look like, girl, and I know you're beautiful. Or you could be beautiful with a little help. Because I'm your friend and I'm being honest. You need a little help. So do most folks. You need to help Mother Nature along a little bit.

I know it.

Start by putting some mascara on, highlight those eyes.

I don't have any mascara.

You ever heard of a drugstore, girl? Go in there, get some Revlon extra-lash-thickening black mascara. Start there, then add a little lipstick after you get comfortable. Are you listening to me?

Yes.

Are you going to do it? I'm going to sit here until I hear yes.

Yes! Nikki, I'm going to do it, I really am!

And what else are you going to do? What else are you going to do to make yourself a winner? I tell you what *I'm* going to do to make you a winner. I am going to sit here while you go get your checkbook and write me a check for forty-five hundred and you're going to tell me the number of that check and the bank it's drawn against and I'm going to give you a Federal Express COA all ready for you to send it because I am not going to sit here and let a friend waste away 'cause she don't feel no better about herself than some picayune termite got to eat rotten wood for its meal in life. I am not going to stand for a friend of mine sabotaging her chance to be a winner just because she don't have the self-esteem to climb that last rung to the top. You are going to climb that ladder. Don't stop me now, girl, don't stop me! If I have to push you to the top on my hands and knees, you are going to climb that ladder! You understand? You are going to make it to the top. Now I'm waiting. Are you still on the phone? I hear you on the phone. You're still there. Why aren't you gone, getting your checkbook out? I'm waiting here, Sylvie, and you're starting to make me mad.

Don't get mad at me.

You are really starting to make me mad.

No, please don't, Nikki.

Well, somebody's got to get mad at you, don't they? Somebody's got to put the worth in your self-worth if you won't do it yourself.

I'll do it, Nikki, I swear. I'm already doing arm twirls with my arms while I talk and I'm going to buy that mascara at the drugstore, I promise, and by the time we meet, Nikki, you won't believe it.

You gonna drive up and pick me up in your new Chevrolet Astro Van?

Yes!

Why are you still on the phone then? Why aren't you getting out your checkbook?

I'm going right now! Don't hang up!

I'll be here, honey, Nikki promises.

Sylvia jerks the lever to open the bus door. She steps on each of the daffodil stepping-stones to the boy and girl birdbaths she bought from Nikki last month. She's stashed half the money under the boy and half under the girl. When she lifts the boy birdbath, something slaps against her nose but it's not too bad, it's got an earthy smell now from lying in the dirt. She knows there's forty-five hundred dollars in there because she's counted it four times and it's like a miracle that it's the exact amount Nikki needs. Somebody is looking out for her, thank God it's finally happened, some angel from the Lord has come down to tell her how much

The Metal Shredders

her life really matters. It's like she's right in the middle of that TV show, *Touched by an Angel*. She's living it but it doesn't seem real but it is real. It's real. Her life is a miracle. Everywhere it's lit up and shining. Everything, her life that's meant to be, her friend Nikki, has a halo glowing all around it.

Her hands are shaking so bad she can barely write down Nikki's instructions. They continue to shake all the way to FedEx where she buys a box and a roll of tape and they say Hurry now we're about to close, and she runs back to her car and shivers beside the popped trunk and pours the money inside. Her hands, trembling worse. She's got to tape that box up good. She sees the man who waited on her strolling in the parking lot like there's nothing important going on. But there is! He's going toward his own car and then he gets in. No! It's only been a minute that she's been gone, maybe two. She runs up to the FedEx building, the roll of tape dangling, still stuck to the box. It's getting cold out but she's sweating, and the thick glass doors to the mailroom thud and thud but they won't open. She pounds on the glass but the glass has got like chicken wire inside it and won't make a noise loud enough for anyone to hear. She presses her face against the glass, witnessing panic, witnessing despair, and witnessing through the little octagons of chicken wire, a dozen goggled angles of the same picture, the blue ocean rolling out of her reach, farther and farther out, swallowing up the island and her statue and the Grecian columns and the way she and Nikki would sit out on their seaside patio having a gourmet breakfast hidden under plate covers of silver. Nikki said get it in tonight. She said get the money in tonight or she couldn't guarantee the top prize.

Now the top prize is going, it's rolling away, and it was almost there for Sylvia to have. Almost.

But almost doesn't count.

She's glad it's dark out because nobody can see her. She's driving and driving and talking away to herself in the car, and now the tears are starting to fall. She thinks about Jesus' torment in the garden. Jesus was in the garden and he was asking God why He had deserted him. She would never of course think to question God; it wasn't until now that she realized He had anything to do with it. And even if she had known, she never would have thought to criticize Him for making her miserable—*never* would she do that (Jesus was allowed to but that was different)—which means she must have passed the test and now she's being rewarded.

Just when she thinks it's all over for her, she drives down a street that leads her to the bright fruity colors of the Mexican restaurant, yellow, orange, and lime, and the shoe-repair store next to it with the iguana in the window, and the dancing-girls place next to that. This is where her daddy's boss took her. This is where she met Amy. Many times she has relived the moment when Amy wrote A-M-Y on the table mat just for her. The others had to read it upside down.

She gets out of the car. The two girls in the window of the dancing place push off their stools and stand up and slink close to the glass, and Sylvia pauses, she can't help it. The girls have seen her and now they beckon. It's like they're underwater the way that they move, undulating and slow. They keep pushing their hips against the glass and motion to Sylvia to move closer, which she does, that's what they asked her to do. Then they both stop without finishing the dance and their arms squiggle down and Sylvia can tell by the way their chins flick that they've caught themselves in a mistake. People do sometimes. It's because she wears her hair so short. And because, too—Sylvia has to admit this and it's not hard since it will soon change—because her stomach pushes out farther than her breasts. The girls have taken delayed notice of her breasts. They pause before going back to their stools; it's like they don't want to be rude to her. They want her to think they do a little dance for everybody.

A third woman is standing in the doorway smoking a cigarette. As she inhales, she raises her jaw toward Sylvia. She takes the cigarette away, exhales, flexes her jaw again. Sylvia raises her hand in a tentative greeting; her fingers curl into her palm.

The woman nods. "Hey," she says, almost a whisper, smoky and low. The two dancers from the window join her in the doorway. They droop into three slinky Ss and stare at her.

Sylvia decides she'll walk to a drugstore and get some mascara before she sees Amy and that way she'll get in her exercise, too. Go on, she hears Nikki's voice telling her. Go on and share yourself with the world. "Is there a drugstore here?" Sylvia asks the woman in the doorway.

"Down the street." The woman waves her cigarette. Sylvia tries to follow its direction, but the path of smoke leads back to the dancing window.

"Okay, thank you," she whispers.

"What you gonna buy?" she hears one of them ask.

"Mascara," Sylvia says. "I have to put some on before I go into the restaurant."

"That one there?"

"Yes, ma'am," Sylvia answers.

"Come here, honey," the woman says.

Sylvia moves forward until she steps into the light. The woman tucks her hand under Sylvia's chin and pulls and lifts and examines her face. Sylvia's not even embarrassed. She likes how it feels. She likes the important look on the woman's face, the way she peers like a surgeon at her face—a face that Sylvia knows, she's not afraid to admit it, is less than perfect. It's the face Mother Nature gave her, but that doesn't mean you just shut up and accept it. Like Nikki says, there's nothing wrong with helping Mother Nature along.

The two dancers peer over the woman's shoulder during the examination.

"Yeah, you got purty eyes," the woman says. "Don't she?"

"Yeah," the two dancers say.

The woman takes her hand away, letting Sylvia's chin drop, and reaches for a coin purse she's got tucked into her belt and she opens it and pulls out a tube. "Look up there toward the light again, just like you was doing."

Sylvia raises her head and the woman's wrist flicks up and down like she's painting a beautiful painting. She feels the feathery kisses of her own miraculous eyelashes. She is watching an artist make a portrait but the portrait is herself, Sylvia Greenslade. She loves this feeling and wishes it would go on forever. She carries the feeling all the way to the restaurant and it gives her the strength to stand, just stand, at the PLEASE WAIT TO BE SEATED sign. The Sylvia Greenslade of the Past would have turned tail and run.

"Hi, Sylvia," calls Amy, rushing by. "Be with you in a moment."

Sylvia reels. Oh my god, she thinks, oh my god. She'd never counted on this. Not only does Amy recognize her, she remembers her name. The pulse in her neck is shouting out to the world. Amy has greeted her like an old friend.

Instead of Amy, a man seats her at the table and he says, "Your waitress will be with you in a moment," and she says, "Is it Amy?" but the man is gone and now all Sylvia can do is wait. She sits back and waits. She breathes deeply to let the noise in her temples die down. She stretches out her palms and fingers on her lap, on the table, on the edge of the chairs where she grasps round the edges and feels hard sticky nuggets of gum. She tries not to crane, to look desperate, she tries to stretch out her fingers to relax herself.

She spots Amy. She watches her. Amy rushes back and forth, and then freezes in midgush at a table. She falls gently to her knees and takes their order. Sylvia loves the way she does this. Amy folding into prayer. Amy who cares about you. Amy who is so sweet to everyone.

A heavenly swish, stride, swish, and there is Amy again. She's down on her knees beside Sylvia, and then her chin is propped on the edge of the table and Amy's eyes are looking up at her. Beseeching her, Sylvia understands, and Sylvia wants to say Yes I'll be your friend, but it's hard with all these people here and it's very loud in here and she would have to shout. YES I'LL BE YOUR FRIEND! is not the kind of thing you shout, unless it's from the mountaintop.

"How *are* you?" Amy asks. She toys with the Navajo bracelet on Sylvia's wrist.

Sylvia is dumbstruck. Forget about saying I'm your friend, she can't even say Hi.

"It's great to see you—oh, you know what, I'm so proud of myself today, I found out I'm going to be accepted to take classes at Columbus State and they'll provide me with a computer and I've already spoken to Enrique and he's told me I can arrange my schedule 'cause I have . . ."

Sylvia can barely follow the words, not because they are spoken so fast or because Amy's words must weave through the tray of beers she has rested on the table. The sweating brown bottles barricade Amy's face and all Sylvia can see are Amy's eyes, neon planets coursing home to Sylvia. Caught up in the enthusiasm, Sylvia says it even though it's probably not true anymore, she says, "Guess what, I'm probably going to win a free van in two weeks." And then she hears herself going further, saying that she could even give Amy a ride to Columbus State. She tells herself to shut her mouth, she brings her hand up to stop herself, and she is almost glad, really, when Amy has to pull herself away to wait on the other tables.

When the food arrives, served by the man, she gulps her burrito even though there's no reason to. She should be killing time, not using it up so fast. After she pays, even leaving a dollar tip which feels weird to leave a tip for your friend, she gets in her car to wait.

It's a long wait. Sylvia can stand it. She's stood for hours with her STOP sign keeping cars at bay, the tar's heat against her back like a bed of nails.

Finally Amy comes out of the restaurant. She's swinging her little knapsack, happy. Sylvia can see that she'll make a good college student. She'll be friendly to all her classmates, and when the teacher is talking, she'll listen with enthusiasm. Sylvia can already picture how the teacher will like Amy the best of all her students; she'll always call on her and when none of the other students has the right answer the teacher will say something like "Let's let Amy tell us." That'll be a really good thing for Amy's self-confidence, because that's all that's missing from Amy's list of talents. When Sylvia picks her up from school Amy will jump into the van bursting with the news of the day—and Sylvia will be right there, sitting next to her. Every day she'll be able to watch Amy take another step forward as she grows into a self-confident, successful woman.

Amy lives only a block and a half away from the restaurant. It's a big brick house she walks into. Sylvia wonders how she can afford such a big place; then she sees another door. The house must be divided up. Maybe Amy has to have roommates to afford the rent. The downstairs light is on and it illuminates the paisley pattern of the sheet spread over the picture window. When Amy moves close to the window, Sylvia can see her shadow.

Why had Sylvia hesitated? Why hadn't she called out to her?

She gets out of the car and determines her way up the walk to the door. She's going to knock. She raises her hand way before she gets there. She tries to be quiet but it's impossible. The porch is wooden. A log-drum of reverberations shakes loose when her foot presses, her thigh follows, her butt and shoulder heave upon it. Too much noise. One of her mother's other complaints: that Sylvia's too noisy even when standing still, that the bus itself makes a racket when she's inside. Her mother says she can't go to sleep because of it. The liar. The mean ugly lady.

Now it's her mother, not Nikki, whispering in her ear. She won't repeat the words even to herself, but she hears them, she knows what they mean to say. Awful things. To the daughter she's supposed to love.

The Metal Shredders

She's retreating down the steps when she hears the shouting. It's Amy's voice, sliding up and down a scale of pain and ending with a pure white out: the screech is so high and wretched it travels into nothing and Sylvia can no longer hear it, but she can feel it stab into her.

She presses her face to the glass of the picture window and peers through the loose threads of the paisley sheet. What she sees makes her cry out in the dark. It's Amy, and Amy has a knife and she is swiping the air, closing in on a figure cowering against the refrigerator, a thick *Vogue* magazine raised as a shield.

Sylvia discovers her own self screaming No, Amy no! and then she's pounding fists against the door and the door pushes open. It's Sylvia who bumps into the kitchen and steps in between Amy and the slashed magazine parrying up, to the side, parrying down. Sylvia hardly registers the boy behind the magazine. What she is aware of is how graceful she is. Her floundering self has somehow darted to the rescue with a marvel of cat-sure speed, and she knows this: it is God's good grace that has sent her here, and she is not afraid.

Oh my god, Amy cries, collapsing into a ball, the knife clattering to the floor.

Sylvia picks up the knife and turns angrily to the boy. What did you do to her? she demands and the boy waves his head and he says I don't know, I don't know. I don't know, his bewildered voice repeats.

Amy is looking up, her face aglow with gratitude, and she says, Sylvia, hi. She says, It's okay. It's happened before.

What has? Sylvia asks.

Never like this, the boy says.

Within these few seconds, or what seems like seconds, the police arrive, and Sylvia, still a marvel of sureness, has the presence of mind to slip the knife into its drawer, and though blood drips from the boy's hand and is smeared on the collarbone exposed by his ripped T-shirt, the boy says he had an accident with broken glass. Amy has not picked herself up from the floor yet and after she babbles happily to the police she laughs without stopping, and after she laughs she cries so hard the police turn to Sylvia and the boy and say, Can one of you get her to stop? An ambulance arrives. Sylvia is starting to panic. Where are they taking her? she keeps asking. Someone says Hilltop and Sylvia knows what that means, and someone else is dangling a white suit jacket and asking if she needs self-protection but someone else decides it isn't necessary.

Sylvia, will you come and visit me? Amy asks politely.

Oh yes, Sylvia says. The boy is crying and can offer Amy none of the support she needs. It's up to Sylvia. Sylvia, calling upon God to give her strength, leans in as two men help Amy to her feet. She says to Amy, You need to look after yourself now. You've got your classes at Columbus State to think of. You've been trying to please everybody but yourself.

Sylvia, you're so wise. You're so right.

I'll come to visit you.

I need to talk to you, Amy says. You're so wise, I need to talk to you!

It's the last thing Amy says before getting into the ambulance.

Sylvia drives away quickly, afraid the police will return for her. What has she done? She needs to stop somewhere and think it over. She is crying. When she looks in the mirror to wipe the tears, she sees someone ugly with black puddles on her cheeks. She needs to stop, but there is traffic here. The crying worsens. She doesn't even try to hide it. Let them look. So many cars. She needs to be alone. She heads out to the country, to the state routes everyone bypasses in favor of the highway. She knows just where to go now. They work so slow they probably haven't moved from the spot where they were working the last time she was there. She gets out and finds her old STOP sign tucked inside a bulldozer. She sits among the slumbering equipment, the dinosaur shadows they throw, but she's not scared. The sky is no longer a bottomless hole. The stars are out. She is alone in her Gethsemane. The stars are watching her. God's twinkling spies—yes, so pretty but they are sentinels of the Bible, mirthless, ruthless, not like Nikki, not like Amy, rules are rules and this is the time she makes her choice and lives or dies by it. It is no accident she has come here. She has been sent here to do something.

What?

Think.

The weeping keeps her warm. The tears flood down her chin and fall to her chest. Her chest warms against the hot wetness. Pain. It's so painful but it's beautiful too. She's above herself, she's not down there trapped inside the muddy walls of Sylvia Greenslade. The stars are calling her. From each star hangs an invisible string and all the strings together become visible and strong and they pull her up, high, she's weightless and flying toward the voice that calls her. She understands now, she tells them. The stars ease her down. Her feet touch the ground. It takes several moments to get her balance back.

She goes to the car and takes out the box of money, the roll of tape still stuck and wheeling out from it. She's happy ripping the box open and pouring the bills over the spongy tongue of road, the tar so fresh it leaves acrid grounds in her nose, and like bubblegum sticks to her shoes. Her shirt is wetter and wetter from soaking up the tears. She empties the box, then throws it blindly into the air. She hears the ping-thud as the cardboard knocks against an orange barrel. She knows where the hide-a-key is and she slides it out from under the bulldozer's wheel well and uses the key to start up the grader. She knows how to operate it. It's something they didn't know about her, like a lot of things. She rolls over and over the money with the grader, flattening the swell of bills into something like a picture. A picture of her past. Her past and her money, they're both part of the road now. She's gotten rid of the money and she's moving toward her future. She's happy. The tears are flooding her body. She feels her shirt. Wetness all over. The clouds shirk from the moon and she holds her hand under the glow. A dark hand, covered with dark liquid. She checks her shirt again, lifts it up. It's wetter on the inside. Her white stomach is covered with it. It's blood. Blood, she finally understands. She lifts the rolls of flesh one by one until she finds it, the wound Amy left there. It's in the same place where the Roman soldier's spear found Christ. The same place, Sylvia whispers. She leans back in the grader and watches the stars. The strings are hanging from them, pulling her up.

Dust to Dust

 Part Three

12

Here it comes, finally. John and Marcus have been standing in the middle of the road waiting for the Nightrider. John spots the mammoth twenty-two-wheeler over the cornstalks. They hear it, too.

It's chilly out, getting cold. Damp. Marcus's breaths come in quick jabs. His cheeks pop. Today is the first day Marcus has donned the wool shirt. John recognizes it from last year. He'll see it on Marcus now all winter long. Every day, to the point that John will forget what Marcus's face looks like. He'll just see the lumberjack plaids. John himself wears a Polartec vest over a cotton shirt. No sweater. Worry keeps the rest of him warm.

"How's your eyes these days?" John asks.

"Doing all right," Marcus says.

The cornstalks are still here, upright but skeletal, begging to be threshed, powdery from brittleness. John can see right through them to the green John Deere centerstage in the field. A wind blows dust in John's face and he knows it's not dirt. It's plant life turned mummy.

"Those drops keep it under control?"

"Oh yeah. I manage."

"That's good you do what the doctor says."

"Well, gotta do what the doctor says."

"Now Dooley, I wish he'd listen. Just does what he wants."

Marcus gives an *Amen* kind of murmur.

"You and Dooley get along?"

Marcus lets out a neigh or something like that. "Ooh boy," he says or something like that.

The Nightrider swings out wide to begin the turn onto their narrow country road. The asphalt is ancient and white, the berm crumbling away. The Nightrider's got the whole road to itself, the intersection coming and going, and still it can barely make the turn without mowing down some cornstalks. John doesn't know how Allman can handle it. The truck is so mammoth it is a parade unto itself, float, marching band, horses, all cemented together, trying to bend itself into an impossible *L*.

A November fog is rolling in, so thick he can almost shuck it. He has that feeling again, that things are falling apart. Too easily John can imagine a phalanx of men materializing through this fog, not gunmen here to save the world but scrap-metal quitters advertising their troubles: Marcus, Dooley, Don Capachi, Joe Greenslade, Worm, Sherry. Blind, dead, or dying. A worst-case scenario. Everybody, all at once, gone from the Shredders.

Yesterday out of the fog there did emerge two people he never expected to see: Rhonda, the Senior's sister, and her new boyfriend. John gave Rhonda $350 out of petty cash, something he could get away with because Ada was gone. Ada's husband has died and she's been out searching southern Ohio, Kentucky, and West Virginia for a good site to dump his ashes. He doesn't intend to mention this $350 to the Senior.

Marcus helps direct the Nightrider. John moves inside and watches the truck make the careful slink through the gates. To move gently, the engine must turn savage. The cab heaves in death throes and he watches Allman rodeo-ride the bounces. Marcus usually directs the big trucks, but Allman pays him no attention. He doesn't need the help. He goes on past Marcus and steers the Nightrider deep to the back and positions it near the Linkbelt crane. Now they're gonna have to wait for Dooley. He hasn't showed up yet. He's the only one who operates the Linkbelt.

Allman cuts the engine and jumps out. He's wearing a sweatshirt of the band. No surprise there. All his clothes are Allman Brothers clothes. Hence, Allman's name. His real name, like the band, hasn't been heard for years. The sweatshirt is greased-up and ripped. A decade of sporadic washing has shrunk it up to his belt buckle. Allman does his own thing, riding by cover of darkness with thousands of overload pounds, doing constant battle with the highway weigh stations. Some scale beds aren't big enough to weigh three axles so they're fined because of the prima facie evidence of bulging tires. Even if a scale bed accommodates them and they come in underweight in total, the weigh stations will grab them for an individual axle weight excess. A two-hundred-dollar fine per axle. It takes a certain personality to run a Nightrider.

John has known Allman long enough to know he's a nice guy (he did, after all, not only attend his grandfather's funeral but donned a white dress shirt as well). He just does his own thing is all, and he's not much of a chatterbox. He triggers a hey over to John and Marcus, then makes his way to the weighmaster station and the coffee setup. No doughnuts with Ada out on her mission. John can see him in there, not talking to Tony either, but not being unfriendly about it.

"Where's Dooley?" John asks.

"Uh-huh," Marcus says. John likes Marcus, wishes he would talk a little more. Marcus shifts around, gives a nod, then scrapes toward the warehouse.

Tony's rattling around in the cashier cage. He's taking over for Ada. Somebody's got to do it since Ada's gone AWOL on them. No one knows how long this search will take. Couldn't scatter him in a normal place. Gotta go on a scouting mission first. John vaguely recalls her telling him one day about cancer or lymphoma or something that was just discovered in Earl, he thinks the third husband's name was Earl. It's terrible to admit, but Ada's yapping, that's how he thought of it, her yapping was something he turned into machine whine in order to deal with it. Machine whine he could handle. He had long since learned how to tune out metal brutalizing metal. He was good at not hearing the shredder, the baler, the shear. A shear going after a tractor shaft was like Zeus taking his fingernail and scraping it down Olympus's blackboard. It could rip you inside out if you let it. So he simply never heard it.

Somebody's staring at him now so he knows he must be talking to himself. He's logged on to the chat room, of course, and he hears Elise telling him how cavalier he is. Not caring about someone's grief. Not listening long enough to a death report to learn the cause of death or even the deceased's name. Characterizing a woman's grief as yapping. It's true; he doesn't need Elise to tell him what a jerk he is. Maybe he doesn't need her at all. He's liking what he got from Crystal. He's liking it a whole lot and he tries to remember if it were ever that intense with Elise before it became the married version that he remembers. If the divorce papers came in the mail today, he wouldn't care. It's not going to work between them, he knows that now. He's done something now that Elise can hate him for, and that's what she wanted. Good for him.

Father and Son Welbarger are watching him. He takes his time and finishes up the conversation. He pretty much tells Elise to go to hell, then wishes her swell times with her new sensitive boyfriend, the English teacher who would not only remember Earl's name (if that's the name) but would write a sad caring poem about his passing. Leaves falling off trees, the usual. That's probably the best he can do. Doesn't she get it? Sensitive men are hustling.

The Metal Shredders

Good luck, he tells her. End of conversation.

He goes over to see what the Welbargers are up to today. This time they have a mother lode of copper gutters and flashing. Must have crowbarred it off some old building in the middle of the night. John weighs it in at the nonferrous scale, which digitizes it down to single pounds. He writes out a ticket to Tony for Birch, No. 2 copper, eighty-three cents a pound. As usual, the Welbargers want to hang around and talk, goofy bragging about how they got the stuff. John is too aware of their disastrous teeth, two matching sets of train derailments. Tony comes out to give the Welbargers some grief, and John takes this opportunity to get away.

Now he sees him: Dooley. Lumbering in late, not looking too good either, and John worries about his blood pressure, or drinking, or both. Dooley swings his lunch pail, carrying an extra thermos against his side. His hooded eyes are dark and insct. He seems to register his surroundings as much as a zombie. John doesn't bother to say hello or anything else. If Dooley bumps into the Nightrider, he'll realize he's got to load it.

It's all just falling apart. John feels it as surely as the start of winter is signaled by Marcus's wool shirt. He scissor-jumps the three feet to the warehouse proscenium. Don Capachi's working the alligator shears, dressed in full-length protection. John sends over a wave, which Don Capachi either doesn't see or ignores. It's sad about Don Capachi—going downhill, like his grandfather. He sees the signs. Going downhill fast. He finds Marcus in the warehouse getting ready to forklift some pig iron and asks him to keep an eye on Dooley ("Uh-huh," Marcus says). He winds through the rest of the warehouse and beyond, to the shotgun addition where the graders work. The place is empty except for Miguel. Annoyed, John spots the basketball hoop. The setup, a $199 hydraulic all-in-one on wheels, has been rolled inside. Now the lunchtime games are played on oil-spotted dusty cement. Now the games have as spectators the unsorted and lethally edged heaves of sheet scrap.

Somewhere there's one of those scoreboards that look like pick-your-number cards at a bakery. Except the numbers hanging on the hook represent the number of days they've gone without an injury. Somebody soon is going to get hurt jumping around playing basketball with a bunch of scrap on the floor.

John goes to find Evert Sheraton to help him roll the system out to the Shredders' parking lot. They can play there on the dirt if they want. Outside, away from sharp edges. If the ball doesn't bounce nice and perfect, tough.

Of course Sherry's no fucking anywhere to be found. John starts rolling out the basketball apparatus himself. Maybe he'll start a babysitting service, too. Maybe he'll start washing their diapers. Who's in charge here? Then Miguel is suddenly there and comes over to help. Miguel is a nice guy as far as John can tell, stocky and unusually short. And passionate about basketball. Sherry told him that after work, Miguel and his compatriots go home, eat, fiddle with their kids, then meet up again at a schoolyard to play some more. John realized, with some embarrassment, that Sherry had bothered to get to know the Hispanics better than he had.

He and Miguel get the hoop outside, as far as the proscenium. The Senior's Trooper is sitting right in the middle of the yard. John wasn't expecting him. John and Miguel topple the post and the Senior is there to catch it. He pulls the heavy post off the proscenium. It thuds to the ground. "Where you going to put it?" the Senior asks, deferential to John when it concerns the most trivial of matters, as if John's not on to that tactic. *My ego is so stroked,* he wants to tell the Senior. *Imagine, I'm in charge of finding a place to hang a basketball net.*

"*Gracias, mi amigo,*" the Senior says to Miguel.

"*No problema,*" Miguel says.

"No problem," the Senior says.

The Metal Shredders

John hopes this wasn't meant as a translation for his benefit. "Okay," he says.

"I'm going to need them for a few days over at my place," the Senior says.

"Who?"

"Miguel. The others, too. I'll be taking them off your hands for a bit." Then the Senior turns away, conversation finished. He goes over to watch Dooley. John hates the way his father is so overly pleased by the sight of Dooley working the Linkbelt.

The Senior sees what Dooley is magging. "Why are you loading up a Nightrider with ferrous?" he asks John.

"I've asked the railroad over and over for lower rates and I've warned them I'm going to do this. So I'm doing it."

The Senior shakes his head. A sigh hardens into a sniff. "Making a day trip with ferrous—who? Allman? He's the only one'd go along with such a crazy stunt. Is that cost-efficient, John?"

"Of course it's not cost-efficient. But I've got to send a message that I'm serious."

"You don't ask these people, you tell them, and then you negotiate from there. *Why* is it in their best interests to lower their freight costs? An-swer that question for them and you're more than halfway home."

"I have. Believe me."

Like an expert fisherman, Dooley whips the cable toward the pile. It's a cable crane attached to a two-and-a-half-ton magnet—not a hydraulic crane, which several of them can run, John included—but a swinging ca-ble with a lot more room for error.

The Nightrider is fixed with a gondola bed and Dooley loads it front to back, laying it down in three layers, and using the dejuiced magnet to compact it. The magnet's five thousand pounds compress the steel as eas-ily as a boot stomping down the kitchen trash.

The magnet juices up another load. As Dooley raises the pile, the magnet hitches: Dooley's expert little pop to shake off any loose scrap. It's a nice sight until the magnet shivers out of orbit and starts a swinging that's not quite right. It begins to leap out of its appointed arc. Instinctively, John's arm reaches out to protect the Senior just as the Senior's arm juts out to protect him. The magnet is high above them, swinging out of orbit. Everyone is running out to see. Almost everyone is there to watch it. Destruction in the making. No way to stop it now.

The two-and-a-half-ton magnet crashes through the roof of a storage shed. John's heart jumps through his chest and he runs over to make sure no one is hurt. As he's returning—everybody safe—he sees Dooley climbing down from the crane. Dooley lumbers over to the Senior. "Swung on me," he says.

The Senior nods. "No harm done."

Dooley lumbers back and pulls his heavy sack of a body back inside the crane. John wants to pounce on him and beat it out of him, this lethargy and gloom, this self-satisfied screwing up, but once started he might go crazy and kill him instead. He's shaking so badly he walks away from the Senior so as not to give himself away.

The Senior follows him. "He's an artist," he explains to John.

John doesn't—can't—answer.

"You have to put up with him," the Senior says.

"That's enough," John manages to whisper.

"What?"

"He just took out a roof. Didn't bother to ask if everyone was okay." He stops himself. One more word and he'll lose it.

His father says, "Let me tell you something, John. The world circles into one: the world's scrap into molten ore, the molten ore into pipes, the pipes run beneath every building in the world. It all starts with Dooley."

John takes a deep breath. "I need Miguel here to be a grader," he says.

"How's Octavia working out?"

"Oh fine, just fine."

"Good," his father says.

"It's just great the way she's learned to do one or two things during the one or two hours she's on-site. It's just great the way nobody's here anymore, Grandpa dead, Rory—though I'm not sorry to see him go, at least he did weighmaster duty for me . . . And you, you used to work here, too."

John knows his father is shocked. He can tell by the stiff way his father turns his neck to look at him with a careful lack of expression. As though his son's deep-seated anger causes him whiplash not tears.

"There is nobody here except me!" John shouts.

"Look over there," the Senior says, pointing to the wet scrubber. The sorter tub is missing, and the fluff is mixed with the nonferrous.

"That's what I mean!" John fumes.

"Your grandpa did it alone. I did it."

"Come on! There's no comparison. The place is ten times bigger. Get me a full-time computer person *at least*. I want to have Tony start doing some of that—"

"No."

"Why not?"

"No."

"Why not?"

"We're not going outside the family."

"Then who?"

"Octavia."

"Oh Christ," John snorts. "Why is this white-goods thing so important? If you only want it to be family, then you've got to be here."

The Senior heads toward the wet scrubber. "I could do this in my sleep," he says. "I don't know what's wrong with you two." He says, "When I look at this pile of foam and plastic, it makes me sick. This is stuff I have to pay to get rid of. And when I look in here and I see metal in here with the fluff, I don't like that. That's thirty cents per pound material I'm paying someone else to get rid of for me in a landfill."

John says, "A man just wiped out my storage shed, could have killed someone, and you're talking about thirty cents."

"I guess it doesn't matter to you. It's inconsequential. But that's how your grandfather got started, figuring out he could sell something for thirty cents that somebody else was going to throw away. And not only that, he could double it by getting that somebody else to pay him thirty cents to take it off his hands. That's sixty cents. That's double out of nothing."

"Wiped out the whole storage shed. One, two, maybe three people could have died."

"Check out that pile over there," the Senior says, pointing out their stash of electrical motors. "From here it looks like a hill. A little closer and I see the individual motors. Is it still a hill? A piecework laborer in Taiwan takes a chisel and hammer to that electrical motor and finds twenty percent copper in there. A chisel in one hand, a hammer in another. I've done it. When I tell you there's twenty percent copper in there, you'd better believe me."

"I know what's in an electrical motor," John says.

"You don't get it, do you?"

"A roof. He took out a whole roof. Does he bother to ask if somebody was standing under that roof? If anyone got hurt? Oh no, cause he's Dooley and without Dooley the world couldn't get out of bed in the morning. He's that important."

"Let me tell you something. People in their houses think they've got it made if they live in some upper-class muckety-muck neighborhood. But the same culvert pipes run through every neighborhood good or bad. Do you want me to describe their world to you? Pots and pans and ironing boards, barbecue grills, lawn mowers, mufflers and refrigeration units, galvanized ducting, ceiling metal, light fixtures, aluminum door frames, the tailpipes of the best and worst cars on the road."

"I know what a neighborhood looks like," Johns says.

"And looking over it all are the zinc grilles of their restored Packards and Mustangs having a big wide grin at their expense."

"I need Miguel here as a grader," John says.

The Senior says, "Throw me out on the street tomorrow, I'd be fine. I'd walk into some office-supply store going out of business and make a bid on their metal shelving. I'd find a bridge that's collapsed and offer to take the broken concrete off their hands. And then what would I do?"

"*Here.* As a grader," John says.

"I'd chisel out the steel reinforcements."

"Here," John says. "Not there at your white-goods wonderland. I don't care if you've invented some way to ghostbuster fluorocarbons. I need him here."

"Go ahead," the Senior says. "Go ahead. Throw me out on the street tomorrow. See what happens."

13

When the Senior physically attacks Worm a few minutes later, John is reminded of the time the Senior went after Tony. It was a couple of years back. John's cousin Rory had been on the job three or four months. Rory was a royal pain with some Bonner DNA. The others didn't like him. Nobody did. One day he and Tony got into it over a cracked scale-louver. Tony's mother was spending the day at the Shredders, her neighborhood having been evacuated due to toxic clouds from a warehouse fire. It wasn't a big deal to have her. She cleaned up the offices and talked to Ada about the time Tony threw a Pepsi can in the school bus, but Rory was being his usual self, and when the mother stepped on the ferrous, twenty-pound increment scale and it registered nine pounds before dipping her like a surfboard into a TILT, Rory accused her fat ass of busting it. That's what he called her, a fat ass, so Tony punched him. The Senior came running to intervene. He threw Tony around in front of everyone, in front of his mother, too, then briefly fired him.

So now the Senior is doing the same thing to Worm. John is struck again by how Worm is such a perfect physical specimen shrunk down to miniature size. He's tight-waisted like a matador. His leg muscles pop against his pants. He's handsome in the face, startlingly so. It's a man's face but it's boy-sized and the beardless skin is boy skin. He'd look good as a dreamboat cover on a teen mag, he's got that kind of beautiful unscary face. The only thing is he's so tiny. Not a midget. Just small. Just this little, little guy. Perfect in shape and feature.

And now John has learned something new about Worm: he's got the emotions of those teen magazines. When the Senior swats him around, he starts to cry. The yard quivers to silence, and everyone listens and watches and in the quiet is the toppling weight of everyone's embarrassment.

What happened came only minutes after Dooley wiped out the storage shed and received praise from the Senior for his artistry. Dooley went back to magging the butte of flattened cars until John spotted an extra movement on top and signaled him to a halt. To the untrained eye it was probably some small animal being ratted out of its hiding place. The dark growth swelled as it wormed out of its spaceless space, and Worm stood up and brushed himself off. He slapped the backside pocket of his jumpsuit to indicate a particularly bountiful booty. Maybe a diamond ring this time, always the grand prize he was after. Worm let Dooley know he was there. He stuck out his chest and signaled that he would *take him on;* then he played a little dodgeball with the magnet.

The Senior hurtled forward, dangerously so, into the crane's still swinging orbit. Dooley wrenched it and the crane grabbed and shuddered. "Get that idiot off that stack!" the Senior shouted.

Worm gave a wave. Okay! He climbed down and hopped toward the wet scrubber shack, where the sorter bin was missing. He was already undoing his jumpsuit. John could see from his lips that he was whistling. His chest was thrust out and he was feeling himself. Must have found something good. The Senior moved quickly. He grabbed Worm from behind.

What the hell do you think you were doing up there? Worm's jockey weightlessness was tossed in the air. The Senior shook him like a child, an extra shake at the important words, *idiot,* shake, if you *ever,* shake, if you *think,* shake.

Worm's jumpsuit fell off and the arms flapped against the ground. Worm had begun to cry and everyone stopped laughing.

And now here they are. Silence has seized everyone in the yard. John is embarrassed, too, but he's embarrassed for his dad, who is hurting someone. Some emotional scar of Worm's has been laid wide open, and John wonders what it is. A mother, a father, some cruelty he can't crawl out of. Worm is crying. John wishes his father would stop. His father doesn't understand what he is doing.

14

A pet-grooming shop gone belly-up. That's what Greenslade's house puts him in mind of. It's a square of flopped-down hopelessness and it sits there all alone, with a snake of creek gravel for its driveway. John gets out and once again finds himself knocking on a door he never expected to knock on even once, let alone in a position of entreaty.

Mrs. Greenslade arranges herself so as to block the doorway as she opens it. After a delay, she registers who he is. "Hello, John Bonner," she says. "Why don't you come in."

Joe is out of bed. He is reclining in a plaid Barcalounger. The TV is on. The room is dark and cold. It smells a little. Nothing to do with the money. It's an odor from lives and houses that can't be cleaned up. It's the smell of being almost poor; it's the smell of body parts growing old.

John feels trapped by the smell. But that daughter, he reminds himself. He coaches himself to be positive. She's different from these two.

"How are you feeling, Joe?" John asks in a careful loud voice.

Joe smiles.

"That flu shot didn't do him no good. Made things worse," Mrs. Greenslade complains.

"Pneumonia," Joe croaks, pointing a single finger to his chest.

"Got it in your chest, do you?" John asks.

"Yeah," Joe says.

John was expecting this. That's why he's here. He's going to offer Sylvia the job of night watchman. He'll offer her good wages, more than she's making on the road crew. She's bigger and more able-bodied than her father. In the dark she'll easily pass as a man. And this way he'll be able to keep an eye on her. Because he knows she's got the money, and he knows he's got to get it back.

"Sylvia ain't home," Mrs. Greenslade informs him. "She's went off to work finally. She's got too much of his side," she adds.

John tries to keep himself from admitting that he doesn't like Joe Greenslade's wife. She has that funny kind of arrogance he sees from time to time in people who've worked hard all their lives and come up empty, the lesson somehow being that those who don't got nothing worked hard and those who got something good didn't work at all—they just sat around, lucked out, and *got*. Joe's wife has that hardworking look to her: a butcher apron is twined around her; her eye bags swing low as hammocks. She's a pillar of strength. Even her hairstyle is strength. The two curls at her temple table out in volutes, like the top of a Greek column (the two brush curlers responsible she crunches in her hand). There's a dawn-to-dusk-clean-sweep-cook, exhausted look to her, meant to excuse her hardness of heart (no time for that mushy nonsense when you're just trying to survive!), but he wonders how much of it is accurate. He looks at the Greenslade's interior—the exposed wallboard, the Pringles cans right where they were last time he was here. The caked-in smell that at one point, spot by spot, could have been cleaned and deodorized. The bathtub and shower curtain—he'd make a wager the scum is junkyard strength. A clock on the mantel works but hasn't been set. The clock ticking out the wrong time tells John this woman has the time to be nice. She chooses not to be.

On the other hand, Sylvia's bus is hyperneat, and although the shimmering, fool's-gold effect might be laughable, he appreciates the effort. Stepping into the bus, he entered into her secrets. Her dreams were naked before him. So was their futility. He was embarrassed for her. But he respected something, too: the desperation to be somebody she could never be hadn't turned her mean. In the romantic yearning of her decor, and then in her eyes, if you isolated those and blanked out the rest, there was something gentle and loving that touched him. After dinner at Enrique's that night, he and Tony and Otty and Hayley Badecker drove her back. The car, a mere toy against her bulk, bounced in ridiculous Slinky boings as she pushed out. He was glad when Tony didn't make a remark. He kept silent. Didn't even seem to be holding it back. He likes Tony, always has— but now, additionally, there's some kind of natural grace in the guy he's starting to admire. Neither did Octavia offer up a comment except to wonder what two medications Amy had been on that made her serve them meals so different from what they had ordered. Hayley Badecker was the one who had said something starting with "What was *that?*" but that was her type, ultrafeminine; naturally she'd be repulsed by someone who looks like Sylvia. He wonders if what Octavia said could possibly be true, that Hayley Badecker is after her, but right now it doesn't matter. Right now he has a job to do: find Sylvia.

He writes down Mrs. Greenslade's directions to the road-construction site.

The roads are mostly empty on the drive to the site, and the fields bare, melancholy, and calm. On the radio is a story about a guy who built a home supercomputer from parts stolen one by one, day by day, year after year, from his place of employment, nothing bigger than what could hide in his briefcase. By the time he got the supercomputer built, technology had far surpassed him. What once took up a city block could now fit on his forefinger, encoded in a single chip.

The Senior is building his own supercomputer except it's a white-goods recycling plant, and he's doing it by siphoning off the Shredders. Today it was Miguel. Every day he leaves with a little of this, a little of that, so that the collapse of the Shredders progresses invisibly but with a minuscule inevitability. And who's to say the idea of white-goods recycling won't find itself already defunct by the time he's finished? The dryers have to be pre-1979 to have a level of fluorocarbons determined to be hazardous waste. It was a good idea, this white-goods recycling, it was a good idea *for a while.*

He pulls out a stick of Juicy Fruit from the ashtray he uses as a coin well and gum-keeper. The mango aroma hits his nose as he folds it into his mouth. Remember Keith, who taught you to fold your gum, who gave you Juicy Fruit and dollar bills like you were one of his pals? Remember the hospital stay?

Keith is Rory's dad. John doesn't know where he is now, heard a while back that he was managing a driving range in Johnson City, Tennessee. Rhonda's been dating versions of Rory's dad for twenty-five years—operators itching to score, who are bound to mouth some ridiculous lie to get them out of a social obligation. *Gotta go cook dinner for my mom,* or some such thing. But it's John the grown-up who has this view. John the kid always liked Keith. A lot. He had a round sweet face. Never got mad or raised his voice—mellow is what they would have called him. Always had a stick of gum on him.

A long time ago something to do with Keith took him and his grandfather to a side of town he'd never been to. It's all pretty dreamy. He had his Little League outfit on. Something to do with Keith (and the adult John knows what that is now) took Rhonda to his father's kitchen and left her crying on his shoulder, the pregnancy ballooning her stomach. *Best not to tell Dad this,* the Senior was saying and Rhonda started screaming at him. *You're supposed to be my brother and you don't even care! You only care about what Dad will say!*

A blackness ran liquid through his scared six-year-old body as he watched his father and aunt, and then again a few days later the same fear flowed through him as he sat in the car with his grandfather. They were on their way to Little League but they had detoured to an unknown part of town and the old man unloaded turkeys, steaks, lamb chops, and a new battery from his trunk and carried them inside a small house. The man who lived in the house went off with his grandfather. John sat with the wife and a boy as small as he, who wouldn't come out from behind the easy chair, and that fear kept bubbling through him and he knew something awful was going to happen. In the car his grandfather said, *No one has to know you were late for Little League.* When John didn't answer his grandfather said, *Isn't that right?* And then Keith was in the hospital for three or four days, and then Rhonda had to go into the hospital, too, and then all Keith had to do was get himself wheeled upstairs to see his new born son.

And now the adult John understands a little more about his own father and that at one point he did try to be a good brother. Yet John feels certain the $350 he gave Rhonda out of petty cash would not go over well. That at one point the Senior said to his sister, *I've done what I can. You've made your bed over and over and now it's yours to lie in.*

John suspects it was his grandfather who stayed a sucker till the end.

He tosses the gum out the window. Up ahead, the road gives up its emptiness to a sprinkle of parked cars. The gaps quickly fill in until the berms on both sides are clogged with vehicles. Sylvia's work site—perhaps. But so many cars. John cranes to see the high orange necks of machinery but he's too far back. The great number of cars is worthy of a festival. Now John thinks he knows what is going on. He's happened onto a flea market. He parks the car and walks closer. A hundred yards, two hundred yards. A quarter-mile lineup of American pickups and sedans.

Now he spots an antenna waving in the air like a lacrosse stick. He steps off the road, climbs a grassy incline away from what's happening, to a vantage point that can give him a view. The lacrosse stick antenna sights down to a Channel 10 News van. Not far away is the Six On Your Side van from Channel 6.

He sees bulldozers and graders so he knows he's at the right place. It's not a flea market. For a moment his heartbeat fumbles. Something's happened—maybe to Sylvia. But no, he knows the answer already. Sylvia wouldn't matter enough for a news van.

Unless it was gruesome.

But they would have cleaned it up by now and people are still looking. Pushing and shoving to get a good look.

He scuttles back and forth on the bank but can't get a glimpse. He jumps upon a lightning-struck tree. Finally he realizes he's looking at the wrong spot. It's not a *spot* at all. It's the whole area. The crowd is not gathering to rubberneck at something, the crowd *is* the something. Enclosed by the orange barrels, the people are crawling along the newly tarred road. All of them are down on their knees.

It's a pilgrimage, Ohio style.

Another Mary sighting, he thinks. The tar in the road is crying real tears, or has melted into the Virgin's face, or something.

But then he sees the faithful beating upon the road. They're raising their knives and garden spades and stabbing the tar. They're tearing the road apart. Why? What is this? They're too lower-income to be ecoterrorists. So what could it be?

The Metal Shredders

He pushes his way to one of the news vans, intending to ask. No one's there to answer him. The rapunzel of wires from the van weaves along the ground through a teeming enthusiasm and ends somewhere he can't quite see. A corner of the cameraman's shoulder is visible; the reporter is not.

John can't get rid of the image of Sylvia's head, all alone, separated from her body, all alone and fused into the road.

He picks out an older pickup and trespasses. He climbs up on the bed, then onto the cab roof. It's nothing so morbid as Sylvia's head. It's so funny he begins to laugh out loud.

The road has been transformed, and the people attacking it transformed. Together it might be called performance art. Or just Mel Brooks.

The people are mostly middle-aged and older, which makes their fervor, the crazy physical gusto of their old-age stabbing, all the more absurdist. The people who would stop them seem afraid to stop them; the flailing with sharp instruments might be directed onto them.

The road has become a parquet floor of money. Embedded into the fresh tar are hundreds of bills. John knows their denominations are twenty, fifty, and a hundred. He knows the burning acrid smell of tar has probably covered their original odor.

He wishes he'd thought of it himself.

15

Tony asks Octavia if she wants to go dog hunting with them. Octavia is watching the incongruous viewing pleasure of Allman. He looks like one of those hippies who look like rednecks. Or vice versa. Allman is very busy teaching them how to roast coffee beans in a hot-air popcorn popper. In the cab of his truck is a sixty-kilo bag of green coffee beans, Brazil Boubon Santos. He has overhauled the popcorn popper with a thermostat and control box for the fan speed and heat coil, but that's just Allman and his overkill. He explains that a simple hot-air popper will do. Five or six minutes.

Octavia is totally enjoying this lesson but none of it is registering and she has no interest in pursuing this obsession of Allman's. She doesn't drink coffee.

Allman says he never goes anywhere without fresh roasted coffee beans and his Chief Special, which Octavia assumes is a type of java liqueur until he pulls a gun out of his belt and displays it across his palm. Oh, Octavia says.

The Metal Shredders

Allman laughs. You're funny. He says to Tony, Let's invite her along on the dog hunt.

The coffee beans spill out on a colander, black and shiny, their oil fired to the surface. So that's all there is to it, Allman says. The smell of the roasting beans is good at first and then gag-level overpowering. We should have used this, Tony undertones to her with a knowing glance. Yes, it probably would have done the trick, but it's too late now. For Octavia the by-product of this whole affair fumigating the money has been to make her hypersensitive to smell. Even good smells quickly turn into bad smells. She can detect the possibility of rottenness in them.

The money is still in her basement, double-bagged in double-reinforced Hefty, four layers of vulcanized plastic. The shape alone, like slumped bodies, sends her running scared. No way she can do her laundry next to those bags. Just the thought that it used the same machine as her clothes . . . Just having to look at the two bags heaved against the wall in body-part mounds . . . She no longer goes down there, instead uses the coin Laundromat down the street. Now all her clothes smell like pizza.

Octavia's been told that she missed some action this morning with John and her father, neither of whom are now here. A near disaster followed by a fight with that handsome little con artist she refuses to call Worm. She doesn't care. She doesn't care at all. She's given up coming in mornings. Soon she'll give up afternoons as well. She doesn't understand what it is she's supposed to be doing here, and she doesn't like sitting up in that little house on stilts, all alone, all day long. Sometimes she stands on the metal staircase, but it looks plain stupid, her standing there outside on a staircase. And now with the cold weather even that will end soon. So she's usurped the mornings for herself. She stays home. Nobody's bothered to indicate that they've noticed. She stays at home and works on new art pieces. She's using interesting morsels of scrap metal. Marcus showed her around in the warehouse and pointed out the things his daughter's

219

school likes to use for their art projects. Octavia is making a dog. She found two shock absorbers for the front legs. It's hard to get back into her art, especially with the memory of her acceptance into the Museum of Bad Art. And Byron's laughter, his infectious laughter and the way it infected her and the way she decided to go along with him and treat it all, herself included, as a joke.

She's been getting these telephone calls, too. At first they were hang-ups she could imagine belonged to Byron. He was suffering without her. Well, she knew that wasn't true. Byron's feelings were like a great big enormous insincere smile at the deli counter. *Hey, Otty! long time no see, didn't know you shopped here, too! I wouldn't buy my maple ham anywhere else! And a pound of the Havarti cheese to finish it up. Great seeing you!* Smile, smile, smile. Byron's smile left behind in a pair of false teeth thrown to the floor.

Pretty soon she figured out who the hang-ups were from. The pressback of a cough was female. And now she could detect it in the slight breathing. A woman's flinch. Hayley Badecker had always been so overwhelmingly direct. This new subtle approach was unnerving. And then one day a man's voice came on the phone and he sounded trashy. He demanded was Hayley there? He went on and on, with the encouragement of a few beers, it seemed to Octavia. How am I mixed up with this? she wondered. Later the man called back and said is she there yet? Where's she at? Tell her I'm coming to get her.

At work Octavia refused to answer the phone. She no longer cared about lower freight costs. Ada helped her out by screening her line. It turned out Ada was an ally after all. She knew Hayley Badecker from before Octavia came on board and didn't much care for her type. To thank Ada, Octavia bought a kachina doll on eBay to go with her collection in the cashier's booth, but before she could give it to her her husband died and Ada took off to scatter his ashes. By then the situation was way beyond screening calls. Hayley Badecker had parked herself in front of Octavia's house. Literally. She appeared to be living out of a Plymouth Voyager (must have traded in her Mercedes). The Voyager had darkened windows for privacy. Every morning Octavia went to one of the upstairs windows (she had the advantage of living on a corner) and found the street where Hayley had parked that night, always within sight of the house, and watched her emerge fully dressed in her business suit. Hayley Badecker then walked toward High Street, and judging from the cup she carried back, she had gone to Basso Bean for coffee but probably the real reason was to go to the bathroom. Sometimes there was a knock on the door and Octavia didn't answer it. When the phone rang, her answering machine always picked up, and if it was Hayley or the man calling about Hayley, all the message consisted of was the male or female version of a frustrated sigh. Once in a while a bark from the man: Is Hayley there? Pick up!

After Hayley drove off in the morning, Octavia went to work on her dog assemblage. She knew how to solder but soldering was about as effective as Elmer's glue. It would hold until it was ready for Tony to weld. Naturally Tony offered to help out with her projects. No surprise there. Octavia knew it was because he liked her, but she also knew he had gone over and patched the Greenslades' carport roof. Therefore, Octavia was free to construe it as *not a come-on* and that's the interpretation she chose.

Now as she sits looking at newly roasted shiny coffee beans, Tony emerges from the weighmaster station and motions her to come with them. She's sitting on the staircase. Fresh cold air that feels good. It's hard to escape the roasting smell, however. Even when they're well beyond the front gates and heading into the woods, the burning coffee odor seems to be getting stronger, as if somewhere along this creek bed, behind a tree with a prime location, out will pop a Starbucks.

She imagines this is how it must be for the dogs. Smells making more smells until they can't stand it. A small piece of meat a mile away bullies them with its stench until they devour it. She can understand that. It's not temptation that attracts them. It's self-preservation. Eat it or keep smelling it. She feels sympathy for these dogs no matter how misbehaving they are. If she weren't so certain about Tony and Allman's ineptitude as fearless hunters, she'd feel bad about having to kill them and try to warn them off in some way. But of course their human encroachment is already warning them. The dogs are smelling them, cringing at the smell of their humanness, gagging. They're already gone, way gone to a place that smells better.

Up ahead Allman sucks in his gut and takes out his pistol and transfers it to his lower back. He's got real long hair, the kind he couldn't grow if he started now. It's not just the length, it's the messiness of it. As it's begun to thin, it has split-ended so much it's almost like a granddaddy's beard. It's just a real mess, and Octavia figures that's how he likes it. It's his badge. If he cut it now, there wouldn't be enough hair to make a mess of, even if he teased it.

Allman's one of these types gotta keep talking. That's okay. He's entertaining. He's talking about this trucker buddy giving him discounts on the coffee beans. Sometimes he gets them free when the bag's been overly damaged and they got to throw it out and take a write-off. Those are the glory days, the Kenya AA from the Kiungu Farm days, the organic Segovia from Nicaragua days. If he's lucky he'll get a Code 53. Code 53—all it says on the bag is Product of Zimbabwe, Code 53, but inside are some of the best coffee beans in the world. They mark it that way to slip it through customs cheap, and if it works, sometimes his trucker buddy will pass the savings on to Allman.

Allman is talking to Tony, but Octavia realizes this conversation is for her. So she says, I love Zimbabwe coffee. He says, I'll roast you some next time.

The Metal Shredders

He turns, flashes her a smile.

Tony stops and tells her that the dogs' nest is just ahead. Octavia didn't know dogs had nests, but then again she's not a professional hunter like them. She tells Tony she'll sit here on a rock and wait. Tony says Well hold on I'll wait with you, and then he goes a little farther with Allman and then comes back. He stands while she sits. She's noticed his body. She's noticed how he doesn't show it off. He seems to try to hide it with his clothes, and not because winter's coming. She likes this modesty about him. It does make her want to see his torso or at least feel it a little bit. She imagines him kissing her. If he kissed her again, she could feel around. She likes hard stomachs. Eventually Tony says Look I got an idea about the money. I'm gonna take it to Las Vegas and spend it on the gambling tables.

She knows what her knee-jerk reaction should be. That's stupid, that'll never work. If you get caught you'll go to jail. She knows this is what John would say.

She says If you get caught you'll go to jail.

I won't get caught, Tony says. If I do, I'll go to jail. You won't be involved, I promise. Do you know how gambling tables work? Have you been to Las Vegas?

So Tony starts to explain it to her, how, say, at a craps table they'll grab your hundred-dollar bills and stamp them down through a slot into a safe box where it's mixed with thousands and thousands of other dollars that're mixed with other safe boxes, with the players jammed around the craps table two- and three-deep on a crowded night, half of them hidden under cowboy hats, so there's no chance really of getting caught. They won't be able to single out the counterfeit bills until it's too late. It sounds pretty good, so good Octavia's soon saying she'd like to tag along. She likes the idea of safe intrigue. Why shouldn't she go to Las Vegas? There's no law against Wellesley grads going there. Plus, there's something about sitting in the woods on a rock that makes all things seem possible. Are all things possible? It seems like a dream just sitting here, and the shots in the distance sound like part of the dream. Weak little pops that could do no damage. And then Allman is back. He doesn't say anything, but he lifts up two fingers. He doesn't seem real happy. She shifts her mind to Las Vegas.

16

John is pulling into the parking apron as Octavia and Tony and Allman return. Octavia watches John notice the gun tucked into Allman's belt. "Do I want to ask?" John says.

"Getting cold out," Allman says.

"It was Tony's idea," Octavia says.

"We went dog-hunting," Tony says. "Two down, some to go."

"You did *what?*"

"The dogs are coming around," Tony says.

John sighs mightily. In the way his shoulders express their burden, Octavia can see her father. She wonders if John is aware of this. She wonders what parental traits he sees in her. Is she acquiring them by the day? She's thirty-four years old. She's at that strange age where some women are thinking about dating, some women are thinking about divorcing. Some women are thinking about whether to breast- or bottle-feed, some women are worried about the big sex talk to their daughters reaching puberty, some women are thinking about the thesis they have to write for graduate school, some women are thinking about meeting someone nice for a change. A strange age, thirty-four. Some women are actually becoming grandmothers. And some women, like her, are just starting to think about growing up.

"Why are you looking at me like that?" she asks John.

"This is not class," John says.

"What?"

"This job. It's not class."

"What's class?"

"You know."

"No, John."

"You don't get to skip it as long as you can pass the final exam."

"I didn't think you noticed," Octavia says. "I'm flattered."

"Not noticed that you're still in bed when I leave in the morning?"

"I don't like to get up that early," Octavia says.

John doesn't answer.

"Stop that," Octavia says. "You're looking at me like Daddy. Stop it. I don't like it."

"Do you want to quit?"

"No."

"Then I'm going to fire you."

"You are so nasty. Here I'm giving you a place to live. Have I asked you for rent? You are such a mean piece of work. Go ahead, fire me. I can go on unemployment."

"Can you just show up in the morning?"

"Not at seven-thirty in the morning I cannot show up."

"Eight," John offers.

"I tried it. It doesn't work for me. Maybe at ten. Can I start my day at ten? Officially?"

The Metal Shredders

"Are you going to work later then?"

"No!" Octavia's voice gives a flabbergasted lurch. "Why should I? I always did my homework in half the time it took you. Half. And got better grades. I don't need to work all day like other people."

"You know, getting out AMM quotes and setting our prices—now that's your job, and it's not a hard one but it's about timeliness, not brains. You could be the smartest person in the world—and by the way, you're not—and it wouldn't matter if you're using yesterday's quotes."

"Oh fuck you too, honey," Octavia says.

"You know what somebody did this morning while you were peacefully sleeping? They ran a truck shaft through the shredder."

"I thought they took out a storage shed."

"That came later."

"I see. And if I had been here, it wouldn't have happened."

"You should have been here."

"Why?"

"Because a truck shaft can't be shredded. So that's got to be sheared or torched."

"Well obviously, John. *I* know that much, but one of your trusted long-term employees doesn't know that much. Talk to Dooley about this. It's his fault, not mine."

"I'm not saying it's your fault. I'm saying you should have been here."

"Why?"

"You're responsible, too."

"No, I'm not. Dooley's responsible."

"Dooley didn't take out the shredder rotor."

"Dooley's in charge of the shredder, so talk to him about it."

"If that shredder rotor's bent—you know how much a new rotor costs? A hundred and twenty-five THOUSAND DOLLARS."

"HOW MUCH DID YOU SAY? A HUNDRED AND TWENTY-FIVE THOUSAND DOLLARS? TALK TO DOOLEY ABOUT IT."

"The bearings alone cost me thirty-five hundred."

"THE BEARINGS ALONE COST YOU THIRTY-FIVE HUNDRED? TALK TO DOOLEY ABOUT IT."

"I've got to shred forty thousand tons before I start making money on that piece of equipment."

"I don't care, John, okay? Compartmentalize, please. It's not my job. I'm not going near THE SHREDDER, THE SHEARER, THE BALER. I don't want to trip and fall, get hacked to pieces. That's not my job. Talk to that little squirmy guy who's always squeezing through the cars. He probably had something to do with your bent rotor."

"People have names, Otty."

"I'm sorry. Worm? Worm is not a name. It's a little boys' club nickname."

"There's nothing wrong with a nickname, Otty."

"It's an insult thought up by a bunch of drunks. Which is okay. I don't want to be in the boys' club. The boys' club meets near THE SHREDDER, THE SHEARER, THE BALER and I'm not going near there. That's your club and if it's also your nonprofit organization, *don't blame me.*"

"If you had been here, I'm sure Dad would not have gone after Worm like he did."

"Who?"

"He beat up on Worm right in front of everyone."

"Who?"

"He wouldn't have done that if you'd been here."

"Okay, so it's my fault. The rotor, and what else, the storage shed."

"Come on! Dad's AWOL playing white goods, Rory's gone, Grandpa's dead. I can't do everything, and you're not doing one little thing to help me out. Not one little fucking thing to make my life easier."

"If you're going to start with fucking this and fucking that, the conversation is over."

John shakes his head. "Whatever self-serving morsel you can find . . ."

"Look, I'm going to help out. I want to help out. All I'm saying to you is that I'm not about getting up at six A.M. That's inhuman."

"Do you want to know how spoiled you are?"

"Do you want to know what a scapegoat is?" She trots next to him as he marches toward the weighmaster station. She jogs in front, then walks backward to face him. "What?" she says. "The conversation is over?"

"Yes, it's over."

"You've decided the conversation is over," Octavia taunts. "I guess that settles it then. Do you know how much like Daddy you are? By the way, how many times did you leave Elise with her mouth open at the bottom of the stairs just the way Dad leaves Mom?"

John lifts his body, readies his jaw to speak. He shakes his head, spins away.

Octavia runs up to him, grabbing his arm to turn him back around. "No, what? What? What? Go ahead, what do you want to say?"

"I don't want to say anything. I don't want to say anything." He starts marching again.

Octavia says, "That's probably why Elise left you." He keeps walking. "Sorry, John," she immediately calls. "No, really, I'm sorry." She trots up to him. "I'm sorry. John, did you hear me? I'm sorry, okay?"

"It doesn't matter," John says.

In the weighmaster station, Allman is boxing up his popcorn popper. He's leaving the coffee beans for them. "I'm shipping off," he says.

"Have a good trip," John tells him. Allman jumps into his cab. This time he uses Marcus's help in backing out. He waves to Octavia. Actually smiles.

"Another admirer," John says. "He never speaks to me."

"Really? He never shut up the whole time. So how mad are you?"

"I'm not mad."

"Yes you are."

"No, Otty. I'm just like Daddy. I don't get mad."

"I'll try to help," she says. "I want to do my part."

"Okay," John says.

Octavia sighs.

"Speaking of admirers—"

"Were we?" Octavia asks.

"Are you going to give Hayley Badecker a call and tell her we're trucking ferrous now?"

"I really don't want to do that."

"I thought you were going to help."

"John . . . it's not that."

"Why not? It's just conversation. Are you afraid of conversation? I see, when it's not your talk show you're hosting . . ."

"Hayley Badecker is stalking me."

"You're just full of one piece of shit after another," John says.

"She's living in a car in front of my house."

"Jesus," John sneers.

"If you didn't leave so early in the morning, I could point her out to you. In fact, I've been meaning to ask you if I can go stay at your old place."

"You really expect me to believe this?"

"It's true. Who do you think is doing all those hang-ups?"

"I guess she must have a car phone in the car SHE'S LIVING IN."

"Ha ha," Octavia says. "And I'm sure she does."

The Shredders is swept up in a grinding roar as the Nightrider inches backward out the gate. A noise so loud to accomplish so little. Three feet. Four feet. Five feet. She wishes Allman would back out already.

Octavia suddenly wonders if she and Elise would have been friends. They might have been alike in some ways. They weren't in totally different worlds. Octavia knows she's past the point of being friends with a woman her same age but with a different life, someone caught up in the loud noise of small things, who has two kids and is worried about socks staying in pairs and what school her kids should go to and what they'll eat for lunch. That just seems so stupid to her. But sometimes she wonders. One lunch, she thinks. Could she prepare one lunch for someone other than herself? She can barely get her laundry done. The small things—they're so noisy in her world.

That's what she hears. Noise. Noise inside her head. Noise outside. Get going, she tells Allman's Nightrider. Back out already. Get going. Leave.

This noise.

Maybe it's the shredder. She hears screaming. She instinctively brings her hands up to her ears. Screaming. The Nightrider cab bucks and lurches. Allman leaps out. Machine screaming? Octavia watches Marcus take off running. Human screaming? She takes a step to follow him. He's way ahead and yet he's moving so slow. Inhuman screaming? It belongs to nothing, to no one. This screaming is like nothing she's ever heard. Her mind distorts the sound until it belongs to something else, a broken throttle. The shredder has broken down. That's what it is. It's that rotor John is so upset about.

Tony bumps her shoulder as he hurtles past her. She looks around for John. He's there on the Linkbelt, pushing Dooley aside. Dooley topples to the ground. Even falling he is slow. So slow, Octavia thinks, focusing on Dooley, that big sack on the ground. From the corner of her eye she sees John squeezing himself inside the Linkbelt cab. Octavia realizes the screaming is coming from inside, that John has discovered the source of the screaming. The screaming continues, but it's something else now. The screaming goes on, but it's an experience of screaming, not really the real thing.

John pokes out his head from the Linkbelt. His face and hair drip red as though someone has poured a bucket over him. He pokes out long enough to shout "Call 911!" which Allman is already doing on the cell phone he pulls from his pocket. Octavia watches Allman, the phone so small it disappears in his hand. The phone so short the mouthpiece stops at his cheek.

The screaming is a sound she's never heard and she's not hearing it. She's already making herself forget about it. She will never remember this sound. Such a sound will never repeat itself in the real world. It will never surface again to remind her she once had to hear it. She finds herself standing next to Don Capachi. The old man wipes his hands on a rag. Over and over he wipes. Then he takes his hands and like a little boy presses his palms against his ears. But the screaming doesn't go on for too much longer.

17

Allman's truck at the gate blocked the entrance and the paramedics had to bail out of the ambulance and dash across the yard swinging their heavy suitcases of medical aids, but it was already over and nothing helped. John was squeezed inside the Linkbelt, his hand clamping the artery at Worm's armpit. He was so intent that he couldn't understand he was gripping a dead man. Worm had bled out. John couldn't hear the paramedics ask him to step aside and let them do their job. Then it became a matter of how to get him out. Dooley was the one clearheaded enough to reverse the gears to disentangle Worm's arm. The glove that had caused it all was unharmed and not even bloody until it dropped down into the mess. Worm had tried to grease the gears with the motor on so the gears would run the lubricant up through the system. An idea they had been warned against, time and again. A tooth bit hold of Worm's gauntlet glove and pulled the arm up and through the gears until the gears jammed.

Afterwards John asked everyone to go home early. Tony stayed to help.

They pulled out a hose and hooked it up. John took off his clothes and stood naked in the yard. Tony sprayed him off in the cold. It was getting colder with the sun going down. John lowered his head and Tony sprayed up there and John kept his mouth shut tight so he wouldn't taste anything. John dried off his hair but it was still coming out red on the towel and Tony sprayed some more. John was freezing and shivering violently, yet a hot syrup kept swishing inside his chest. He threw his clothes away in a Dumpster. He put on the clean extra pair he always kept on-site. He washed his hands and scrubbed them hard with a nail brush. In the bottom file-drawer he found an extra pair of sneakers.

Tony was already spraying the inside of the Linkbelt. He hooked up a soap attachment. John got out a wheelbarrow and loaded it up with sawdust. He took it over near the Linkbelt and dumped it. It would take several loads, he could see. He spread it out over a section of the bloody dirt and shoveled and raked and mixed it all in till it disappeared. When he turned around, he saw someone standing in the middle of the empty yard, watching them. He was not himself, and even people he knew looked like people he had never seen before. It took him several moments of squinting. He walked toward the person. A man. No, a woman. He had to think for a minute who she was. Greenslade's daughter. Sylvia. John realized he was still shivering. His body was knocking against himself. When he called out to her his voice was shaking. It had trembly extra sounds within. He sounded like an old tin can.

He took her upstairs and showed her his former office. There was a kitchenette for her to use. He told her he'd buy her a little TV. She said she had a book to read. He said I won't lie to you, there's been an accident. He told her he'd talk to her more tomorrow about what the job entailed if that was all right. He could hardly talk because of the shivering. He went back downstairs. Tony was still spraying. The inside of the Linkbelt continued to drain red, then pink. He wondered if it would ever get clean.

The Metal Shredders

Tony put away the hose and helped him shovel sawdust and dirt. The sun was down and they were trying to finish but they ended up working in the dark. The yard lights came on. They did the best they could. He went up and told Sylvia he was leaving, to call the number he gave her if she had any problems. He heard something against the front gate just as he was about to open it. He knew it was dogs. They were out. It was the first time he believed in them enough to be scared. John could see it happening. Sylvia might open the gates to get something out of her car. Anything bad seemed possible now. John went back up the stairs and told Sylvia maybe she should drive her car right into the yard and lock the gates behind her, but Sylvia said no, if she had a nice Astro Van she would, but she didn't care about that car. He warned her not to open the gates until somebody got there in the morning.

Tony waited for John, protection in case the dogs appeared. John got into his pickup shaking and freezing. He remembered as a little boy being picked up from the outdoor ice hockey rink, cold beyond belief. His dad would always pick him up and ask how did it go and his teeth would clatter together as he tried to answer. He clenched and held his breath until the pickup's heater began to thaw some of the ice from his veins. At home he found Octavia sitting in front of a big fire in the fireplace. She had a robe on and smelled of bath gel. Her face was flushed and dewy. Her eyes were drained out and dry from crying. She was leaning almost prone in the easy chair, staring at the fire and drinking wine from a second bottle. He went looking for some whiskey, found some vodka and gin and tequila, all of which he didn't like. He started in with some beer. Octavia had the TV on and the channel showed an aerobics class on the beach. The man leading the class wore a unitard, and his chest and legs were hairless though he looked like a hairy man even without the hair. After a while there was a quiet knock on the door and John opened it to find Tony standing with a six-pack. He smelled of strong cheap deodorant soap. John inhaled, taking it in. John asked him if he had any whiskey and he did, back in the car. Before John got too drunk, he and Tony got Octavia off the chair and half-carried her upstairs to bed. He told Tony he was taking a walk and he looked for a warm coat but his winter stuff was back in his apartment. He put on a sweater and borrowed Octavia's down vest. Tony asked if it was okay to stay and he said yes.

John walked to his own apartment. He passed the townhouse where Crystal was inside. He stood for a moment. Her lights were on.

But he would have to talk to her and he didn't want to have to talk. Not a single word did he want to say.

To her.

He cut through Goodale Park and stumbled upon two panting men whose frigid breaths were bright as flashlights in the dark. In his apartment he found his coat. In a few minutes he felt warm. He steadied himself. He talked to himself, Hello, this is John, testing his voice to make sure it had evened out. He dialed Elise's number in Telluride. He recognized the almost-Elise voice that answered. Elise's sister said Elise wasn't there. John could hear her two kids in the background. He could hear the sister's husband on the edge of the other sounds. John asked the sister to tell Elise to call him. To please call him. He hung up and waited in the dark. He sat on the painted wood floor, huddling under his coat. The floor dipped down right where he sat, as if the floor were an old squashed-in mattress.

He heard sirens far off. He heard the descending motor of the police helicopter, flying low with searchlights. Whenever he thought of Worm it was mixed up with the aerobics class on the beach. Worm the little boy crying as the Senior shook him got mixed up with that man in the black unitard whose white smile seemed as unreal as his muscles got mixed up with Worm's crooked smile got mixed up with himself being picked up from the hockey rink teeth clattering so hard he could barely speak.

He heard Kevin, downstairs, throwing something heavy against the wall, his bicycle perhaps. John went to the window and looked out. Now Kevin was outside. Kevin was yelling at a woman. John couldn't see if it was his wife or a new girlfriend. The woman got in a car and squealed her tires and tried to go fast but there was a STOP sign two houses down. Kevin got on his bicycle and chased her. John expected to hear a crash or shouts and screams, or something, but didn't. He looked at his watch. It was one A.M. Eleven P.M., Elise's time. Still time for her to call.

Thanksgiving

 Part Four

18

Octavia. Not the eighth child as the name implies, but the firstborn. The first of two. It was her father's choice of names. Octavia, to mean the eighth wonder of the world. That's what he had in mind. Sweet of him.

Stupid of him.

The eighth wonder of the world is feeling more like an insignificant eighth note. Up before the crack of dawn. Again. For the past two weeks this is what she's been sentenced to. It's right on time, her punishment. The earth rotates, then wakes her up at five A.M. She can't lie there and drift through it. A headache sees to that. The same headache every morning. And a vague nausea that's worse because it's so vague. She gets up and takes Tylenol Sinus for the headache, hoping there's a Thanksgiving version of hay fever, that this is all she has. She doesn't know what to do for the nausea. She sits, waits for it to pass. Wide awake, she gets to experience every minute of what she dreads most: the early morning. She hates it, the smell of a newspaper she won't open, the neighborhood like a spooky empty gym, the kitchen lights and the weird visibility they give. Most of all she hates where thoughts lead you on mornings like this. Too much time to sit alone and think about that little boy-man. Worm. What an awful name. She always refused to call him that. She wasn't going to call anyone Worm. Instead she called him *that strange little creature,*

that on-the-job toker,

that guy,

that pretty little thief.

Or nothing at all. Because usually she didn't call him anything. Usually she didn't think about him.

That guy. He could flatten himself thin as protoplasm and slide through the stacked mountain of scrap, lost, sometimes for hours, as he milked himself impossibly through one flattened car after another, through fossils of Skylarks and Chryslers, and emerged from the geomancy of crushed doors and hoods with jewelry, money, and drugs—especially money and drugs—books, pens, candy bars, and even an unbroken, unopened bottle of Glenlivet, which he gave to that other strange little man, Don Capachi. She knows. It's all there written out on his wall, the graffiti list of items and the hash marks keeping score. All there on his hidden wall behind the mountain of cars, next to his two lounge chairs and cigar box of dope and rolling papers.

She sits at the kitchen table, John not up, John now the one who's sleeping late, and she tries to think herself through it. She tries to get free to the other side. And each time she comes close. A deep breath of relief as she realizes that yes of course he went into instant shock and perceived nothing, felt nothing, was not scared, it was over the exact moment it began. Every time she gets right to this edge and is about to make the last push—home free—when the sight of Allman bouncing up and down in the Nightrider swims before her. And then come the sounds. She can't hear them yet but everyone else does, she can tell by the stiffened postures. Allman is rising up, his chin lifting. She smells the stench of roasting coffee beans. Allman is jumping out of his twenty-two-wheeler, the brakes screeching. She can hear the brakes. That's the one thing she can hear. Everything else is on mute. And the noise the brakes make is terrible. Terrible noise. How terrible. Her brain is about to wrap itself around these screeching brakes when the noise veers off from the truck and travels elsewhere. She tries to catch it and fuse it with another piece of machinery, the cracking rotor of the shredder, that's all it is, it's machinery, just machinery, but again it separates out. Like a darting sprite the noise flies out and fast-loops in the air and then rushes to its home in the mouth of someone screaming—who? That little guy, that handsome artful dodger—she thinks it's him. Maybe it's just a noise. His arm is being kneaded up through the gears. But maybe not. Maybe not.

And then her heart begins to thud, and in the predawn it makes her sick to her stomach. The extra smell visits her, the smell from afterwards. She runs to the toilet, but like every morning these past two weeks it doesn't come up.

Now her brain has to start over. Her head is in her hands to help her think. She has to go through the whole scenario again and clear out the debris. She'll have another morning and yet another to find her way to the right ending.

John Bonner & Son Metal Shredders. It may not be her first name but it's her last. She feels responsible. It's strange how she won't assume responsibility for her own life but she will assume responsibility for someone else's death. She went days at a time without giving him a thought. She made the mistake of joining the others around the paramedics and looking. Now she can think of nothing else.

At his memorial her father gave one of the eulogies in a string of otherwise bizarre testimonials. He put high class and grammar in, took profanity out, in a service shaken by loudspeakers of Godsmack and Outkast and Insane Clown Posse, devil rock, fuck-the-world lyrics, what his friends called good funeral music. Her father looked so out of place among the eulogizing buddies, the way Octavia remembered him in the wine store when her mother went off wine-tasting with the owner. Her mother, whose gregariousness always seems so promiscuous. Her father was deserted; he stood alone in the store.

A small moment, totally minor, but it keeps replaying. Octavia peeked over the gourmet mustards to spy on him. He looked off-balance, not so much out of place as usurped, and Octavia viewed him then as a dinosaur and snob unwilling to go with the flow on any level. At the memorial service, watching his interaction among that little man's hell-raising friends, she viewed him in a different way, and what she perceived was a natural elevation in his being, a sense of propriety that steeled his spine and couldn't allow him to bend, his own way to be honorable. A mild smile and mild refusal to act like the others carried him through the deranged stations of the memorial service where no parents of that handsome little thief were around to issue controls. No older folks to curb behavior. Octavia got to witness firsthand what happens to a funeral when it's left up solely to your friends. Everybody went wild, howling and drinking like it was a Harley Davidson mating rite. She wished she could have carried herself the same as her father. Instead she began drinking with the others and it was Tony who carried her home. They were alone in the house and she knows she would have done anything with him, though she didn't, and she knows fucking would have been exactly what it was, a Godsmack Insane Clown Posse fuck-you version of making love. Which is the way some thirty-four-year-old women get themselves through a hard day. The question this morning is, which thirty-four-year-old woman is she?

From the refrigerator she takes out the pumpkin pie she promised her mother she'd bring. Her mother will be disappointed it's not homemade. She won't say anything but she'll be able to convey the message. She'll say something. Something like "Oh yes, Kroger is such a good brand." Octavia won't be able to tell her the truth: "Well, I would have made it myself but I can't stand the smell. I can't stand any smell."

She opens the box, takes out the pie. The filling has shrunk away from the crust. There's a widening crack down the middle. Maybe she can eat a piece. She's always loved pumpkin pie.

She puts it back in the box.

Padding of footsteps on the ceiling. Above the kitchen is John's bedroom. She can hear him peeing. She can hear the lid going up, then down. She can hear the cascade of a dog chain, not just from outside, but from way down the street. She can hear everything. She hears a woman clear her throat. When the shower goes on, she hears John stepping inside. She hears the flood rushing into the wall pipes. The doorbell rings and she jumps.

It rings again. She opens the door and Hayley Badecker is standing there.

Octavia says, "I thought you were gone."

Hayley Badecker says, "Happy Thanksgiving!" She holds out a pumpkin pie.

Octavia says, "Great. Kroger is such a good brand." She closes the door on Hayley to complete the joke (the joke only she understands), then opens it. "That was fun," Hayley says. Octavia tells her, "Normally I wouldn't ask you in, but John is upstairs and he'll be coming downstairs with a gun to shoot you."

"I can't wait!" Hayley enthuses.

"Why are you here?" She gives Hayley the once-over. Hayley is dressed down in brown slacks, silk shirt, silk sweater, calf-leather black boots. Her van has been gone from the neighborhood for several days.

Hayley's soft lips lean into her forehead. Suddenly Octavia feels like crying.

"It's warm out there," Hayley says. She ambles through the living room. Her fingertips sweep the tops of the two leather chairs. She takes a seat in the kitchen. Octavia is still standing at the front door. She can pretty much guess this chummy self-confidence is the only thing Hayley has left. That's all right, Octavia thinks, that's all someone like her needs. She'll begin again, start her own telemarketing firm, get an infomercial, turn the prompted applause into real applause, get rich, go on the road, write a book for women about climbing to the peak from rock bottom.

She can't feel sorry for Hayley Badecker. After all, Hayley Badecker is still alive.

"What happened to you anyway?" Octavia moves into the kitchen and stands before her.

"Did you miss me?"

"I noticed you were gone."

"I've been staying at a motel off and on."

"No, I mean how did you hit rock bottom? One minute to the next, without warning."

"I would love some coffee," Hayley says.

"I don't have any."

Hayley's lips pout in the direction of the coffeemaker in full view.

"I don't know how to make it. I don't drink coffee. Hayley, I'm not in the mood, okay."

"But you started out so well. Lots of rapid-fire digs masking your true feelings." She moves over to the counter and begins rummaging. "This is the first time you've answered the door."

"How was I supposed to know it was you?"

"You knew the other times."

"I was watching."

"I know," Hayley says.

"How's your job?" Octavia asks.

"I'm going to get a new one."

The Metal Shredders

"Oh. Are things that bad?"

"How does this work?" Hayley mumbles. She brightens and says, "Have you ever noticed how everyone can run their own coffeemaker but no one can run anyone else's? I'm going to manufacture a coffeemaker that's universally understood by every guest."

Octavia feels herself go limp. It's not in her this morning to answer such stupidity.

"That of course is a little bit down the road. First things first." Hayley turns, arching her back over the counter, a beauty pose. "But I'll get there." She studies Octavia with a feline smirk. Studies her like this is her nice big house and she doesn't live in a van. Then unaccountably her face relaxes into a normal expression. "I heard you had an accident," she says.

"It was bad, and if you say one more word I'm going to throw you out the door."

Octavia briefly needs to cover her mouth. The retching that fools her every time is making another visit. Every time she thinks this is the time it will really happen. She's about to run to the bathroom when it passes. Sitting at the table, she rests her forehead against her fingertips.

"I didn't mean it that way," Hayley says. She is standing behind Octavia and Octavia is aware of the hands that are stroking her hair. How long they have been stroking she doesn't know. The fingertips comb along her temple and then through her hair.

Hayley pulls out a chair and sits before her, knee to knee. Octavia finds herself wanting a confrontation, she's just itching for it. She brings her hand to her face and pushes away the tears that are falling so fast she can't possibly hide them. She's aware of Hayley staring at her. She can already predict that Hayley will lean over to kiss her tears away. She can already feel Hayley's hand wiping them away.

But Hayley does nothing. She watches her in a mild way. She makes no move. The two spots where their knees are touching grow hot.

"Is it okay if I sit here with you?" Hayley asks.

"Do what you want," Octavia mumbles, everything all congested.

John comes hopping down the stairs. He's wearing a suit and tie. "Good morning," he says. He takes in Hayley Badecker's presence, takes in Octavia's red eyes. "Thought I heard talking."

"Happy Thanksgiving," Hayley says.

"Hayley's off to the convention center for her big dinner," Octavia says.

"That's funny," Hayley says. "As soon as I have coffee I'm going to start laughing."

"I've thought about volunteering myself," John says. He begins to make coffee.

"Thank god," Hayley sighs.

"Joke, John." Octavia blows her nose.

"What is?"

"Oh, I'm not volunteering at the convention center," Hayley says brightly. "I'm one of the homeless."

Octavia listens to John take a deep breath, a long intake to buy him time. "You're welcome to join us," he says. "We're going to my parents'."

"I am such a big fan of your dad's," Hayley says. "A nice, nice man."

"He's a big fan of you, too." John turns to Octavia, suddenly remembering.

Octavia sends out a dismissive, okay-with-me sweep of the hands.

"You sure?"

She shrugs again.

"Thank you, darling," Hayley says. "You're so kind."

John gets the coffee started while Octavia covers her nose. From the fridge John takes out a milk shake, a nutritional supplement from the GNC store, and pours it into a glass. He hands the glass to Octavia. "Try," he says.

One sip is all she can manage. It should be every woman's dumb luck to find herself not able to eat, but once it happened for real she found out there was a difference. As long as you're forcing yourself not to eat, your health is working in your favor. Every time she tried and failed to force herself *to* eat, her health was working against her. She wants her health back.

Hayley stands behind her and begins to massage her neck. "Maybe this will help."

"Oh stop," Octavia says, swatting her away.

John asks, busying himself with coffee pouring, "Hayley, is there something wrong?" He stays turned away from her. "Otty has said some things. About living in a car, that kind of stuff."

Hayley happily scoots over to John's side, takes her coffee, and leans back against the counter. John in his embarrassment stays pointed toward the wall. Hayley gives his shoulder a meaningful squeeze but her eyes are serious and they are on Octavia. Octavia's eyes are on Hayley. "Things are a little so-so," Hayley finally says, sounding like a resolute financial analyst. "I've been run out of my apartment by a violent boyfriend. I have a lease so I'm paying the rent and I can't afford two places. So," she concludes with a jaunty sigh, "I live in my car, sometimes, and when I can I stay in a motel."

"Sounds like you're down and out," John says.

"There's been a downturn, John Junior," Hayley agrees. She rests her head romantically on his shoulder. "But I'm certainly not out," Hayley concludes. The words are still showy but the eyes on Octavia are not.

"This will just be chapter one of her best-seller," Octavia says, wondering at her own too-showy sarcasm.

"I do want to write a book when this is all over. I do I do I do—I sound like the Cowardly Lion, don't I? But I do. By the way, am I dressed okay? Do I need to spruce up more? I can't get to my clothes very well. Octavia says you have a gun, by the way."

"Octavia says a lot of things."

"The man I was with does have a gun and he does feel like shooting."

"How dramatic," Octavia says.

"So you're hiding out?" John asks.

"Until he moves on," Hayley says.

"They don't move on," Octavia warns. "Only unless you don't want them to."

"Oh, he will."

"Get a restraining order."

"We haven't been together long. He'll find someone else. In the meantime I've got to think about saving my life."

Saving My Life. Good title for the first chapter. Naturally the book version will be more exciting and desperate than the petered-out version before her. Living in a van was just a bit of research. Octavia wonders if she herself is just some footnote Hayley is playing around with, or whether there's real emotion there.

"Why are you so dressed up?" Octavia asks John. "You don't need to get dressed up for Mom and Dad."

John pours his coffee into a travel mug. "Gotta meet someone about the rotor."

"On Thanksgiving?"

"I'll be back."

"They want us there at noon."

"I know," John says.

"Am I okay like this?" Hayley asks.

"You're perfect," John tells her.

Perfect! Hayley mouths to Octavia.

"Say hi to the rotor repairman," Octavia calls to John's retreating figure. "Weird," she mumbles. When she looks up, Hayley is still posed on the counter. Octavia imagines her in a couple of years, up on stage, taking her infomercial on the road. By then she won't have that long blond hair that's getting kind of dry from bleaching. She'll have a signature coif, something short and free, and women all over the country will be rushing to their hairdressers for the "Hayley Pixie," and she'll have her own signature clothing line too, something balletic. Maybe she'll wear those soft rock-climbing shoes. Good symbol—*climbing up from rock bottom*—and good-looking to boot, ha ha, to boot. Constantly interrupted by applause, she'll perform her life, the way she's performing it now. She won't have to sing or dance. She'll just empower. Whether she'll address her act to women loving women or to women loving men who don't love them back the way they should or to women loving men who treat them so badly they wish they were women loving women will depend upon the demographics. If she's smart enough, and Octavia knows she is, she'll manage to appeal to all the categories. She has the benefit of being a total contradiction. She has the decided advantage of being nuts.

Octavia wonders if Hayley Badecker will ever think of her after she's famous. How long is it before everyone disappears from your thoughts? Octavia wonders how long before she stops thinking of Worm.

The first time she has said his name.

She supposes that was his name.

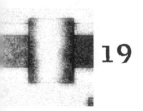 19

It's stupid, he knows it, but he stands there anyway in his suit and tie. The lack of traffic has silenced the park and he can hear the birds. He ambles down to the pond. Mossy lily pads half sunken. A centerpiece of dry rocks where the fountain doesn't shoot. The Kendo group isn't thunderclapping their fighting sticks under the gazebo, barking out commands in Japanese. Thanksgiving morning and just one person jogging in the whole park.

He gave it a shot. He sat in his pickup (that vintage eight-cylinder so conspicuous), drinking coffee, hoping he'd see her. The T-shirts in numerical order told him if anyone wouldn't give up her routine for a family holiday, it would be her. He spilled coffee on his pants when he saw her march out of the townhouse.

She did stretches at the gazebo, checked in all directions, craning her neck. *Not a soul around*—that's what he imagined her thinking. She took off, veering from her usual loop and heading down a side street. His heart fell. He got out of his pickup and walked up and down the sidewalk, still hoping for a casual interception.

The Metal Shredders

He's standing there idiotically when he sees her coming. So it will be an interception, but it won't be casual. It's obvious he's waiting. She trots to a stop beside him, her skin warm and sweating. Her hair is a Paul Revere lava lamp. To the bangs and ponytail she's added streaks of purple and magenta. They walk through the park to cool down.

"Can you believe this weather?" she says. She throws her leg on the gazebo steps and stretches. Half-naked, her body shows all its cuts. "You look nice," she says, reaching toward her toes.

He says, "Plans today?" He doesn't want to invite her but he knows he'll have to. He knows she'll take his suit and tie as an invitation. They continue through the park on a walk. A black man, young, with matted Rasta hair, sits at a picnic table, staring into space. He doesn't take any note of them. Crystal tells him she's eating with her mom at a restaurant. "Just you and your mom?" he asks.

His Ford sits alone by the kids' play area, the slides and monkey bars made from recycled plastic, painted primary blue and red and yellow, and cushioned with a floor of mulch. For a second he sees himself and Crystal rolling in the mulch. He opens the door of his truck. He doesn't want to go to her apartment. He puts his hand on her slick waist and moves inside the lycra. "I'm so sweaty," she says.

If the Rasta man turned around he could see them. "I'm all sweaty," she repeats and he knows what she's trying to say. Neither one had a condom before, but she seemed to like it that way. She liked what he did without himself inside her. He has a condom now but he doesn't say anything. She says, "Maybe I should just do you."

"All right," he says, trying not to agree too readily.

20

Is this their house?" Hayley asks.

Octavia turns off the car and they sit for a moment. She checks her watch. Twelve noon on the nose. "We're early," she says.

"We'll help out," says Hayley. "Is your mother as nice as your dad?"

"I don't know how to answer that," Octavia says. She gets out and retrieves the two pies from the back seat. Not three steps into the open garage, Octavia has already burst into a cold sweat. She starts to gag on the smell of roasting turkey. Rushes back out to the sidewalk. Holding it back makes her sweat more, and she can tell her neck is streaked with red. Hayley Badecker is studying her, but for once the woman has decided to shut up. She hands Hayley the pies. "Introduce yourself," she says. "I'll be back in a minute." She tries to act normal, but that makes it worse.

The large backyard, secluded by a medieval fortress of bushes, has several hidden wrought-iron benches. She sits in a niche and puts her head between her knees. She breathes. She instructs herself to feel better, feel better. She checks her watch. Hardly any time has passed. There is nothing she can do. Taking a breather down the street won't help. Even with the houses set so far back from the sidewalk, it would still be a gauntlet of Tudors clubbing her with roasting turkey after roasting turkey.

From the kitchen comes her mother's laughter, almost always a grating sound, like a cold engine cranking. Hayley has her mouth stuffed with crackers and cheese when Octavia walks in. The unexpected guest doesn't seem to have thrown her mother at all. Octavia kisses her mother on the cheek, takes off her shoes and tosses them in the corner. Her mother is in her robe, but she has coifed her hair and applied makeup. On the kitchen TV is the Macy's parade.

"Go say hi to your father," her mother says.

"Hi," Octavia mumbles.

"He's upstairs watching football."

"All right. Hi . . ." Octavia makes it to the living room, then collapses on the couch. The turkey has permeated the house. The retching starts again. It will be her luck . . . and on her mother's newly shampooed carpet. But then it stops. Again. Like always.

Covering her nose doesn't help. Breathing into the sofa cushions doesn't help. By now her forearms and the backs of her hands are damp with perspiration and she slides off the sofa for fear of soiling it. Her silk pants are sticking to her shins. She can hear Hayley and her mother laughing in the kitchen, her mother's slutty gregariousness on full display. Her mother is one of those types who love the transfusion effect of an unannounced body. She knew her mother would go for Hayley. She likes weirdos. They release her repressed personality.

Every breath brings turkey with it.

She realizes she is going to faint. She is relieved at least to do it alone. She gives herself up to it, lets it happen, whatever *it* is going to be. She wakes up on the carpet an eyeblink later. She hasn't fainted at all. Of course not. Just the next step to torture her in a downhill recovery process. A pair of feet are eye-level with hers. Hayley's expensive calfskin boots. She can smell them, too. "Do you shoplift?" she asks as Hayley bends down with a cold washcloth. Her voice is a whisper and she realizes she shouldn't have asked that: the words are too sensuous and flirtatious. She wakes up again, coughing up turkey smell. Her mother's and father's faces are bobbing upon Hayley's shoulders.

Octavia grabs the washcloth that Hayley has laid upon her forehead. "It smells like turkey!" she screams and tosses it across the room. Her mother's head is whisked off Hayley's shoulder, then reappears a minute later. A frozen ice pack knocks against Octavia's nose and brow. "Too cold!" Octavia yells and hurls it away.

"Come on now," her father says. "No tantrums."

"John, let's be accommodating," her mother says. "I did get it from the kitchen after all. Does it smell bad, honey?"

"I just don't want her breaking something."

"Oh John. Really."

"You don't think that ice pack is heavy enough to break something?"

"Since when do you care about anything in this house?"

"I know that you care. I don't want to deal with two women and their tantrums today."

"Do you have any idea—"

"I'll get a washcloth from upstairs," Hayley offers.

"I'll show you," her mother says.

Octavia is left alone with her father.

"I'm not having a tantrum," Octavia says.

"Mom thinks you have the flu," her father says, patting her shoulder.

"It's more than that."

"I haven't told her," her father says. "She wouldn't understand. Let's keep it between us."

"You didn't tell her?"

"Octavia . . ."

"What about the funeral?"

"Your mother doesn't handle death well."

"It's not a secret. The whole yard witnessed it. We all got to see it."

"You'll be fine."

"Up close and personal. Except you, Dad. You didn't get to see it."

"It'll pass."

"It smelled so bad," Octavia sobs. "Even worse than . . ."

"It's all right."

"How it looked." Octavia gulps deep breaths. "Oh god."

"You can't let it get to you like this. You can let it . . ." he begins.

"I can't help it," she says. "You weren't there. I can't help it."

"These things happen."

"No they don't," she says.

"Sometimes they do. It's unfortunate and tragic, but sometimes they do."

"No they don't. They don't sometimes happen. Sometimes they never happen."

"You've got to let go of it."

"No I don't," she says. "You weren't there, you don't know." Her crying breaks loose but it releases in jags, and her father thinks she's choking. "Dammit," he spits out. "She would have to shampoo the rug. It's making things worse." He tries to sit her up. No, no, she wants to tell him through her jags. She can smell his deodorant and even the OSU logo sewn on his polo shirt and it's like someone taking chunks of soap and jamming them in her nostrils. She smells deodorant and red logo threads and the room goes spinning. Hayley is there to lay another washcloth over her forehead. Detergent odor rises from the cloth. A retch bursts in her throat.

"This rug shampoo is the culprit!" Eyes closed, Octavia can hear how her father spews the remark toward the intended guilty party. "For god's sake, Janet, what's the point?"

"John," her mother says. "I'm really quite sick of you."

"I feel better now," Octavia tries to tell them. "It's all right. It's not the rug shampoo."

Her father has thundered away, her mother after him. He stomps back into the room. "How are things?" he asks.

"We're okay now," Hayley tells him. "Not to worry."

"I'm better," Octavia says. "It's okay. It's not the rug shampoo."

"I'm so sick of you." Her mother's repeated remark is now a hiss; the politer version went unacknowledged. As will this one, Octavia imagines.

"Are you getting all this?" Octavia undertones to Hayley.

"Where is John!" her father demands before stomping away again.

"I've never seen him this upset before," Octavia whispers to Hayley. "Yelling."

"He loves you. That always yanks a chain." She pats Octavia's forehead with the cloth and then her throat and then her cheeks and then she strokes her hair. "Does this feel good?" she asks.

"Hayley," Octavia whispers. "What are you doing?"

"I'm ministering to the sick."

"Is that all?"

"No," Hayley mouths and keeps on doing it. Octavia keeps on letting her.

Her father returns. "John is here," he announces.

"Dinner's ready!" her mother calls.

John declines the crackers and cheese but accepts the whiskey his father offers and takes it upstairs. He expects his father to follow him, but at the top of the stairs he is alone. His father always follows him. This time he actually hoped he would. They need to talk. Here, at the top of the stairs, he has this one moment to be a loyal son and tell him: how things have changed for him, how he's gone ahead and made a plan. He has this one moment which is quickly moving away and out of reach. John hears them all downstairs, hovering around his sister. His father is not coming up. The moment moves past. John moves from being a loyal son to a traitor.

He takes his whiskey outside. A second-floor deck stretches out from the upstairs living area. The day is balmy in a crazy way, records being set all over the country. Lying back on an Adirondack chair, legs propped up, he smells burning wood. Someone has their fireplace going, determined to treat this Thanksgiving like the crisp autumn day it is supposed to be.

Despite the eerie springlike warmth, the sky's light is tired and winterish and it casts his recent pleasure in a dream. He begins reliving the fantasy of an hour ago and now his body is acting as though it never happened. He unzips. There are women out there, women who look like Crystal, women who are built like her, who will let you do this. He feels like somebody who has robbed a 7-Eleven and discovered how easy it is. Why would you stop? Why would you ever go back? For meaningful conversation? For a relationship?

He's never going back.

He checks around for a Kleenex box on the deck; there isn't any. He goes to one of the bathrooms and grabs some toilet paper. He hears them downstairs. The worry about Octavia is gone from their voices. His mother, laughing like a ghoul. Either that or she's frozen stiff. He doesn't really get her, tries not to think about it. Maybe that's what Elise would have turned into.

He steps into his father's study, finds the upstairs liquor cache and pours another whiskey. On his father's desk is a barometer, colored balls floating in a cylinder. He wonders if his father sits alone in the middle of the night, staring at these balls. Red, blue, yellow, green worlds bobbling in their watery tube. Does his father ever try to figure things out? On the shelves of plaques and photos and trophies, he sees a photo of his grandfather and grandmother, with his father and aunt as children. He remembers it from somewhere. Maybe it used to be on his grandfather's desk. His father somehow looks just the same, like a tough little orphan kid from Boys Town. Everything figured out, even at age nine. Rhonda, however, is totally unrecognizable as a little girl. He remembers out of nowhere that she was named after Rhonda Fleming, his grandfather's favorite actress. She starred in some pirate movies but that's all John knows about her. His grandfather was watching one of her films when he died, a bit of funny symbolism he hadn't caught until now.

He looks down and sees that all this time his penis has been hanging out of his pants and that strikes him as almost funny. He goes back out to the deck. The colored balls, his mother's laugh, the cocky nine-year-old stare, his sister on the floor and Hayley Badecker leaning over her like the prince over Snow White. Pirates and the face of Rhonda Fleming, which can be any face he'd like. It all gets thrown into the orgiastic pile and then it just becomes wood smoke. When he finishes, he finds to his surprise that he is sweating.

Octavia takes a spoonful of everything that is passed her way. Turkey, sweet potatoes, mashed potatoes, cranberry sauce. Beans. Dressing. Corn, too. A roll. Some gravy. She takes it all. She doesn't look at any of it.

She actually manages two or three bites, and in between she's lifted up her fork at regular intervals as a disguise. Her mother is refusing to acknowledge that her two children are ruining her Thanksgiving. John is asleep on the upstairs deck. Her mother refused to wake him, just so she could keep the ruined Thanksgiving intact. Only Hayley, enthusing with every bite and pouring more wine into the suffering hostess's glass, is the object of her mother's smiles.

As if anyone would want one of those isometric smiles directed at them. Octavia wonders whether plastic surgery ruined her smile or if it was always like that.

Across the table is the ant farm built into the wall. All the ants are long dead and dried up. Octavia gazes with satisfaction upon the glass block, still filled with rolling hills of aerated soil. It calms her stomach a little bit to see the dairy farm motif, the grain silo, the white-trimmed barn and the plastic cows. Her grandfather, unlikeable and nuts as he was, had something going with this idea. She uses the gravy to stir the mound on her plate until it's a Pollock glob of stuff. It's still food, it just doesn't look it. At least it's not making her pass out. She's making progress. Still, she wonders how she will manage the nine-o'clock flight to Las Vegas tonight.

"Dessert?" her mother asks.

"In a bit," her father says.

"How about now," her mother says.

"In a bit," her father says.

Her parents eye each other like gunslingers, their glances darting to the weapons that present themselves on the dining table. Rolls, carrot spears, the potentially lethal serving fork invitingly sprawled across the platter of turkey. Both twitching gazes are fixed on the mashed potatoes, however.

Hayley's hand is resting on her thigh.

"Let's do it now and get it over with," Octavia says. She removes Hayley's hand and gets up from the table, leaving her mother to compose a polished stare at her father. Hayley follows Octavia into the kitchen. Octavia opens the refrigerator and gets out the pies.

"Is there whipped cream?" Octavia asks.

"Here," Hayley says.

"Looks like you two were busy."

"Your mother is a nice, nice lady," Hayley says.

Octavia pulls out the silver bowl where Hayley or her mother hand-whipped the cream. She cuts the pie into slices, dishes them out, and shakes out gobs of sweet white clouds on each piece.

"What if they don't want whipped cream?" Hayley asks her.

"Tough."

"What if they don't want so much whipped cream?"

Octavia shrugs. "They can throw it at each other."

"Might lead to something," Hayley says provocatively.

"I doubt it." Octavia puts the whipped cream back in the fridge. Hayley closes the refrigerator for her and traps her against the door. Not really traps her, but Octavia plays it that way in her mind. She feels Hayley pin her against the freezer door and she feels the warmth of a woman's hands upon her shoulders. They stare at each other. "I don't fall for your act," Octavia tells her.

Hayley looks at her.

"I don't understand you," Octavia whispers meanly.

Hayley looks at her.

"Do you hear me?"

"You invited me to come."

"That was John."

"You're the one who wanted me here."

"Quit looking at me," Octavia says.

"Leave. Then." Hayley is still pinning her shoulders. Not really pinning, but Octavia plays it that way.

Hayley's face is close to hers but she hasn't floated any closer. She isn't moving in for the kill. Her lips are plump, but not too plump, and soft. The lipstick is still fresh. Everything on her face is soft and pretty, softer and prettier than any face Octavia has kissed before.

"If you knew how to kiss better," Octavia says.

"I kiss fine."

"You kiss like a man. You kiss awful."

Octavia sees a quiver of hurt on Hayley's face.

"If you have two pairs of soft lips, you might as well take advantage of them," Octavia says. Her own lips reach out and find Hayley's. She keeps her head perfectly straight, in keeping with the lesson she's giving. She bestows upon Hayley what she hopes is a revelation.

Hayley receives Octavia's mouth-to-mouth limply. She doesn't kiss back. Octavia draws away, checks her reaction, Hayley refusing to give her any, then pulses her lips gently against Hayley until Hayley's lips pulse back. Octavia smells her mother's fragrance. She pulls back and they stare at each other.

"See what I mean?" Octavia asks.

"That's how I do it, too," Hayley finally whispers.

"Hmm." Hayley's hands are still on Octavia's shoulders, but there is no pressure in them; she's simply holding on. Octavia could slide away, she begins to slide away, her hands reach out to Hayley's belly but she doesn't push as she had intended. Her own hands stay on Hayley's hips, lightly, but they are there. She looks off to the side. "I can smell my mother's perfume on you."

Hayley watches her without moving.

"Don't," Octavia says.

"What?"

"What are you doing with her?" Octavia asks. Where once she could never have envisioned it, now she can see her mother going for it, living some kind of Thelma-and-Louise fantasy, one more way to throw the mashed potatoes into her father's face.

"With who?"

"With my mother." Octavia is acutely aware of the warm lack of pressure on her shoulders, how easily she could escape. How her own hands have grown tighter around Hayley's jutting hipbones.

"Kiss me again and I'll tell you."

"No," Octavia says. They have their standoff, eye to eye, nose to nose, and then Octavia gives in and this time she angles her head. Hayley lets her be the one to open her mouth. Octavia withdraws to let Hayley's tongue find hers. Hayley kisses Octavia's ear and then her throat. Octavia listens to the way Hayley breathes. To keep herself from pulling Hayley against her she has dropped her hands but now she finds them traveling to Hayley's neck, stretching tightly across throat and chin, while her tongue explores. Hayley's hands mimic her own, two pairs fighting through a narrow passage to cup chins and entwine necks, and their increasingly fervent knot requires extra heartbeats to unravel when someone walks through the kitchen door.

The feet coming through bounce backward and retreat.

Octavia turns around and gets the whipped cream out of the refrigerator.

"It was just John," Hayley says, removing the whipped cream from Octavia's hands and putting it back.

"I guess he's awake," Octavia says. She grabs the pieces of pie and heads out of the kitchen. Her mother and father are still sitting there, across from each other at the table. The mashed potatoes haven't been thrown. They're politely silent, sending up damaged, unhappy fumes.

Rolling
the Dice

 Part Five

21

Even after the sun sets the day remains mistakenly balmy. John takes advantage of the deserted Shredders to inspect the yard and give the place a homemaker's once-over. It's not like it's a house for sale getting ready for the Sunday realtors, all the vases and flowers in place, but John wants it to look nice nonetheless. He turns on the yard lights.

He sits inside his pickup to wait. He told Octavia he'd fly into Las Vegas tomorrow, but he doesn't know if he'll keep that promise. It's not as if he has to meet up with them. Tony's got it all figured out, his latest plan to trade in the money. They all stay in different casinos and gamble in different casinos. Tony's already there, gambling at Caesars Palace and staying at Barnaby Coast. He wanted to take advantage of the sports book on Thanksgiving. John is supposed to stay at Bally's and gamble at MGM. He forgets where Octavia is supposed to be. That's sure to be a laugh. He would love to be a fly on a wall watching her try to figure Las Vegas out. Octavia, who thinks she knows everything. They'll love her in Las Vegas. Love her.

He eats at his doggie-bag Thanksgiving dinner that Hayley Badecker secreted away for him, including a bottle of wine. He has no idea if Tommy Landers's nephew will even show up. But he'll wait for an hour. Maybe he'll wait for two hours. He's sleepy again. He's felt so sleepy lately. He drinks the wine from his coffee cup as if it were coffee, a gulp followed by another gulp.

The silver vehicle that pulls in is a Cadillac SUV. A man named Bob Dunning is behind the wheel. Kids in the car. Lots of kids. John wonders if it's a second marriage, kids before, kids after. Nobody looks too happy. They're on their way back home to Weirton, West Virginia.

Bob Dunning is Tommy Landers's nephew. Last week John called up the Senior's archrival in Indianapolis, made some small talk, thanked him for coming to the funeral. Wouldn't have missed it for the world, Tommy said. Your grandfather would have loved it. He loved trouble.

John said, I want to sell out.

And Tommy said, I heard about the accident. Maybe you need to get back in the saddle.

No.

Give it some time.

No. No, John said.

It's nothing that can't wait.

I've waited too long as it is. Do you want to take a look?

I'll take a look, John. Sure. And then he said the one thing that was uppermost on both their minds. Your father know about this, John?

No.

Well. Well, I'll do this for you, Tommy Landers said. But let the blood dry, John. Let's take it one step at a time.

The kids pile out.

Bob Dunning immediately begins to shout. Before they can do anything he yells at them not to do it. The wife finally uncoils from somewhere inside the SUV. Dunning is flapping his arms like someone wronged by the referee. "Get back here!" he screams.

John would like to be able to say oh it's all right, they can't hurt themselves, but it's not true. They can't go running and jumping wherever they please. Especially in the dark. He remembers the basketball and retrieves it from his office, and the kids move out to the parking apron. Already he doesn't like this nephew whom Tommy Landers has sent in place of himself. His coarse behavior matches his looks. He's got a lower-species build, a fast-food soft face. John instantly takes ten years off the age Dunning appears to be in order to guess his true age: thirty-five, he decides. All those kids at age thirty-five. Someone who goes headlong into things, then keeps starting over, dragging a maze of false starts behind him.

This Bob Dunning has none of Tommy's (albeit aging) golden-boy charm. John much prefers the Jewish recyclers. He feels in the presence of culture and heritage, he looks into eyes that might read books at night. It might be his own projection. But he at least knows he doesn't completely understand the Jewish brotherhood that dominates his business, and he likes that. He likes not knowing, he likes a little mystery. Every day he's smack in the middle of a culture he knows too well, the white lower-class Ohio culture. He's suppressed his hope for a pleasant surprise. Everyone turns out the way you expect.

"Do you have a bathroom we can use?" the wife asks.

"For Christ's sake."

"The kids need to go, Bob."

"Fine," Dunning spits out. *Fine*, he says, like *Fine, ruin my day*, like *Fine, ruin my life*. Dunning and his wife retreat to a darkened niche to get their business straightened out. John slips away to give them some privacy. He's headed toward his office when he sees a note taped to the weighmaster window:

Never heard a word of sorry deepest sympathy from a single one of you except Tony the only man here with some breeding to him. 25 years and nothing. You showed your true colors. One of you gets killed, though, that's all you hear. I'm not surprised Worm got himself shredded but you might of told me so I could pay the proper respects you never gave me or my deceased husband. I know all your secrets. Good ears and a little woman's intuition.

Ada

There's nothing he can say to her except, *You're right.*

"There you are," Bob Dunning calls.

"Well, let me show you around," John says when the couple reappear. The wife heads to the parking apron, calling after the kids.

"Got a list of things Tommy needs me to check on," Dunning says.

"All right. You the one going to be running the place if he decides to buy?"

"Means moving family. Might do. Columbus a nice place?"

John is pleased at the thought of a dunderhead taking over the business. He won't do as well as the Bonners did. John doesn't want his family surpassed.

"How are the schools here?"

Better'n West Virginia, is all John can think to say, so he says nothing.

"You and your wife pretty satisfied with the schools?"

Again, John can think of no reply.

"Maybe you homeschool," Dunning says.

"What about Weirton?"

"Well," Dunning says.

"I wish I could tell you something, but I don't have kids. Haven't paid too much attention to the schools. Some people seem satisfied."

"No kids?" Dunning looks mildly shocked.

The Metal Shredders

John shakes his head.

"Married?" Dunning asks.

"Technically."

"That there's my high school sweetheart," Dunning tells him.

John waits for some kind of remark, a crude or coded comment he knows is coming.

"Today's Thanksgiving," Dunning says. "Sometimes I forget what all I got to be thankful for."

John is completely taken aback by the comment. He has to walk away. When Dunning follows him, he keeps moving. Dunning detours to check out the baler. He writes something down on his list. John keeps moving. His life has proceeded normally since the accident. He never thinks of Worm and the blood that poured out. Except sometimes he wants to hit people who look like Bob Dunning; except sometimes he wants to kill them; except sometimes people who look like Bob Dunning make his eyes well up with tears. He's lost all clear vision. He's walking around like a blind man. His dad said accidents happen, you have to move on, you must, but his dad wasn't there, and his dad wasn't there twenty-five years ago when the shredder swallowed a human soul and spat nothing out. If his dad had been on-site that day, if he'd been an eyewitness, if he'd tried and failed to stop the guy, as Don Capachi had tried, he would have done what John is doing now: he would have walked away. He would have sold the place out from under *his* father.

John moves over to the shredder and stands below the wet scrubber. Stands there. Just stands. Every day cars chewed into pieces emerge from the shredder's maw and travel along the wet scrubber. The magnet intercepts the iron. The rest travels to the Stafford Slide. The Stafford Slide does nothing. With its funnel shape it has found the perfect form to stay at rest and still enact its purpose.

Its uncomplicated employment of physics has served to John as the wrong kind of beacon. He has thought that doing nothing was the answer, that somehow he could be a form at rest and find the answer. That his own response to Elise should be a lofty inertia.

Sometimes standing under the shower he still expects Worm's blood to rinse out. Worm, who was not too young to die alone. He's sorry about Ada's husband, but sorry in a way that doesn't matter. It's Worm he thinks of.

Bob Dunning walks up and stands beside him. John doesn't sidle away. "This is a nice operation." Dunning's shadow nods.

"Yes," John says.

"How come you're selling? Just because of that accident?"

"Lots of things."

Dunning's shadow bounces in sympathy, but he says nothing.

John knows that it will always be in his blood. Nobody would understand this. Nobody but his grandfather and father. You want to dig your fingers into the earth's topography and pull it away. You want to pull back the continents floating on the oceans and take a look. It's all scrap inside, guardrails and piping and nothing else.

"I just can't do it anymore," John says to Bob Dunning.

It's over.

22

Octavia sits on the edge of a Las Vegas hotel bed; it's hard and bouncy like a trampoline and that doesn't help the seasick roiling that has arrived right on time. The early-morning curse continues. Except that because of the time change it's two A.M. instead of five. She looks around at what she's got herself into. A knight's coat of arms is carved on the bedboard. The purple cushion of the desk chair is embroidered with a king's crown. She's staying in a castle. When she looks out the window she sees illuminated turrets, shining pink and blue. *It looks like Sleeping Beauty,* she thinks. And then, *Oh, right.*

The room is not that small for a hotel room, but it feels closed in, and she doesn't like the lighting and the way it casts the palace wallpaper as mausoleum brick.

The silence is tomblike. That strangling heat on her neck begins. Then nausea. A cold sweat. She's prepared to throw up right there at the window, but nothing happens. Nothing ever happens.

She staggers into the theme bathroom and in more ways than one sits on the throne.

Sits.

Sits and leans her head on the sink counter. Her hand reaches out and plays blindly with the faucet. Splashes cold water on her forehead. Better now. A little bit.

The telephone rings next to her ear and she leaps screaming against the shower curtain. She picks it up, expecting Tony. She can picture him calling from a phone booth, playing super spy. Julie! the voice shouts. Wrong number, but would she like to party anyway?

She pulls down towels for a shower. Searches for the bath mat. Can't find it and throws a regular towel on the floor. She doesn't know how she managed the four-and-a-half-hour flight from Columbus. Well, actually she does know. Lots and lots of vomit bags but nothing ever in them, just the relentless urge to fill them. Everyone was kind. They assumed she had morning sickness.

She has slept in her clothes. She begins to undress, unable to escape the pallor-intensive mirror. She leans in close. Is that true what she sees? Her shirt collar is stained with lipstick. Undeniably a lipstick stain. She can see the tattoo creases, a perfect set of red lips, right there, kissed upon the cloth.

Hayley Badecker.

And she did this on purpose, that woman. Octavia knows it. All through dessert her mother and father staring across the table at the maroon imprints of her make-out session. Her mother, cheeking that side of her face when they departed, no doubt for closer inspection. Her mother's hand straightening her collar no less, a sadistic grace note for Octavia to remember later.

And yet her mother's big air-smooch to Hayley was undeniably lively. Smooch smooch, Hayley and her mother. The whole time Hayley's arm

The Metal Shredders

was linked through Octavia's and Octavia had to wait until they were outside before swinging Hayley in a circle and wrenching her arm free.

She finishes showering, dresses in clean jeans and a blouse, only then looks down and sees the bath mat folded over the tub side, soaking wet from the shower. Her blouse hangs out over jeans. It's a pastel blue, a color as safe as a Crock-Pot. The blouse tails are prim and girlish. It has waist darts. A bolo tie looped around the collar would complete the Western-housewife-at-the-roulette-table look.

She tiptoes out into the deserted hallway. There are room service trays in front of some of the doors. It's 2:45 A.M. Las Vegas time. Everything is quiet except for the faraway retch of an ice machine. She takes the elevator down to the casino, embarrassed that she's wandering around in the middle of the night like an addicted gambler, or a prostitute, or an ex-cowgirl in search of a husband who promised to come up hours ago. She wants to hide. But when she steps out into the casino, she discovers the great thing about insomnia in Las Vegas. You get to share it with hundreds of others. The place is so bustling it's like stepping into afternoon. The brooding nature of predawn is left behind. As soon as she realizes she'll never have to be alone at any hour of the day or night, she decides she is staying right down here in the gambling pit.

She wanders, scoping out the place, afraid to touch. She roams from one slot machine carousel to another, each round-up of machines topped by a flashing medieval centerpiece. Heralds blowing their trumpets announce one carousel. The centerpiece of another is fire-breathing dragons. Charging steeds gallop across strobing Blazing 7's! Blazing 7's! Blazing 7's! When she strolls over there to check it out, she discovers Blazing 7's is just another name of a slot game. And then there's another kind of slot game and then there's another. They're grouped together, little hamlets where you can settle in and feel at home. Some hamlets are really popular, not an open slot left. Old people, young people, fun people, handicapped people. Frenetic neon announces the dollar progressive slots. There's twenty-five-cent ones, and nickels. A cherry-red sportscar rotates atop another carousel. Why, she wonders, why not a horse-drawn pumpkin carriage? *Because the car is the jackpot prize.* She figures it out. She's starting to figure out this Las Vegas scene.

Like any overkill, she soon stops taking it in. In five minutes it's old news. But not the fact that she's spending the grim early morning with a loud crowd of revelers. That still seems so wonderful, such a great way to spend the dead hours of the night. She doesn't have to think, she doesn't have to talk to anyone, and yet she's not alone.

She goes over to some nickel slots tucked into a corner. It's mostly senior ladies in decaled sweatshirts, and their less noticeable retired husbands. Octavia pulls out one of her special twenties. It's making her nervous; she doesn't know what to do. She sees the automatic bill taker on the machine: 1s, 5s, 10s, 20s, 100s. She's afraid to put the bill in. Afraid some alarm will go off. She's heard the new twenties are woven through with an infrared thread to prevent counterfeiting. But you can still use old twenties, presumably. Hers is an old twenty. An old, smelly twenty. She smooths the bill, pushes it in. The bill is swallowed, then coughed out. She grabs it back, jerking in both directions to see if anybody witnessed.

Visible above a bank of slots is a pennant flag announcing CHANGE. The flag travels down one row, turns down another; it wavers invitingly near. CHANGE.

"Change over here, please," Octavia calls out loudly, surprised at herself. When the flag emerges from its row, a pushcart comes into view. The pushcart is all brushed steel. It's like one of those old Popsicle wagons, a giant steel thermos, handles for pushing, topside drawer to dig down to the frozen treasures within.

Octavia's hand trembles as she turns over her festering counterfeit bill.

The Metal Shredders

She sees herself being strong-armed by Las Vegas security, mobsters of course. *Thought it was mildew,* is what she'll say.

They won't buy it.

Damn you, Tony, she thinks.

But the Change Lady at the pushcart barely takes notice of her or her wrinkled twenty. She opens the drawer and digs down into the core. Briefly, Octavia anticipates a Popsicle. And it is cold, what she receives. The Change Lady begins loading chilly, heavy fingers onto Octavia's hand. Octavia's hand drops with the weight. The woman must sense Octavia's confusion. She glances again at Octavia's face, then explains: "Ten rolls of nickels for twenty dollars." Octavia nods sickly.

The woman whips off a thirty-two-ounce change cup from a stack and drops in the remaining rolls. The change cup is brightly colored with a mural of a madrigal feast. Sort of like the Last Supper with mead and dice.

"First time to Las Vegas?"

Octavia nods.

"Good luck," the Change Lady says in a not-insincere way.

Octavia stares down at twenty dollars' worth of wrapped nickels in her hand. She tears at the paper covering until she unearths a dull nickel lid, the first of forty coins. She looks around for somewhere to deposit the paper crumb, finally rolls it up into a spitball and drops it into her change cup. Okay. Well, she's figured out that the change cup can be used for trash, too. Next, she pries the first coin from its bound stack and aims her single nickel at the slot machine before her. Her fingers inch closer to the machine's tiny mouth (sort of like her lips toward Hayley, she suddenly thinks. And how exactly did that make her feel?). She lets the coin hover in the slit. A pulse of her fingertip and the nickel falls inside.

Now what?

Got to study this thing.

Square buttons have lit up in front of her.

How did she feel?

An older man leans over two empty seats and offers some friendly advice. "It's better if you play three nickels."

"Why?" she asks.

Why does she keep thinking about it?

He explains it to her. You have to play the maximum to get the maximum. He points to the PLAY 3 COINS button. She pushes it obediently. Nothing happens.

"It's not lit up," she says, poking at it again.

"You only have one nickel in."

"Okay," Octavia says. She picks at her roll, prying out another coin. She fits it into the slit, lets it drop. She pushes the PLAY 3 COINS button again.

"One more," the man encourages.

She pries out another nickel and slides it into the machine. The PLAY 3 COINS button lights up.

"Oh!" Octavia exclaims.

"There you go," the man says. "Now you're all set. Now all you have to do is push it. This one here."

Octavia pushes the lit-up PLAY 3 COINS button. The reels spin round, then stop. "Nothing happened," Octavia complains.

"You didn't win anything on that one. Keep trying."

"All right." Getting out another three nickels from the paper tourniquet in her hand requires the fingernails she would like to have. (The fingernails that Hayley has. Never did she think those painted atrocities would come in handy. So it would be nice if she were here, but only for that reason).

The man leans over again and says helpfully, "I just crack it like an egg." She has no idea what he is talking about until he takes one of her coin rolls and cracks it over the tray rim and a chute of nickels pours from his palm into the well.

"Thank you. That's clever."

"You were never a cashier, were you?"

"No," Octavia says.

She puts in another three nickels, hits the button. This time she gets one nickel back, which is strange, she doesn't know why that should happen, but she doesn't want to bother that man again. She plays another trio of nickels and then another. Eventually she has gone through two rolls of nickels. Though she doesn't want to make the mistake of overconfidence, at the end of just four dollars' worth of nickels she's feeling comfortable enough that she thinks she can handle these slots on her own. Any slot. She gets up to go elsewhere. She turns to say good-bye and thank you, but the man is busy with his machine and doesn't notice. She waits a few moments. She doesn't want to be rude. Then she moves on.

She gathers all her rolled and loose nickels into the madrigal feast cup and wanders around until she spots a CASHIER sign. The cashier's booth is enclosed in castle mortar and castellated trim. She gets twenty dollars and thirty-five cents back.

She's only been here forty minutes and already she's made thirty-five cents. She roams over to a crowded carousel of quarter slots where things look serious. The theme of this carousel is nonmedieval, just a fountain spewing neon streams of light. Yes, this is a serious one, too serious for a playful Dark Ages motif. Maybe these slots will be over her head but she'll give them a try. She maneuvers through the tightly bunched entryway, squeezes past a wheelchair, and trips toward the empty seat she has her eye on, but a woman's arm backs her away. The woman is playing two slots, one with the left hand, one with the right. "Sorry," Octavia says. She leaves this too-serious group and drifts around some more.

Now she notices something very interesting. Some of the slot machines are upright; others are banked. And her preference is immediate. She's going to like the banked ones where you can lean over on your elbows and peer down. So she can hide her face and have some privacy. So she can sometimes close her eyes and rest, especially if she feels the nausea coming on. She chooses a banked Double Diamond slot and takes a seat. Ah, and something else. The chairs are more comfortable, too. They have backs to them. She puts in the real twenty the cashier gave her, and begins. After a few pushes the machine doesn't work anymore. She starts to tap the call button to summon management, but then notices 0000 on her credits. Already? Twenty dollars gone? She uses a false twenty to get change from another CHANGE cart ("Good luck," says the Change Lady) and this time monitors the machine to make sure it's not cheating her. It is cheating her, but, well, in a legal way. Anyway, she's really getting the hang of it now. In no time she's starting to lose like a pro. She settles in and for the next few hours feeds it twenty after twenty. The crowds disperse somewhat, then build back up as the official morning arrives, what others would call morning anyway, those silly people who don't live in Las Vegas. Morning —just another marketing concept made up by TV. Morning, afternoon, evening—Good Lord, what will the media think up next?

By now she has made friends with one of the strolling cocktail waitresses. The waitress manages, in her black hose and a skirt no more than waist fringe, to take the sex out and show the outfit for the worn-out camping gear it really is. She's not too heavy for the costume, like some; she's not too old for it, like many; she's not too unpretty for it. She's just not a match. The other waitresses took their orders on the run; Octavia had no time to think. For she doesn't know quite what she wants; she needs time to think out loud. This one stops to listen and Octavia explains she'd like something that would help settle her stomach. The waitress coos sympathetically, says let me think about it honey. She brings back ginger ale, comes back in a bit to check, and Octavia says no, that didn't work. The waitress tries drink after drink, finally comes up with a virgin margarita, and the lemon-lime does the trick. The waitress high-fives her in triumph; she is genuinely happy for her, so it seems. Octavia tips her a twenty. She likes how that feels. Tipping a twenty. The second margarita the waitress refines with fresh slices of lime. Octavia tips her another twenty and finds out her name is Robin. She decides her mission here is to tip Robin as many twenties as she can before she leaves. She goes upstairs to lie down and when she comes back, everything is the same except Robin is off her shift. She heads over to the other casino where she remembers she was supposed to be playing all along. Tony's instructions were to play at a casino different from the one she's staying in. She's staying at the Excalibur. She's supposed to play at the Luxor. Or something like that. All these rules.

She follows a connecting tunnel of stores and eateries until she gets to the next casino, the Luxor, where the walls are a desert clay, and promenading bodybuilders are costumed in cobra headdresses with gold bands around their biceps. Why is that? she wonders. Why the pharaoh look? Okay, stupid question, she gets it now. Themes. Each casino has a different theme. That's why they have those names. Caesars Palace, for example. She never thought about it before. She would bet money that Caesars Palace has lots of Roman pillars and waitresses in togas. And that also explains why Merlin's Magical Keno Kave is back there in her castle casino and the Pyramid Party Zone is here in the Luxor's Ancient Egypt one. All right, she gets it, a little tardy, admittedly, but she gets it. This Las Vegas thing—piece of cake.

She spends a while checking out the new casino. A hieroglyphic-looking sign points the way to King Tut's pyramid. It has her fooled for a minute, all these new bells and whistles, but a few more minutes and she feels like she's been here before. This casino is but an adobe rerun of where she's been and, frankly, she prefers her Excalibur. She's developed a loyalty to her little medieval home. She meanders back toward the castle, stepping into stores along the Giza strip to kill time. She buys a fanny pack just like the women in jogging suits have. Good snug place for the money. She feels better from her nap attempt. Back at the Excalibur, she goes into Lance-A-Lotta Pasta and manages some plain spaghetti and a slice of Queen Guinevere's homemade bread. She heads to her Double Diamond machine, invitingly banked, seat backed in cushy vinyl, and settles into her new home and she's happy not to think about anything else.

She's still at the same machine although it's the next day. She's been playing for hours in a blissful blankness. She tried going to bed around midnight not expecting anything. Was prepared to commit to memory the coat of arms on her headboard. She woke up nine hours later. It wasn't two o'clock, it wasn't five o'clock, it was nine A.M.! She wanted to lead a cheer for herself right in front of one of those gumdrop-shaped Snow White mirrors. Her day was already a success. Anything else that happened was gravy.

Now at midday she looks up from the Double Diamond and it's a man she's about to recognize. "Tony!" she exclaims after a beat.

He sits down next to her. "Here," she says, scooping out a handful of quarters from the tray for him.

"I've been looking all over for you. You're supposed to be playing at the other casino."

"I like this place better. It's homier."

Tony slips three quarters into the Red White Blue machine before him. "Quarters," he says. "You're playing quarters?"

"So? That's all I can afford. It eats up the money like that." She snaps her fingers. On Tony's machine a balloon on the payline acts as a wild card to two single bars and pays out double the usual ten coins. See, she's got it all figured out. "Look, you won," she tells him.

The Metal Shredders

"Octavia." Tony catches her eye.

"You just won twenty dollars."

"Twenty coins. Five dollars." He tries to gaze some sense into her.

"Oh," she says after a while. It's been quite some time since she remembered her original purpose for being here. Except for the fact that it wasn't bothering her to lose hundreds of dollars, she more or less completely forgot the money was counterfeit. She wasn't even smelling it any longer.

"You're not supposed to be here anyway," she says. She leans over. "It's dangerous. Remember? Have you heard from John? Is there something wrong?"

"Everything's fine. Haven't heard from him, which is the way it's supposed to be."

"Then why are you here?"

"I guess I'm here to help you. You still have a lot of money to unload."

"The quarter slots will eat it up in a hurry."

Tony says, "I'm finished."

"Congratulations."

"Couldn't resist seeing how you're doing."

"As you can see, I'm doing quite well on my own."

"I'm done," Tony says. "It's gone."

"All of it?"

"I have five hundred dollars. Real money. I thought . . . We could take a taxi somewhere. We could have a nice dinner."

"Oh, I—" She starts stuttering. "It's not that I don't want to. I appreciate it, I do. I don't have much of an appetite right now."

"You aren't feeling any better? Maybe you should go to the doctor."

"I'm feeling better."

"Are you eating?"

"They have a spaghetti dish here at Lance-A-Lotta Pasta that I like. I was looking forward to that. So see I'm feeling better, but that's about all I can handle."

"Let's do that then," Tony says. "Is that okay? Do you want to?"

"And then . . ." Octavia tries to put a gentle warning into her voice. "I thought I might go over and find John."

"Okay."

"Do you know how to get to his casino?"

"I can take you," Tony says.

"Do you know what casino it is?"

"Yes I know."

"Because I forget."

"I'll take you," Tony says.

"Thanks."

"Can I buy you a drink?" Tony asks.

"Tony . . ." Octavia chuckles in disbelief. She sees her waitress friend and waves her down. "You don't have to buy me a drink. Don't you know?"

"Another regular?" Robin asks Octavia.

"Yes. And how much are your beers?" Octavia asks mischievously.

"All our drinks are complimentary," Robin says, turning to Tony.

Octavia smirks triumphantly. "This is Robin. She gives me all my drinks free."

"Yeah, I—Never mind," Tony says. "I'll have a Bud."

"No, it doesn't have to be a Bud. Does it have to be a Bud?" she asks Robin.

"Your pleasure," Robin says.

"I'll have a Corona," Tony says.

"All right, sugar."

Octavia offers her approval. "Might as well get the best, right?" She lays a twenty on Robin's tray. Robin gives her arm a special pinch.

The Metal Shredders

Tony mutters, "That's a nice tip."

"She's nice," Octavia protests. "She was nice to me before I tipped her."

"I hope it's a real one."

Octavia squirms. She digs into her fanny pack and pulls out a bill and asks Tony to go get a hundred dollars' worth of quarters for her.

"How much do you have left?" Tony reaches for the envelope. "Look how much you have. Come on, we gotta spend this." He pulls her up.

"Where are we going?"

"Dollar slots. Come on."

"Wait, I have to tell Robin where we'll be."

"She'll find us."

"I'll wait here for her and bring the drinks over."

"Come on," Tony says. "She'll find us."

Octavia is led to a carousel of Elvis slots. Tony buys three hundred dollars' worth of coins. The cashier hands him three heavy trays of Excalibur silver dollars. He drops in three coins, pushes PLAY MAX CREDITS. Above them is a small video screen of Elvis looking the best he ever did—starve-dieted into the black leathers he wore for his TV special. Tony spins the reels. Nothing happens over and over. Octavia's mind spins its own tumblers, racing ahead to predict the nothing that will happen, the non-matches and the blanks—she correctly pictures losers at each spin. Her brain is anticipating, her optic nerve sends her the preview. Magically an Elvis logo drops onto the payline and shocks her system.

"What happened?" she says.

"We won something."

"I don't believe it," she says. "How much did we win?"

"Now we do this." Tony slaps the Elvis logo button. They look up at Elvis in his leathers. A video square pixelates out of his crotch and swells into an Elvis dance number. Then "Don't Be Cruel" or one of those songs blasts out and then Tony hits another button and the gold record above

285

Elvis starts spinning around, numbers popping up, blacking out, popping up, slower, forty dollars, popping up to a hundred and fifty dollars, blacking out, slowing down, slower, a thousand dollars,

"thousand dollars! thousand dollars!" Octavia shouts,

slower, popping up to three hundred dollars. Stop.

Thunk thunk thunk.

Octavia locates the sound on the credit line. Thunk thunk thunk. Three hundred dollars are thunking into place.

"That was great," Octavia says.

"Told you I was good."

"Let's get the thousand-dollar one."

Robin brings their drinks over. Tony lifts a row of silver dollars from his rack. They're heavy. He's about to put them on her tray, but sees her apron and slips them in there. She bends over and pecks him. When she's gone, he hands a row of dollars to Octavia and expectantly raises his jaw for another peck. It's so stupid it's halfway funny. She halfway laughs. She takes the coins he's placed in her hands and feeds them three at a time into the machine. She waits till each coin plops before inserting the other.

"Too slow," he criticizes.

"I'm better at the quarter machines," she says.

On the third feed she runs out of coins. Tony adds a dollar from his stack to complete the threesome. His hand quickly moves to cover her hand poised over PLAY MAX CREDITS. He is going to kiss her, she knows it, her optic nerve sends her this preview. The pressure of his hand as he leans over pushes her palm against PLAY MAX CREDITS. This is when the jackpot will burst sirens over their heads, right? A thousand dollars will shower their kiss. But it's quiet and growing quieter. It's very quiet where he's kissing her. His lips against hers and the way she feels it deep in her throat, on the outside of her throat, and then the way it travels down her chest. She's starting to breathe heavy right in the middle of a kiss where there's no breathing at all, and his mouth is chewing on her, a little bite before he pulls away. It makes her feel good. It makes her feel sad. She can't bring herself to look at him.

He feeds more dollars into the slot with his left hand, his right hand knotted around hers. He's not going to let me go now, she thinks. When he leans over to kiss her again, she imagines Hayley's lips and her lips push back and her tongue is in his mouth. His hand is tighter around hers but they don't go exploring; they just grip tighter and tighter and tighter and when his tongue finds her mouth she has to pull away and shake out her hands.

"Sorry," he whispers. His other hand keeps her waist warm. His thick hand is so close to her breast, but it stays put. She can feel how thick it is. They kiss again and just the thumb moves higher and the underside of her breast grows hot. He pretends to kiss her ear, but really he wants to talk to her. Really, she knows, he's embarrassed for her to see his face when he says, "The good thing about playing here is that your room is so close by." Her ear tickling up and down his lips registers her nod. "Should we leave?" he asks and she says, "No," because she doesn't know who she would be leaving with.

She turns around in her seat to watch everyone else.

"That was nice," Tony says.

She turns to smile at him.

"Are you all right?"

"I'm fine," she says. His hand is crunching all over hers. She keeps her back to the machine, to him, so she can watch the people. She likes watching the people. She likes the way there are so many gamblers in wheelchairs and the way nobody pays attention to them. The way there are fat people and grotesque people and nobody cares. Nobody cares if you're a good-looking knockout, nobody cares if you're an old hag. Addiction is a great equalizer. She likes that about addiction. That is a great selling point about addiction.

"There's so much I like about you," he says. He leans in to kiss her again and when it's only the softness she feels and not the stubble above his lip it's Hayley she finds herself kissing and she raises her hand to Hayley's throat and strokes hard jaw muscles and rough skin, but that's nice too, but it's also what she's used to. Tony pulls away with a gulp and imploring look. But he won't ask again if they should leave. She understands that about him. She clears her throat. He touches the fanny pack stretched across her stomach. "Better give me some more money," he says.

"You know, I'm actually getting hungry," she says. "Keep playing," she says. "We still have a ways to go and I'm getting hungry."

People are lining up to eat at the Sherwood Forest Café. There are a surprising number of gamblers who have brought along their children. Two little boys languish against the walls, keeping a place in the long café line while their mother plays a Wheel of Fortune slot. She plays standing up, turning to check on her boys and the line's progress. She leans on a stroller with a baby in it. The woman looks about her age.

When Octavia's father and mother were her age, their kids were already preteen and starting their own identity crises before the parents ever had a chance to have their own. So maybe that's why they act the way they do now.

They never went off gambling, she'll give them that much.

There's a price to be paid for not making decisions about yourself. But deciding too quickly—that's just as bad. It's hard to get the timing right. When is it premature? When is it too late?

There are hard questions that need to be asked. Not all of them need to be asked every day. But all of them need to be asked and answered at least once. She wants to tell herself that she'll go back to the Shredders and with an Unsinkable Molly Brown enthusiasm make that place the best gosh darned Metal Shredders the world has ever seen! But she's not Molly Brown and she's not that woman at the Wheel of Fortune slot with two kids and a baby and she's not her mother either, or her father. She's not the lady in the wheelchair she sees laughing with Robin. She's not Robin. She's not a metal shredder, not even a beginning one. She's not old. She's not exactly young. She's thirty-four years old and she's still in the kissing stage of her life.

She says to Tony, "Have you noticed something? Everybody here is having the time of their lives."

Who is she? It comes down to this: she needs to stop answering the question in the negative. It also comes down to this: she won't easily be made happy. But she might as well try.

When Tony kisses her again and her back is pushed against the metal edges of the slot machine, she sways into Hayley's kiss and then back into his, and she realizes there's one more question to be answered.

He says, "So are you having the time of your life?"

"I'm having a good time," Octavia says.

Epilogue

All distant places seem romantic until you get there, and then it's just a place. Until it becomes a somewhere that's here in front of you, it could be anything. It could be the place where your wife forged a new life. It could be the place where she met a new lover and forgot all about you. It could be the place where she's the happiest she's ever been before.

As soon as John sees it he knows none of this is true. He knows that Elise is as lonely as he is. He knows that Columbus is now a distant place to her, perhaps a romantic place, and that he is here to return her to it. Maybe. Maybe not.

He stares through the rental car windshield at the house. A normal house, clapboard, two floors, beleaguered from the traffic, the window lights fighting a winter of darkness ahead. It sits on a hill in the brew of an intersection. A rim of iron mountains in the distance. For two hours there has been nothing but these window lights to see. Never changing. Not flickering out in one room, flickering on in another. No shadows in the windows. No blue light of a TV.

The Metal Shredders

It's been a long ride, 576 miles from Las Vegas.

He remembers what his grandfather used to say: *What is a fair price for scrap? The question is irrelevant.* And what his grandfather meant was that a couple of decades ago zinc was worthless; now it sells for eighty cents a pound. Are memories just scrap? The question is also irrelevant. Because they will continue to have whatever worth you assign to them. And at least Elise has taken him from the literal to the metaphorical. At least she has done that.

He gets out of the car and crosses at the intersection and walks down the drive, and who he wants to be knocks on Elise's door.

Who he really is waits for her to answer.